MOBASHAR QURESHI

R . A . C . E .

A MYSTERY

MERCURY PRESS

The publisher gratefully acknowledges the financial assistance of the Canada Council for the Arts, the Ontario Arts Council, the Ontario Media Development Corporation, and the Ontario Book Publishing Tax Credit Program. The publisher further acknowledges the financial support of the Government of Canada through the Department of Canadian Heritage's Book Publishing Industry Development Program (BPIDP) for our publishing activities.

Canada Council for the Arts　Conseil des Arts du Canada

Canada

Editor: Beverley Daurio
Cover and text design: Gordon Robertson
Cover image: iStockphoto
Printed and bound in Canada
Printed on acid-free paper

1 2 3 4 5　　10 09 08 07 06

Library and Archives Canada Cataloguing in Publication

Qureshi, Mobashar, 1978-
R.A.C.E. / Mobashar Qureshi.

ISBN 1-55128-124-4

I. Title.

PS8633.U74R32 2006　　C813'.6　　C2006-904327-2

The Mercury Press
Box 672, Station P, Toronto, Ontario Canada M5S 2Y4
www.themercurypress.ca

To my mother,
Munawar J. Qureshi
For her unconditional love and support

ACKNOWLEDGEMENTS

I would like to thank the following people: my sister, Wajeeha, for always believing in me; my brother, Furrukh, for pushing me to make the novel better; my father, Faiz Qureshi, for being my motivation; my best friend, Kam Joi Chu, for always being there—always; my assistant publisher, Angela Rawlings, for finding different ways to promote the book and for answering all my questions and concerns; my editor and publisher, Beverley Daurio, for taking a chance on the book and doing an awesome job of making the manuscript publishable; and in the end a person whom I consider a true gentleman, Mike McElroy, without him this book would have never existed. Thank you all.

R . A . C . E .

1

I lifted my head from the pillow and squinted at the clock. It was time to get up. Five more minutes, I warned myself.

Twenty minutes later, groggy and bleary, I sat up on my bum, my feet dangled over the bed. I yawned and then yawned longer and wider.

I'm not a morning person.

In fact, I'm not even a night person.

I'm a sleep person.

Wrap and seal me in a coffin and leave me alone; that's what I'm talking about. And no need to dig me up, as I would still be sleeping. But, like three million others in Toronto, I am forced to go to work.

I rubbed my belly. It was soft and natural. I once dreamed of having six-pack abs. It turned into a nightmare when I realized I had to actually do something. I *was* able to manage a two-and-a-half-pack. No more than that.

I pulled myself up on my feet. I felt along the walls and found my oasis: the bathroom. I finished my task and then moved to the kitchen, following my morning routine. A sweet smell seeped into my nostrils. My state-of-the-art coffee maker had spurted the last drop twenty minutes ago.

I grabbed my favourite cup, a picture of a mouse snoozing in bed, and filled it with the dark liquid.

I strolled to the second-floor balcony and inhaled the morning air. It smelled of . . . um . . . let's see . . . well, it just smelled.

Below, Gerrard Street bustled with the early morning commute. Cars, minivans, and SUVs maneuvered around the white-and-red streetcars, afraid of getting stuck behind one.

Across, a brown tow-truck parked in front of a gray Honda Civic. The Civic had already been tagged; a yellow ticket flapped underneath the windshield wiper. The driver emerged from his truck and swiftly began securing the vehicle.

It was the most beautiful sight in the world. Justice was being done right before my eyes. At this moment I could have shed a tear or two, but I wasn't.

The name on my Toronto Parking Enforcement badge reads: Jonathan Rupret—not *Rupert*—but Rupret. If there's ever any confusion, always remember, R *before* the E. Jon Rupret is my name, parking tickets is my game.

I had arrived from Guelph two years ago, as a mild-mannered college graduate. Now, I was a superhero in a parking enforcement uniform.

As I am an only child—with no siblings and not many friends—my Mom wasn't too happy with me coming here. She thought I'd be lonely. A superhero was never lonely. His friend was his duty and my duty was to keep the parking in Toronto efficient.

The Civic was now secured.

"Keep up the good work," I yelled across, saluting with my cup.

The tow-truck driver waved back, approvingly. Two law enforcers sharing a Kodak moment; it was priceless.

I have to say I cannot stand violators. They never seem to understand that the roads are for everyone. There are city-parking laws and they must be enforced.

Obviously, the owner of this Civic had no regard for the law. Parking wherever and whenever he wanted. He probably even thought he was above the law. While everyone else got up early to move their cars, he could sleep in and not worry. That crook!

The tow-truck driver was inside his truck and was now easing it into the road. The Civic trailed behind.

I took a sip of my coffee. My senses flooded back. Everything seemed much, much clearer now.

Wait a minute . . . I squinted . . . that Civic looked familiar . . .

"Hey, wait," I yelled. "That's my car!" The cup slipped out of my fingers.

I skipped down the stairs and was out onto Gerrard Street in no time. But I was too late. The tow-truck dragged my car into the distance.

"Not again," I mumbled.

This was the morning rush hour and it was tag-and-tow time.

I decided to go back inside. I was attracting too much attention in my Toronto Raptors pajamas.

My building had one parking spot and my Filipino landlady, who, by the way, lived below me, occupied it. Her son lived a block away and I was allowed to park in his driveway any time. But last night I was too lazy to drive over there. Come to think of it, what had I done last night?

I stomped up the stairs and was ready to slam the door when I realized my landlady would hear me and come up to see if everything was okay. I didn't want to spend the morning explaining why I didn't drive that one block.

I nearly screamed when I saw my favourite cup in pieces on the floor. I was ready to shed a tear now.

Would this mean I had to give up coffee? Who would replace the snoozing mouse? Could I ever get over the snoozing mouse and continue on with my life? There were too many questions running in my head, with few answers.

I cleaned and then had breakfast—without coffee. I wasn't going to replace the snoozing mouse so soon. I had to give myself time to mourn.

I changed into my Parking Enforcement Officer (PEO) uniform: light blue shirt with black tie, black pants with blue stripes on the sides, a black police cap, and a handy-dandy radio. Half an hour later I stood on the sidewalk waiting for the streetcar.

It was embarrassing. Here I was a member of the police force, looking exceptionally fine in my uniform, waiting for transportation.

If only I'd come to my senses sooner, I would have yelled at the tow-truck driver and would now be in my car. Instead, I had saluted and congratulated him for taking it away. The only thing left was to give him a box of Turtles and sing him a song.

Crap.

Rain pelted my shirt. I was wet.

You cannot trust the weather in Toronto. It could be bright and sunny one minute and pouring the next. That's why the weatherman always says it like it's a guess or a possibility: *Today, it's going to be sunny, partly cloudy, thirty per cent chance of precipitation, some mild wind, slight chance of humidity and maybe some snow.* In Toronto, you wake up and take your chances. I've had days where it's freezing in the morning and damn hot in the afternoons.

The rain was soaking my uniform, and not to mention, wrinkling my beautiful black skin.

I could walk five steps left and save myself from the rain in the bus shelter, but there were already four people inside it. Two teenagers, an old lady with a dog that looked like a raccoon, and a guy in a business suit.

Civilians.

Officers don't share bus shelters with civilians. Never. Okay, technically, a Parking Enforcement Officer is also a civilian. But I'm a civilian with a cool uniform.

I pushed my police cap lower and stuffed my hands in my pockets. Eventually, this rain would stop or the streetcar would come.

Ten minutes passed and neither happened.

My stubbornness was going to get me sick. Abruptly, I turned left and took the five steps.

The inhabitants of the bus shelter made room as I took my position in the corner, dripping and wet.

I tried not to make eye contact with anyone, especially the dog, but I did. It was staring up at me. Then his or her—I can never tell the difference—tongue came out.

Fine. *Mock me.*

You don't even look like a man's best friend. You look like a large rodent.

When no one was looking I stuck my tongue out. The dog's tongue instantly went back in.

That's right. Now who's the man?

The streetcar approached.

I went up the steps and the driver nodded. Officers of the Toronto Police Services do not have to pay fares while using public transit. The Toronto Transit Commission or TTC allows officers to ride free of charge; it deters crime while they are on a bus, train, or in my case, streetcar.

A punk kid snickered at my wet uniform and I was ready to arrest him but seeing that he was only six years old, I gave him a warning look and moved to the back of the car.

The ride was uncomfortable. I kept my focus on the advertisements plastered above, but I could feel eighteen eyes on me. The passengers were probably wondering why I wasn't prepared like them and carrying an umbrella. This was Toronto, they'd say, you should know better.

I didn't make eye contact with any of the passengers. I was happy reading the ad about how, I, too, could be debt-free. Being debt-free was on my list of things to do.

2

Between his thumb and index finger, Armand Dempiers held a small tablet. It was oval and smooth, and resembled an over-the-counter medication. But it was not. It was far more dangerous than anything available in drugstores.

He returned the tablet to a tray and slid it into the dryer-oven. As he moved away, the door behind him flew open.

"Joey, what do you want?" Armand said.

"Is it ready?" Joey looked too young to shave.

It would never be ready, Armand wanted to say. Not if he had anything to do with it. "A few more minutes."

He moved across the windowless room, no bigger than a two-car garage, passed a large motorized ventilator and slumped on to a chair behind a battered steel desk.

He shoved a stack of books and note-filled binders aside and rested his head on his palms. Through his fingers he caught sight of a picture frame with gold borders, half-hidden underneath the pile of material.

He squinted at the photo inside the frame. Four smiling faces looked up at him. Three children and one . . . he stopped. One, a man he no longer knew. The man's smile was, perhaps, the widest. He seemed healthy and full of life.

Through the cracked glass he saw his own reflection. The man looking back at him was weak and exhausted.

How did his life end up like this?

He caught the three smiling faces again and he couldn't help but smile himself. His children brought him immense joy. His smile drained when he thought of the person who had taken the photo: his ex-wife.

He was glad she was not in the picture. How he hated her. It was her fault—all of it. She wanted to take the kids from Toronto to Vancouver. How could she expect him to see them over the weekends when they were that far away?

He closed his eyes. This drug was a mistake. A mistake he no longer wanted to be part of.

What was he thinking, creating this drug? Was it that it would bring instant relief to whoever used it? Or was it that it would make *him* instantly rich?

This was supposed to be for his children. Once he was rich, he would give them everything they'd ever want. He'd buy a house so that they wouldn't have to move to Vancouver.

So, what was wrong with providing relief and profiting from it? He wanted to shout. Nothing. Except when the user has no choice but to want more, and more, and more . . .

This was Bantam's fault, as well. He'd worked for Bantam Pharmaceuticals Limited for over fourteen years, giving them the best years of his life. He'd been working on a painkiller that would irrevocably change the drug industry. But, just as he'd discovered a revolutionary, instantly absorbable version, Bantam had cold feet. It was dangerous, they said; it had potential for something sinister. It wasn't finished, Armand retorted, there were tests that still had to be done. Give me more time, he begged. They didn't. They down shut his project, and when he protested, they fired him.

He stole the designs and was here, working for *them* in completing his masterpiece . . . except, he had realized, his creation could one day cause so much misery that it could even affect his children. So now . . .

"Armand, it has to be ready by now," he heard Joey say.

Armand shut his eyes tight; deep lines etched his pale skin. His wiry fingers moved in a circular motion around his temples, trying to alleviate the pain in his head.

After tonight he would do what he should have done months ago. Call the police and give himself up. He would confess. Surely, they would be lenient; after all, he would save them a great deal of trouble.

"I think it's ready," Joey said.

Armand lifted his head, rubbed his eyes, and took a deep breath. For now, he had to continue this charade. He had to show the kid—a chemistry student whose job was to watch over him—that the drug they had been labouring over for the last three weeks was capable of doing what it boasted: providing such intense relief, the body couldn't help but crave more.

He went over and pulled out the tray he had been examining not two minutes ago. Two dozen, identical, yellow tablets lined perfectly across the tray in rows.

Joey rubbed his hands. "We have it. I know we do."

"Armand will never have it," said a female voice from behind.

They both turned.

She stood near the door with one hand on her hip. Her auburn hair flowed down her back. Her lips were parted slightly, revealing glossed teeth. Her emerald eyes bore into Armand.

"We have it, Ms. Zee," Joey said, moving his hand through his shaggy hair. "Don't we?" He turned to Armand.

Armand didn't meet his eyes.

"Armand never had it," Ms. Zee said. "And he never will."

"But . . ." Joey started. "We've been working . . ."

The look on Ms. Zee's face was both menacing and disappointing. "Joey, get out!"

When the door had closed behind him, "Kong!" she commanded.

A massive figure emerged behind her. Veins throbbed from the side of his shaved head. His black t-shirt was ready to tear from the bulging muscles. His neck was the size of a tree trunk and his chest the width of the door.

The tray in Armand's hand shook; a few tablets fell. "Ms. Zee, I will have it. I just need a little more time."

She shook her head. "No."

Kong moved toward him.

Armand lifted the tray over his head—tablets scattered to the floor—and threw it at Kong.

A loud metal thud reverberated as the tray hit Kong on the forehead. Kong stumbled back, jerked his head and clenched his jaw. His nostrils flared.

Armand grabbed a binder and a book and threw them at Kong.

Kong was ready. He flicked them aside with his massive hands as if they were nothing. He charged.

Armand moved backward, slipped on the tablets, and fell sideways. His head hit the edge of the desk with a loud crack. His body slumped to the floor awkwardly, his right arm underneath him, his left turned upward, his legs spread apart, and his neck twisted to one side.

Bone protruded from the side of his neck, revealing a lump underneath the skin. His chest was still. His eyes, empty and hollow, stared up at the ceiling.

Armand Dempiers was dead.

3

When I reached my destination, I exited the streetcar but was greeted by the bright sun. My eyes took a second to adjust to the glare. Hadn't it been raining just a short while ago?

The Toronto Parking Enforcement Unit is inside the Toronto Police Headquarters, located on College Street.

The salmon-coloured building has a twelve-storey tower and a ten-storey-high atrium. From far away it looks like someone stacked granite cubes and glass blocks on top of one another, something like those Jenga shapes, where you stack wooden blocks as high as possible until they fall. Lucky for me, this building was not made out of wooden blocks, so I felt pretty secure going in. Plus, it had a cool domed roof atop the elevator lobby.

I got off on my floor and was stopped by the front desk officer.

"What happened to you? You're all wet," she said.

I shook myself slightly, like an animal coming out of a lake, but better.

"What happened?" she asked again.

"It's a long story," I said, wiping my hair, which was now pretty much dry. "You wouldn't want to hear it."

"Try me," Roberta Collecci said.

Roberta is in her late forties and has been with the force for twenty-two years. She was looking at me with one eyebrow raised.

We were alone. I was cornered. I had to make something up. And fast.

I lowered my voice, like a broadcaster: "Last night, after I left here, I was driving and minding my own business when I see I'm out of gas. So I go into this gas station and park behind this Mazda. This is when I see this one kid."

"Just one?" she said.

I eyed her suspiciously, "Were you following me?" I cleared my throat and lowered my voice again. "So this kid is sitting in his car while I'm pumping my gas, right. I could see the kid look at me through his rear-view mirror. He keeps staring.

Maybe my uniform made him nervous. But I just keep pumping, when suddenly I see a second kid run out from inside. He jumps into the Mazda and they drive off. I knew something was wrong. So I dropped everything and chased after them."

"You didn't pay for your gas?" she said.

My eyes narrowed. *She was right. I didn't pay for the gas.*

"I know the owner so it wasn't a problem," I said.

"The owner was certain it was your car that drove away—in pursuit—of the robbers?"

My eyes were now slits. "You *were* following me, weren't you? Anyways, the robbers realized I was following them so they started speeding, going through red lights, and changing lanes with no signals. I did the same. I had no choice. I had to catch them. I drove like a demon. This divine force had control over my body."

She raised both her eyebrows.

"Deep, I know," I said. "So, here I was changing lanes, crossing over, edging past minivans, waving at little children along the way."

"You had time to wave?" she inquired.

"Yeah, but I always kept one hand on the steering wheel. You know me, safety first. Anyways, we did this for almost twenty minutes, them crisscrossing lanes and me in hot pursuit, until, luck would have it—they got onto the highway. That was my chance. I drove up straight beside them, swerved left and slammed into them, trying to push them to the side." I placed both of my hands on the desk and demonstrated my daring heroics. "I ended up shoving them to the side and arresting both of them. My car is in the shop getting fixed."

"You're a hero," she finally said.

Of course I was. No one appreciated me.

"They should give you a medal."

"They should, but they won't," I shook my head as if I was being discriminated against repeatedly. "Politics, bureaucracy, you know how it is."

"So how much did they steal?" Roberta asked.

"Who?"

"The robbers."

"Uh, lots. I don't know off the top of my head. Maybe five hundred, maybe more."

"So let me get this straight," she started. "You damaged your car—"

"—It was a piece of shit, anyways."

"Risked countless lives, just for a couple of hundred dollars—"

"—It was probably in the thousands. Definitely in the thousands."

I took a big gulp. She had me.

"Car towed again?" she said.

I lowered my head and whispered, "Yes."

But she wasn't done. "Isn't it ironic the person who gets other people's cars towed has his own car towed? Tragic."

"Not for long." I smiled. "If the sergeant listens to me I'll be out of Parking Enforcement as soon as permitted."

"Jonny, you keep bugging him. Sooner or later it will happen. Now back to work, hero boy." She smiled.

Roberta Collecci was like my guardian. She had taken the responsibility—a very hefty one, if I may say so, to watch over me. She kept me out of trouble.

I decided to meet the staff sergeant, but first, I needed to get dry. My light navy blue shirt had dark blue patches all over. I headed for the men's washroom and inside allowed the hand dryers to blow over my body.

It was surprising for some to enter the washroom and see me dancing sensually in front of the dryers. I just smiled and they quickly left.

When I was all dried off I stood in front of the mirrors. My shirt was back to its original colour. My pants, which are black, stayed black but were more comfortable. I placed my cap on my head and took one last look. A handsome man looked back and grinned. I was grinning, too.

Once ready I went through a set of doors and into a hall with rooms on either side. Important people had offices here. Not sure why I didn't have one yet. I stopped and tenderly tapped at the glass beside the door.

"Come in," said a voice.

I entered the office of Staff Sergeant James Motley, who was in charge of the Parking Enforcement Unit.

"Jon, come in," he said. Motley was unlike the sergeants you see on television. He did not have a belly, did not smoke a cigar, and he hardly ever swore. There was a book on spirituality sitting to the side, and last week he was reading Native history.

How he ended up at PEU, I don't know.

"Sir, have you ever thought about watching those cop shows?" I said, standing.

"Jon, what can I do for you?" he said.

"It's about any openings . . ." I let my words trail.

Motley did not look surprised or interested. He knew I wanted to move on and gain other experiences.

"Yes, I know, Jon. You have asked me six times this week and today is Tuesday."

"Tuesday?" I said, looking around. "Time drags."

Don't get me wrong. I liked being a PEO but I felt I could better serve society if I were a detective or a lieutenant. Maybe even a commando, but that would mean joining the army. Discipline, hard work, and respecting authority were not my strong points. So the army was out.

What about the navy? No, water equals sharks. Sharks equal missing limbs.

How about the air force? No, flying equals gravity. Gravity equals falling thousands of feet to your death.

Parking Enforcement? Hmmm, now that's something I could do. Wait a minute. I was already doing it.

Motley leaned back in his chair and said, "Jon, I have my eyes open, you know that."

"I just thought, y'know, I'd remind you."

"If it were up to me, I'd have you transferred immediately." He gave a short smile.

"Thank you, Sir," I said, about to leave.

"Jon."

I stopped. "Sir?"

"If and when something does come up, you'll be the first to know. I promise."

That was the sergeant's polite way of saying "Don't call me, I'll call you."

"Thank you," I replied.

I went down to the parking lot to retrieve my marked cruiser, a Dodge Neon parked in the corner. It was white with blue and red stripes across the sides. It had the words TO SERVE AND PROTECT/ WORKING WITH THE COMMUNITY on the side doors, and PARKING ENFORCEMENT on both front sides.

I eased the cruiser out from the parking lot and headed in the direction of my route. This may be a good time to explain what I do. I know, I know, most people think we, PEOs, just go around giving parking tickets. That's somewhat correct. We do give a Parking Infraction Notice or PIN whenever a vehicle is illegally parked, but that's not all we do. We help keep the streets safe and clean.

How? Whenever someone is walking around and they see a uniformed officer, be it a traffic cop, or even security guard, they do try to be on their best behaviour. *Right?*

If someone is about to commit a crime or is thinking about it, he or she will, at least, think twice if they see us driving by. We help deter crimes.

Not just that; without us the city would not move. Think about it. Why would anyone want to move their car if they didn't have to? They could just park and leave it for the entire day. Imagine if someone had to take their grandmother to the doctor for a checkup after she'd had a hip replacement and they couldn't park anywhere because some jerk parked his car on the street and gone to work. Now imagine if they had to park two blocks away and carry their dear old grandmother just because there was no turnover of parked cars. Now wouldn't they be pissed off?

Our main job is to keep traffic flowing.

I parked behind a row of parked cars and pulled out my little black book.

I checked the first meter: seventeen minutes left.

Second: three minutes. I should see the owner any time soon.

Third: fourteen minutes.

Fifth: expired. Oh, goody. On the ticket I wrote down the date of infraction, time of infraction, license-plate number, vehicle plate, checked off box with code number one, placed my signature at the bottom, entered the unit and employee code, and gently placed the banana-coloured ticket under the windshield.

Sixth: no fee deposited. Good, another one.

Seventh: fifty-two minutes left.

Eighth: broken meter. I wrote a fifteen-dollar ticket.

Whoa! The meter is broken! The owner should not have to pay for the ticket, right? Wrong. Parking at a busted meter is illegal.

Some people tamper with meters on purpose in order to avoid paying the fee. It's quite easy to sabotage a meter. It can be done with a piece of paper, by jamming the mechanism and fishing out the parking fee with a paper clip. But I'm not going to say exactly how.

As I was on my twelfth someone ran up. "I was *only* gone for two minutes," he said.

"Sorry, Sir. I see an expired meter," I said and moved on. It's always *two* minutes. The man muttered something under his breath.

I've been called many things: Meter Maid, Green Hornet, Vulture, and other lovely terms that I didn't know existed in the English dictionary.

The first couple of days on the job were terrible. The things that were said to me left me scared. I stopped sleeping, and I love to sleep. I dreaded going to work and having to confront these types of people. The looks they gave, the upstanding middle fingers, the curses. Now, I'm immune to it. In fact, I think I've become cynical.

If they say, "Screw you," I say, "Thank you." That pisses them off.

If they say, "Kiss my ass," I say, "Sir, it'll take me a whole week to kiss all that."

I keep smiling and that truly annoys them.

I remember once this nice lady placed a spell on me, saying I'd die a horrible death in ten days. That was eight months ago, and seeing that I'm still alive, the spell didn't work.

Maybe someone has a voodoo doll of me. Every so often they poke needles into my head. No wonder I can't think straight. Maybe . . . just maybe, they place a pillow over my head and . . . yes, now it makes perfect sense, that's why I feel sleepy all the time.

I drove into a more upscale commercial street. This street had something that made all PEOs' lives easier: pay-and-display kiosks. Each of these babies replaced ten parking meters. Plus, these high-tech solar-powered kiosks were reliable and difficult to vandalize.

All I had to do was look at the receipt on their windshield, and if it was expired I gave them a PIN.

I drove to a public parking lot and made a quick round when I saw a car parked in the disabled zone. I scanned the vehicle and found a placard hanging from the rear-view mirror. I went back into my cruiser and contacted the communication dispatcher. Parking Enforcement vehicles are not mobile workstations, meaning we have no access to police information systems—at least, not yet. The dispatcher, linked to police systems such as CPIC (Canadian Police Information Center) and MOT (Ministry of Transportation), responded to my query over the radio network.

This disabled permit was on the wrong vehicle.

Beautiful.

I wrote a ticket for three hundred dollars and placed it under the windshield. I was about to leave when the owner showed up.

"What are you doing?" he yelled from a distance.

I did not answer.

"Hey, man. I'm talking to you. What the hell are you doing?" He hobbled toward me.

"I'm giving you a ticket, Sir," I said. What I really wanted to say was: *Don't mind that, that's just a flyer.*

"You can't give me a ticket," he said, waving his hands.

I hate people who abuse rights that are for the disadvantaged.

"Can't you see my foot?" he said, pointing to his right foot.

I looked at it carefully and I didn't see anything wrong with it. It looked like any other foot. Maybe it was shorter than the other one, but I didn't want to mention it.

"It's broken," he said.

"Sorry to hear that, but that placard is not registered to your vehicle, Sir," I said.

"The permit belongs to my aunt and since I broke my leg she lent it to me."

"That's not how it works," I said.

"What do you want me to do in this condition? Park at the end of the lot and walk?"

"I'm sorry, Sir," I said. "I'm just enforcing the by-laws."

"You can't do this," he said. He was in my face.

"I just did," I said.

Veins popped up in his forehead.

"You can't," he repeated. "I know my rights. I'm gonna take you to court."

There was a crowd gathering around us. This was going to get nasty.

A woman carrying way too many shopping bags said, "This man is hurt. There should be a law against you guys."

Everyone approved.

I wasn't about to start a verbal tennis match with the woman, so I pulled out my cell and dialed a number. I said a few words and turned to the violator.

"All right, Sir," I said. "Please follow me."

I led the man away from the crowd. He hobbled alongside me. We stopped at a spot where, in the distance, his vehicle was clearly visible.

"Now, Sir," I said. "I think we should discuss this in a civilized manner."

"Yeah," the man said.

"How did you break your foot, Sir?" I asked.

"I dropped a bowling ball."

"Sorry to hear that. It must have hurt. Shatter your toes?"

"Huh?"

"I mean, broke your foot terribly?"

"Yeah, hurt like hell,"

"I bet it did, Sir. I'm just doing my job. I checked the permit records and it does not belong to your vehicle."

"Yeah," he began to stumble. "It belongs to my dad."

"You mean aunt."

"Yeah, aunt. She's actually my dad's aunt. After I broke my foot she lent it to me."

I nodded.

"I was gonna get my own, y'know," he said, as if he could walk into any store and pick a disabled parking permit off the shelf.

"So what do you want me to do?"

He cleared his throat after seeing I was willing to compromise, which I was not. I was buying time.

"I don't think I should get the ticket," he said.

"You want me to take back the ticket?"

"Yeah. I got witnesses and I'll take you to court."

He would do that, after he saw I'd given him a three-hundred-dollar ticket.

I lowered my voice and leaned in. He got closer, too. "Sir, this is what you're going to do. You're going to keep that ticket and you're going to pay it within fifteen days."

Veins popped up in his forehead again.

"And Sir, you're going to run. Run as fast as you can."

"What?" he said perplexed.

I turned and looked in the direction of his vehicle; he instinctively did the same.

A tow-truck was getting ready to haul his car.

The man forgot about his injury and dashed. I never knew someone with a broken foot could run that fast.

Now let's see those witnesses.

Some days my job was so much fun.

I went to a fast-food restaurant, the one with the golden arches, but I'm not saying which one. I sat in my cruiser and ate away at my chicken burger. We're not supposed to eat in our vehicles, but who would know, right?

What else do PEOs do? Give tickets every minute of every hour? No. Like I mentioned earlier, we deter crimes. We've recovered stolen goods, assisted police officers in arrests, and even prevented robberies.

A few months back I had chalked the tires of a vehicle parked in a non-metered space. I recorded the time and a short while later, when I returned, I saw a kid trying to break into the car. He had slid a metal coat hanger through the side window, and was, unsuccessfully, trying to unlock it.

I walked up beside him and watched. He was perhaps thirteen or fourteen, definitely not driving age. I knew what he was after, as I had scoped it out before: a brand new Yamaha five-disc car stereo, with two-hundred-watt speakers and subwoofers that were powerful enough to shake this car and the ones around it.

The kid was sweating and he was becoming impatient. He would slide the hanger down the window slit and fish it up and down. When he didn't get the desired result he would pull it out and curse.

The kid wasn't even looking up. He was focused on the task at hand. After a few long minutes he had the door unlocked. I could tell he was glad. So was I.

I placed my hand on his shoulder and spun him around.

"All right, Son," I said imitating my father's voice. "You're under arrest."

He didn't wait. He darted. I went after him. We raced, maybe a block and a half before I finally caught him.

"Why bother running?" I said out of breath. "I saw you break into the car."

The kid shrugged.

"Let's go," I said.

During our walk the kid kept his head down.

When we got back I saw the car's door open and the stereo, speakers, and everything else of value missing.

The kid looked at me and said, "I didn't take nothing."

I had been duped.

The kid was a decoy and I was the bait. While I was running after the kid his buddies cleaned out the car.

Obviously, I didn't see the kid take anything, so the judge gave him some community time. He and his buddies got away with thousands of dollars worth of goods.

Even now I laugh when I think about it.

It goes to show no matter how smart you think you are, someone is always smarter.

It was almost the end of my shift and close to rush hour. I drove to a tag-and-tow street. I stopped behind a gray Plymouth Voyager and wrote a ticket.

"Hey, wait. Stop," said a voice further away.

I turned and saw a man in a robe running towards me. He stopped and caught his breath.

How do people know I'm about to give them a ticket?

"Hey, please. Don't give me a ticket?" he said.

"You're not supposed to be parked here. Rush hour," I said.

"I know," he pleaded. "I'm having a bad day. My girlfriend left me. I was up all night. I didn't even go to work . . ."

People tell me their life's history hoping I'll change my mind, and in certain situations I do.

"I'm sorry, Sir," I said.

I placed the ticket on the windshield.

"Haven't you ever had a bad day?"

"Every day," I said and moved to my cruiser.

"Haven't you ever been too busy to move your car?"

That stopped me.

He said, "Come on, can't you give me a break?"

"I did," I said. "You're lucky I didn't have your car towed."

I headed back to headquarters with forty-seven tickets and two tows.

After my shift I took the subway to Joe's Towing. Inside the impound shed, mighty Joe Coultier sat behind the counter.

Behind Joe was a huge sign that read: WE DID NOT DRIVE YOUR CAR, WE DID NOT PARK YOUR CAR, WE DID NOT TAG YOUR CAR, WE DID TOW YOUR CAR, SO WE DESERVE ONLY 1/4 OF THE ABUSE.

"License plate?" Joe asked a gentleman in front of me.

The man gave him the plate number, paid, and left.

"Next," Joe yelled.

There was no one else in the impound shed.

"Jonny," he said in a deep voice. Joe is massive; he has big hands, big chest, big feet, even a big head.

"Hello, Joe," I said, embarrassed.

"License plate?" he asked

"Come on," I snapped. "You know my car. I've been here many times."

"Too many times," he said, clearly enjoying this.

"Yeah, all right," I said and gave him my license plate number.

He looked through his records as if it were a technicality. "The usual spot."

Something was different. "What happened to Marcie?" I asked.

"She got tired of the yelling and swearing—"

"—From you?"

"Funny guy," said Joe.

"I always liked her," I said. "She had a beautiful smile."

"Yeah, well," he shrugged. "There's a vacancy if you're interested."

"Funny guy," I said imitating him. "How much?"

"The usual. Forty-nine dollars."

"Come on," I said. "I'm your best customer. You must have a super-customer rate."

"Sorry, I don't."

"You know what you need?" I said, getting excited. "Those coupons like in the grocery stores. After five tows the next tow is free."

"Not interested," Joe said.

"How're you supposed to attract customers?"

"I don't need to."

I leaned closer. "You know they'll go elsewhere."

"No, they won't. I have the contract to this district for another three years. They have no choice but to come to me."

I stood up and waved my finger, "That's monopolization and that's illegal."

"Go fight the system."

"I intend to," I said. I pulled out my chequebook, ready to pay and get out of this place.

"No cheques from you," Joe said, shaking his head.

"Since when?" I asked.

"Since the last time your cheque bounced."

"I had to pay my cable bill."

"I don't care." He pointed to a piece of paper, stuck on the wall, behind him. It read: DO NOT ACCEPT CHEQUES FROM THIS PERSON. Underneath was a smiling picture of me.

"Where'd you get that?" I exploded.

"From your driver's license," he said, laughing.

"All right, you giant clown, take it down." After paying, I said, "I'm going to be back in three years and Marcie and I are going to open our own little towing company. And we're going to offer discounts to our loyal customers."

I went to the back end of the lot to where my car was, in the dark corner.

I patted my baby. "Sorry you have to come to this awful place," I whispered. "Daddy will be more responsible from now on."

For a brief moment I thought my car sighed. It had been a very long day.

I got in my car and drove into the sunset.

I drove to my landlady's son's house.

He came out as he saw me ease my car into the driveway.

"Jon," he said. "Mom told me your car was towed."

"How did she know?" I'd been certain she was sleeping when the towing occurred.

"She saw you standing on the street, waiting for the streetcar."

"Yeah, well," I shrugged.

"You should've parked it here," he said.

My landlord's family was from the Philippines and some of the nicest people I knew.

I walked the block to my house and with the key opened the main door. As I was walking up the stairs my landlady appeared from behind her door.

"Jonny," she said in her native Tagalog accent. "I was so worried. You get your car back?"

"Yes, I did," I said. Whenever something happened to me she got worried. "It's okay; I parked at David's."

"You should do that every day. Okay?"

"Yes, every day," I said in resignation.

I unlocked my front door and entered.

I was greeted by a life-size cut-out of Michael Jordan, wearing his No. 23 Bulls jersey, hands clasped to his sides and smiling radiantly.

"Hi, Mike," I said, in customary greeting.

To this day Mike has never answered back, but his smile always reassures me that he is listening.

I had arrived in my one-bedroom castle. The king had returned from giving parking tickets to those who chose to break the municipal parking by-laws.

I washed up, warmed my TV dinner and placed myself in front of the television. Nothing beats coming home and watching a basketball game.

Like most nights, I was asleep before the start of the fourth quarter.

4

I rolled to the other side of the bed trying desperately to block a sharp noise. Every few seconds the noise emerged again and I placed a pillow over my head. I opened my eyes and looked at the time: 7:34 a.m.

I removed the pillow and realized the noise was the ringing of the telephone. Who could be calling me this early in the morning? I don't get up until almost eight. My voicemail should have picked it up by now. I waited, but the ringing started again. Why did this person continue calling me?

Annoyed, I answered it. "Jon Rupret."

"Jon, sorry to wake you up so early . . ."

"Roberta?" I said. "It's 7:30. I've just lost twenty minutes of my beauty sleep."

"I know . . ."

"Is everything okay?"

"The sergeant left me a note to tell you to come to headquarters early today."

"Early? What for? I didn't do anything, Roberta. I swear. They always blame the black guy."

"Don't get paranoid. It must be a shift change or someone called in sick. I don't know. Just come in early."

"How early are we talking about?"

"Jon, now!" she nearly yelled.

I hung up and sat silently.

This wasn't right. Not that I haven't been called at inappropriate times to fill in for a colleague before. But I had a bad feeling.

I changed into my uniform, ate my favourite chocolate cereal, said my morning goodbyes to Michael Jordan, and left to pick up my car, all in less than my usual time.

I drove to the department, which took almost twenty-five minutes because of the morning rush.

"Thank goodness," Roberta said, seeing me come through the doors. "You're late of course."

"Good morning to you, too," I smiled.

"The sergeant is waiting impatiently."

"What did he say?" I inquired.

"He said, 'Wake Jon up and tell him to come to the department right away and see me first.'"

"Did he say that while he was smiling?"

"He seemed happy."

"That can't be good," I said to myself.

"Jonny, go," she said, pointing in the direction of the sergeant's office.

"Do you think I should buy him some roses?"

"Go."

"How about dandelions?"

"Jonny!"

"All right."

The door to Sergeant Motley's office was open and I found him reading a piece of paper.

I tapped at the door and said, "Sir."

He instantly got up. "Jon, come in." He walked over and slapped me on the back as if we were good friends. "Have a seat."

I sat.

Motley went around and sat behind his desk. He smiled broadly. He was beaming, in fact. "How long have we known each other?"

"A year and a half, I think," I said.

"That long, wow," he said as if he was pondering the date. "Jon, let me first say that I've always enjoyed having you work under me. Always." He paused. "In fact, it's been a privilege. That is why it is with great sadness that I have to see you leave."

"Leave?" I was shocked. "I'm being fired?" My mind jolted to our union, the Toronto Police Association.

"No," he said waving his hands. "Transferred."

"Where?"

Motley went silent. His face turned grave.

He slid the lone piece of paper in front of me. Without touching it, as if it might bite me, I scanned it.

"Drug squad!" I shrieked. My voice was so loud I bet the whole department heard it. "I'm being assigned to the Central Field Command Drug Squad?" I asked, still not sure if this was happening.

He nodded.

"You can't do this," I said.

"Take it easy, Jon," he said. "It can't be all that bad."

I gave him a hard look and Motley went silent again.

Almost a year ago, when I was in my fifth month as a PEO and new to the department, I was given the night shift. I was very naïve. One night on patrol, I saw two vehicles in a supermarket's parking lot. There were three people in one vehicle with two sitting in front and one in the back. The other vehicle was unoccupied. I had a feeling something wasn't right. I drove up in my marked cruiser and parked right behind the occupied vehicle. I got out.

My radio crackled but I turned it down. It was rattling my nerves. I pulled out my flashlight and approached the driver.

I flashed my light into the driver's window and motioned him to roll it down. Reluctantly, he did. He was Hispanic with a heavy moustache.

"Good evening, Gentlemen," I said as I flashed the other two passengers: one white, the other black.

"May I ask what you gentlemen are doing here?" I said. My radio crackled again, but I ignored it.

"Just talking, officer," the Hispanic driver said. "That's not illegal, is it?"

I smiled. "Of course not, Sir."

"Do you want to check my driver's license?" the driver said, offering it to me.

I flashed the passengers again.

The other two were getting nervous. But the Hispanic driver calmly offered me his driver's license again, "Go ahead, officer. Check it out."

I said, "I don't think that'll be necessary. Just checking to make sure you guys aren't dealing any drugs."

As I finished the last sentence the two passengers bolted.

Within seconds I was surrounded by police cruisers and unmarked cars. Two cruisers cut off the other car.

"What the hell are you doing?" said the Hispanic driver, turning to me.

I was confused.

"That was a crack bust," he said.

"Crack . . . bust. . . ?" was all I could utter.

Detective Constable Mark Lopez had been under cover. He had arranged to buy a large amount of crack from a local dealer. He needed to make a physical purchase in order to charge the two dealers with trafficking. Prior to my arrival at the scene, he was about to gain possession of the goods, but when my cruiser pulled up behind them the one dealer became frightened. Lopez assured him that he'd take care of it and was hoping that I would check his driver's license in order to find out who he really was.

Across the parking lot, members of the drug squad were waiting for the exchange to take place. Detective Ronald Garnett saw my cruiser approach the lot, and had me radioed. Instead of contacting the dispatcher, I had to be the hero.

Next day the front pages of the major newspapers read:

Toronto Star: DRUG BUST FOULED BY PARKING ENFORCEMENT OFFICER

Toronto Sun: TORONTO POLICE BLAME FAILED DRUG BUST ON PARKING ENFORCEMENT OFFICER

Globe and Mail: FAILED DRUG BUST: PARKING ENFORCEMENT OFFICER AT FAULT

I had screwed up.

It was embarrassing for the force and especially embarrassing for me. My face was on all the papers with my name misspelled as John Rupert. It was a tough period, and I was not prepared for it.

I was lucky that I wasn't charged. The entire drug unit hated me. I didn't blame them. I would have hated me, too. I had destroyed four months' worth of investigation.

I stared at the piece of paper lying in front of me. I closed my eyes and opened them, hoping that the words Central Field Command Drug Squad might morph into . . . the Prime Minister's Office.

"Sir," I said, my eyes pleading. "Please, tell me this is a joke."

"Come on, Jon. It happened almost a year ago. It's all forgotten."

"Forgotten?" I snapped. "These guys are professionals. They never forget." I started talking to myself. "Maybe it's a trick. Yes . . . yes . . . it's a trick to get back at me. I screwed them and now they're going to screw me." Then it occurred to me. "I'm not qualified."

Motley opened a drawer and pulled out a manila folder. "According to your file, you kind of are."

My face said: how?

"You worked in the Guelph Police Services?"

"Yes."

"And according to this you worked in Drugs and Intelligence."

Uh? "Sorry, what was that you said?"

"The file we received from Guelph Police Services said you worked in Drugs and Intelligence."

"It does?" I whispered.

"Yes."

It must be a clerical error. Someone had made a mistake.

Was it that assistant who had dozens of trolls on her desk? Was she getting back at me for calling her trolls miniature freaks of nature? They were tiny people who had black eyes and permanent smiles on their faces.

"Actually, Sir . . ." I started.

"The information provided by them assisted greatly in your transfer over here."

"It did?"

"Is something wrong?"

"No, no, no," I waved my finger. "That information is absolutely, positively, without a doubt . . . information."

Something occurred to me. "I can't be in the squad. I'm not even a constable."

"Under certain situations, exceptions can be made. I received the letter from Detective Sergeant Andrew Aldrich and the Deputy Chief of Central Field Command backed it up. Important people, Jon."

"What if I wrote to the Chief," I said. "She'll do something."

"You don't want to involve her, Jon. I don't think she'll override the Deputy Chief's authority."

Motley stood and walked up beside me; with his voice low, soothing, fatherly, he said, "Jon, you can always come back if you screw up, you know that."

I could always come back. Tears welled up in my eyes, "Yes, I know."

After collecting myself, I said, "When do I leave?"

"Now," he said. "You're to be briefed at eleven at the Central Command Headquarters."

I took a deep breath. "I won't let you down, Sir."

"I know," he said. "And Jon, you better go plain."

Without my uniform.

I left his office and headed out. Roberta saw me.

"So, what happened?" she said, a worried look over her face. "I think everyone heard you scream."

"I'm going to be in the drug unit," I said.

"Oh, my . . ." she covered her mouth. "But . . ."

I held up my hand. "But there are always exceptions."

"When do you—"

"Right now."

She got up, went around her desk, and hugged me. "Good luck. Call me if you need me."

Ms. Zee looked out onto the silent street. Every so often a car would drive by. She had counted three in the last ten minutes. The neighbourhood was quiet, which was why she had chosen it as their so-called base. So far they had had no trouble.

Kong was in the room, and Joey was still in the adjacent room. They would not tell him about Armand's death, but he was smart, and when Armand did not return . . .

Joey. It had been a mistake bringing him into the operation. He was supposed to watch Armand. Instead, Armand had played them like fools.

When they met, he had promised so much, a product that would revolutionize the drug business. It was only when he kept asking for more time that she became suspicious. She had the previous batches tested and found that each was missing a component.

She sighed.

This was not going as planned. She knew they had successfully created the drug at Bantam, and she'd been certain they'd have the prototype by now. Different versions were already sent out to potential buyers. But nothing could happen until she had one that was as potent and lethal as they had claimed it would be.

There were so many pressures. She rubbed her temples. So many forces were pushing her in all directions. But if her plan worked, she could control the entire city.

Kong crossed his arms. She understood. He was unhappy about Joey.

"No, Kong," she said, still not looking away from the window. "We cannot kill him."

Kong snorted his disapproval.

"Not just yet. We need someone else who can continue the work."

Two men entered the room. She turned. One was white and the other brown. The white man had limp blond hair, as if he'd just come out of the shower, and a long goatee. He looked like someone who was used to taking orders. The brown man had a flat boxer's nose and earrings in both ears. He looked like someone who would rather spend time with his car than people. "It's done," said the white man.

She had sent them to dispose of Armand's body.

"Where?" she asked.

"Scarborough Bluffs," the white man answered.

"Good."

Another man entered. He was wearing a blue striped business suit; stylish round spectacles were propped up on his nose, and his hair was gelled back.

"Ms. Zee," said Martin, her lawyer and business advisor. "You do remember your meeting today?"

Ms. Zee nodded. "Yes." She turned to the white man. "Hause, you'll be with us and," she turned to the brown man, "Suraj, you'll follow behind."

Kong made a noise.

"Kong," Ms. Zee turned to him. "You'll stay here and watch Joey."

He grunted.

"You *will* behave yourself," she said.

He was not happy.

"When I come back Joey better be in one piece."

5

I looked at my watch and realized I had only forty minutes. I drove back home, changed quickly into a blue shirt, cargo pants, and a brown jacket, and left without saying goodbye to Michael Jordan.

As I was out the door I saw my landlady on the roof.

What the hell?

"Morning," I yelled.

"Hello, Jon," she said, waving.

"What are you doing?"

"Cleaning the gutter, too many dirty leaves is not good. Rain makes problems."

I understood. Leaves were clogging the trough.

"Be careful. You don't want to fall."

"I'll be okay." She smiled.

Damn. Damn. Damn.

My mother always taught me to help others, especially if they are your sixty-one-year-old landlady.

I grabbed the ladder and got on top of the roof.

"Where's David?" I said.

"He's gone to work," she replied.

"You go down," I said pointing.

"No, no. It's okay. I can do it."

"No. I'll clean everything but you don't come up." I felt obligated to do it right then because earlier I had complained about a leaky roof. She climbed down.

I grabbed a plastic bag and gathered all the nearly decomposed leaves. Once I was satisfied the trough was cleared I came down.

"Jon, I can do it," she said.

"You call David next time," I said and left.

I drove straight to the Central Field Command Headquarters. Inside, I was directed to a room.

I gently tapped.

The door swung open and a huge man with spiked hair stood facing me. "You're late," he growled.

"Old lady . . . roof . . . leaves . . ."

"Get in," he said.

The room was bare, with ten or twelve chairs facing a large board. At the front, a man paced impatiently. There were six other people sitting, as if waiting for something . . . or someone.

The man stopped pacing and stood with his chest and shoulders high, like a proud general before his troops. He had blond hair, a thin golden moustache, and an upward pointy nose.

"We can finally begin," he said, looking in my direction.

What a happy start.

I took the nearest seat.

The blond man crossed his hands on his back and began, "I'm Detective Sergeant Andrew Aldrich. Last night I received a call from the chief to lead a new task force. Most of you know that our drug squad is going through a tough period and will not be fully functional until the Royal Canadian Mounted Police completes its investigation. But that does not mean our battle with drugs and narcotics ceases. That is why you were called in to this new task force—to stop this new group that threatens our fine city. You're all here because you've shown interest in fighting drugs . . ."

I looked around. What interest? No one had asked me.

". . . You've shown interest in being part of this unit. While others." He looked in my direction. "Needed to be persuaded."

I was so tempted to give him the middle finger.

Aldrich turned and nodded. The guy with the spiked hair removed a large piece of paper from a yellow file and stuck it on the board.

"Thank you, Detective Garnett," said Aldrich.

Garnett? *Ronald Garnett?* This was going to be exciting. I could see he and I being great friends.

It was a blown-up photo of three men. One was white; the second looked Asian and the third brown. They were standing outside what looked like a dance club.

"What's wrong with this photograph?" Aldrich asked. "Please raise your hands and introduce yourself first."

A hand shot up. "Constable Clara Terries, Community Patrol, 51 Division. The three men in question are dealing drugs," she said.

"Good guess, but not quite," replied Aldrich with a smile.

Another hand shot up. "Constable Michael Barnes, Neighbourhood Crime Unit, 31 Division. They are recruiting."

"Definitely no. "

A third hand shot up. "Detective Carlos Herrera, Street Crime, 41 Division. They belong to a gang."

"Yes, but something else."

I could tell Aldrich was enjoying this.

There were three people left and I was one of them. I had no intention of raising my hand.

Another hand came up. "Detective Simon Nemdharry, Plainclothes, 21 Division. They are looking for potential areas to set up shops."

"That is definitely a possibility, Detective. But not quite what I was looking for."

Aldrich was waiting for me.

His stare was burning into me. I slowly raised my hand. "Jon Rupret, Parking Enforcement, no division. A black guy is missing."

My answer was not very popular with Sergeant Aldrich. "Not even close, Officer Rupert."

Rupert? I exploded, "It's Rupret. R *before* the E."

"Yes, that's what I said." Aldrich's features remained calm. "And the next time address me with *Sir*."

He waited. My beautiful black skin was turning an ugly red.

"Yes, Sir," I said between clenched teeth.

"Good."

My middle finger was itching to introduce itself to Aldrich. Such an introduction at this stage would be damaging to my career. So I controlled myself, and my finger.

Aldrich smiled at the last person, who was sitting behind me. I turned to have a look at him. The man was wearing a brown three-piece suit, had dark, neatly combed hair and a trimmed beard. He looked snobbish to me. Come to think of it, everyone who wears a suit looks snobbish to me, so what do I know.

He responded in an accent I couldn't figure out. "Detective Phillip Beadsworth, Plainclothes and Drugs, 23 Division. The three individuals come from different ethnic affiliated gangs and are now members of this new group."

"Very good, Detective." Aldrich smiled.

Jeez. I could have thought of that.

Aldrich said, "At first glance you wouldn't think they are associated. But they are." He paused. "We are used to dealing with the Colombian Cartels, the Chinese Triads, the Italian Mafia, or the Jamaican Posse—with individuals who associate themselves with a group, most of the time race being the main factor. You were only allowed to join if you were of certain class, certain colour, certain religion, or from a certain country." Aldrich turned to the picture. "This group does not discriminate. We have been able to gather some information on these individuals—but nothing too conclusive, I'm afraid. The gentleman on the far left goes by the name of Hause." Aldrich was referring to the white guy. "He used to belong to a group of skinheads, who, a few years ago, were involved in massive robberies of retail stores along Yonge Street. The second individual." Aldrich was now onto the brown guy. "Goes by several names, some of which are Mandeep, Suraj, and Brown Sugar." Aldrich raised his eyebrows. "Mr. Sugar belonged to a group called Desi Thugz. They primarily sold drugs to high school students in Scarborough. The third individual . . ." Now we were at the Asian guy. ". . . goes by the name of Kong, but we do not have any relevant information on him." Aldrich turned back to us. "My guess would be he worked with the Chinese Triad, but that would only be a guess."

Aldrich nodded to Garnett. Garnett placed another sheet of paper on the board. The paper contained four letters: R.A.C.E.

"Radical Association of Criminal Ethnicities," Aldrich said. "Hence, welcome to this new task force: Operation Anti-R.A.C.E."

Aldrich paused and let everyone digest this new wave of information.

"We believe this group was started right here in Toronto. The organizers are from this city—*your* city. We believe this organization will expand within weeks, even months. It will move to other major cities in Canada. Montreal, Ottawa, Vancouver, all over. It could even expand to the United States. Our mandate is to quickly search, locate, and shut down this group. The pressure is on us. If this group expands there's no telling where it'll go. Right now, this group is small."

A hand shot up. Carlos Herrera. "What does this group deal in?"

"A very good question and I'm glad you asked it," said Aldrich. "Gangs prefer to have a niche in the market and they protect this niche. The Italian Mafia deals in gambling and prostitution; Colombian Cartels: cocaine; Jamaican Posse: crack; Chinese Triads: Heroin. They don't and won't allow anyone to enter their market. When a new group tries to enter their turf, there's a war. Gang wars are part of their business. R.A.C.E. knows and understands this very well. They're not interested in marijuana, crack, cocaine, heroin, Ecstasy or any of the existing drugs. No.

"They're interested in creating their own niche. They want to be the sole providers of a new product. They want this new product to be bigger than Ecstasy. Our sources, which I'll mention shortly, tell us that this new drug will be sold like a pill, similar to Ecstasy. Which means, once manufactured and distributed, the drug will be harder to catch."

Aldrich took a few seconds to collect his thoughts.

This was way too much information for me. I needed a day.

"As you all know, the two major stock-market busts in Canada were Nortel and Bre-X. You take the first letter of Nortel and the last letter of Bre-X and you get N-X, or on the street it might come to be known as Nex." Aldrich picked up a manila folder and retrieved a sheet from it. He glanced at it briefly and then spoke again. "Once swallowed, Nex takes immediate effect. Sources say it explodes inside the human body, similar to how the finances of Nortel and Bre-X did in the stock market. The human nervous system then becomes paralyzed or numb for a short period, maybe seconds, maybe minutes. But for that brief time, the user will feel such relaxation that I cannot possibly describe it without having experienced it myself.

"Such a drug can be compared to a painkiller. But it is not. It's far more dangerous. The sudden shutting of the nervous system can cause heart attacks or seizures. Also, the human system eventually becomes resistant. It takes more and more pills to get that sudden effect. Slowly and gradually the human body begins to lose sensation. The mind and body eventually become anaesthetized, and the habitual users die a slow and horrible death.

"It's like a person who has Lou Gehrig's disease, Alzheimer's, and multiple sclerosis all at once."

I listened attentively. This was serious. What the hell was I doing here?

A hand shot up. Clara Terries. "Who are the target users?" she asked.

"Everyone," answered Aldrich, as if he was proud of this knowledge. "Anyone can use it to cope with stress," Aldrich continued. "A CEO, who is putting in seventy hours a week, stressed out; he might take a pill. A single mother, unable to handle three children and two jobs, might take one. Teenagers who just want to experiment might take a few and in doing so get addicted. Movie stars, athletes, singers, anyone might be enticed to use it."

"How do you know all this?" asked Simon Nemdharry.

Aldrich crossed his hands behind his back. "One of our undercover officers stumbled upon R.A.C.E. At that time the drug squad was maximized in its resources. New investigations were not a priority. But this undercover officer was resilient. He felt that this new discovery could pose a real threat. I authorized the officer to investigate. In a span of four months he began to uncover the inner workings of R.A.C.E. They were working on something big. Nex."

With a hand raised, Simon Nemdharry said, "Will the undercover officer brief us?"

"No. There will be no direct contact with the officer," replied Aldrich.

Simon Nemdharry waited. We all waited for an explanation.

Aldrich said, "We will continue our investigation. I know and understand that most of you, except for Detective Beadsworth, are not familiar with drugs and narcotics and, if it were up to me I would wait until the probe into the drug squad was completed before establishing this unit. But, time is not on our side. We believe R.A.C.E. will bring out Nex into the market within the next few weeks. Once out it'll be very difficult to control. The chief has requested that this task force be set up and officers outside of the drug squad be brought in.

"Two weeks ago we received information that prototypes of Nex were produced in the basement of a house in Mississauga. Officers were sent in but found nothing. R.A.C.E. had moved their laboratory. We believe they are relocating every few weeks until they have a fully potent and effective product.

"With the internal probe filling the front pages of the newspapers, we cannot let any information regarding this team be known to the public. You are not to contact any officers of the drug squad regarding this unit. This is a classified investigation. You are to report directly to me. Detective Garnett will be assisting me during the investigation and in certain situations he'll be accompanying you."

He looked at the clock and then at us. We were all beat. Or, at least I was.

"You're dismissed for lunch. We'll go over certain things afterward."

I looked at my watch. It was after twelve. My stomach was making ghoulish noises.

Everyone prepared to leave.

"Before you go, pick up these at the front," Garnett said, holding papers in the air. "These forms state that you agree to be part of this new unit. Human resources has requested that they be filled out. A technicality. Bring them back after lunch."

They all lined up. I waited till the end. I went up and Garnett's face turned foul. I slowly picked up the forms. He was staring at my every move.

"Officer Rupert," I heard Aldrich say.

I faced him. *It's Rupret, you blonde pompous jackass.*

"Sergeant Motley spoke highly of you," Aldrich said.

I bet he did.

"I like you," Aldrich said.

I didn't like the sound of that.

"You're young."

Uh?

"Imaginative."

I narrowed my eyes, trying to fully understand what was coming out of his mouth.

"Creative."

Where was he going with this?

"Bold."

He had lost me.

"You possess the qualities this unit requires."

Oh, *right.* Why didn't you just say that?

"That is why you were chosen. Contrary to what Detective Garnett believes," Garnett turned his head away, "I think you did the right thing. You showed initiative. Your instincts told you something wasn't right and you acted. Foolish—procedures are procedures—but gutsy. There will be a lot demanded of you here and I hope you are prepared for it."

I nodded, not sure what to say, and left. I went out into the hall and saw the other members gathered together.

Barnes said, "Come join us for lunch."

"Um . . . I have to make an urgent phone call," I said

"Okay. We'll be in the cafeteria," he replied.

With the forms clutched in my hand I headed to the washroom. I splashed my face with cold water and took a deep breath. This was not happening to me.

6

They were in a white Lincoln with Hause driving and Martin and Ms. Zee in the back. A few cars behind, Suraj was following in his red Sundance.

"It was difficult to arrange this," said Martin in his business tone. "He is very anxious."

Ms. Zee stared out into the passing streets.

"It wasn't wise to get rid of Armand," he said.

"He was playing with us," she said.

"Who will continue the work?"

"We'll find someone."

"Ms. Zee, we've built three samples, and each time we have failed. It's bad business when you don't deliver on your promises."

"This is different," she said.

"No, it's not. Business is business. Our associates want to make money. We want to make money."

She understood, of course, but had no answer. "How many employees do we have?" she said, to change the subject.

"Almost twenty. I've personally screened each and every one of them. Not one has a criminal record. I've registered companies under different aliases and have rented several stores all over the Greater Toronto Area. This will keep the police busy if they are ever onto us. But." He raised an eyebrow and smiled. "We know that won't happen, thanks to our friend inside the force. And they are too busy clearing up the mess of the drug squad."

"Yes, by then our product will be everywhere. Are the machines in place for mass manufacturing?"

"They will be in a few days. All we need are the ingredients."

"We'll have them soon." She was certain. It was a matter of finding and persuading the right person. She was also certain that she was the boss. She was the one who was financing this venture and she was the one who had employed Armand.

"We're here," Hause said.

The Lincoln turned left into a narrow street inside Regent Park. There are twenty-five hundred units in Regent Park and all are social housing.

They parked and got out. A small group of children was playing games: skip-the-rope, hopscotch, marbles—kids' games. They moved past the children, Martin in front, Ms. Zee in the middle, followed by Hause, who kept his eyes on the area like a bodyguard. They went inside a building.

On the second floor they knocked and a woman answered the door. She got out, locked her apartment, and took them down to the laundry room. The worn-out door was shut. She tapped twice and a skinny black man answered it, suspiciously eyeing the people behind the woman. He nodded. They were allowed to enter. The woman left.

One man was standing beside the washers. He wore an expensive fur coat.

"Marcus," Ms. Zee said.

"I've been waiting," the fur-coat-man responded.

"The laundry room," she said. "How ingenious. Doesn't anyone here wash their clothes?"

"Do you have it?" asked Marcus.

"Not yet," she answered.

"Figures."

"Why, because I'm a woman?"

"Hey, no," Marcus began to explain. "All I'm saying is that if I had to get it done, it would have been done by now."

"It will be done."

"You could . . ." he paused, dramatically scratching his chin.

"Give you the formula," she said, knowing what he was about to say next.

"No. Sell me the formula. If this thing does what you say, then I'll buy it from you."

"It's still not complete," she said. She knew these people. They never spoke straight.

"Yes, but it has potential."

She listened and then said, "No."

"You haven't even heard my offer."

"No."

"If you hear me out I promise you'll be interested."

"No."

"Then why don't we talk about how we are going to do business together? Partner to partner."

"We're not partners, yet."

"Yes, but you need me more than I need you," he smiled. "I'm already well off with my current venture." He meant selling drugs to the innocent children of Regent Park.

She said, "When the product is ready the demand will be too much for even your *little* venture."

He tried to read her. If this product was going to be bigger than Ecstasy then he better play his cards well. "No matter," he shook his head. "Let's say fifty-fifty."

"No."

"That's reasonable. Considering I'm putting blind faith into the product."

"Seventy-thirty. Considering I'm paying the start-up costs."

"All right. But negotiable in the future, of course."

"Of course." She didn't really care for the future. If the product spread as it was expected to then she wouldn't need him.

"Agreed. Once you provide me the goods I'll have my boys get to work."

When Ms. Zee was gone, Marcus smiled. Once he had the product he'd have some of his experts analyze it and make another brand—*his* brand, which would mean one-hundred per cent profit for him. In the market of illegal goods there were no such things as patents.

I left the Central Field Command Headquarters and went to my car. I needed to get away. I needed to drive.

Behind the wheel I relaxed. This is what I'd done for the last year-and-a-half. Drive and give tickets.

I drove along Eglinton.

I was born in Nigeria, in Benin City. I was the only child, and as my mom told me, she was in labour for eighteen hours before I arrived.

We moved to Canada when I was five. My mom worked dead-end jobs while my father went back to his studies. He soon became a lawyer. Life was good. After he left us life became tough.

But my mom was tougher.

She and I moved to a nice neighbourhood, where she became a grade-school teacher, and I went to some of the finest schools.

My childhood was strict. I was not allowed to get an earring like my friends. I was not allowed to listen to rap music or anything with explicit lyrics. I was always told to behave. My childhood was firm, but I don't blame my mom. After Father left us, she became extra protective of me, trying to shield me from everything. She said I was the only family she had, and she was right.

My mom always wanted me to grow up and get a job where I could wear a tie and people would respect me. She wanted me to be someplace safe. Instead, I joined the force. I'd already spent a year-and-a half as a PEO and I didn't know how many years I'd spend as a narcotics officer before I could tell . . . my mind trailed off.

I should quit and do what my mom always wanted me to do. I could get used to wearing a tie. Quitting seemed right.

I picked up something to snack on and drove back to headquarters.

Inside the meeting room I found Garnett standing in the front. "Your forms," he said.

"Not filling them out," I said.

He looked at me as if I had just told him off.

"Why not?" he said.

"Personal reasons," I said. I wasn't going take his abuse. It no longer mattered what he thought. I was going to quit.

He wasn't happy with my answer. But I wasn't going to back down. He smirked, the kind of smirk that said *You'll be sorry*.

I went back to my chair and sat down.

A few minutes later Sergeant Aldrich entered the room. Garnett whispered something to him and he turned to me. "Officer Rupert, can I have a word with you?"

We went out into the hall.

"I've just been made aware," he started, "that you haven't filled out your forms."

"That's right," I said.

Aldrich's features did not change. "Why is that?"

"I'm quitting."

"Operation Anti-R.A.C.E., you mean?"

"Yes."

"You do realize that if you quit you will not be allowed to go back to Parking Enforcement. I assure you of that."

That was a threat. But I didn't care.

"I'm quitting the force all together."

I saw a slight jerk under his eyelid. For a brief second I had taken him off guard. But the next second he was calm and collected again. He raised one eyebrow.

"There isn't anything I can do to change your mind?"

"No."

He went silent for a minute and then I saw what looked like a smile. "What would you say if I told you after this operation I could put in a good word for you in the intelligence unit."

Damn.

I'd always wanted to join that unit: Detective Jon Rupret, Intelligence. I liked the sound.

"You know I want to be part of that unit?" I said.

"Officer Rupert, it's my job to know everything."

I felt overwhelmed. There could be a possibility for me to achieve something. Maybe this wouldn't be such a waste. Plus, I hadn't seriously thought about what I was going to do next.

I looked at him hard.

"My recommendations are always approved," he said, as if he knew what I was thinking.

“Under one condition,” I said.

“Yes?”

“It’s Rupret. R before E.”

“Fine, Officer Rupret.”

“Thank you, Sir.”

I was beginning to like him. Maybe, after all this was done, we could go fishing together. First, I’d have had to learn how to fish.

“Good. You have precisely three minutes to fill in those forms and hand them to Detective Garnett.”

No. I was wrong. I really didn’t like him.

I scribbled onto the forms and handed them to Garnett. Garnett gave me an *I thought so* smile.

Aldrich was back at the front. “Now that we have everyone on board. Your main objective: find where Nex is being produced. There is a clandestine laboratory producing this lethal drug. We need to find and destroy it. Constable Terries, Constable Barnes and Officer Rupret, you’ll be partnered with a senior member of the unit. They have been provided with leads and they will guide you.

“Constable Terries, you’ll be with Detective Nemdharry. Constable Barnes, your partner will be Detective Herrera. Officer Rupret, you will be with Detective Beadsworth.”

Great. Mr. Uptight.

I turned and looked at him. He didn’t look back. He was going over a file.

“You’re dismissed. Keep me posted.”

7

Everyone immediately stood up and began to leave the room. I got up and went over to my new partner.

"Hi, I'm Jon Rupret, R before E," I said.

The man did not look up, nor did he respond. He continued going over the file. He was carefully going over each page. I looked around the room and it was empty.

I coughed, hoping to get his attention. I did not.

I looked at the file and on top of it was the name: Jonathon S. Rupret.

He was reading a file on me.

He closed the file, got up, and looked at me.

With an arm extended he said, "Detective Phillip Beadsworth."

I shook his hand, "Officer Jon Rupret—"

"—R before the E. I heard you the first time," he replied in an accent I still couldn't figure out. It was a mixture of British and American.

"Follow me, Officer Rupret," he said leaving the room.

"You can call me Jon," I said, following behind.

"I suppose you'd like to call me Phil," he said and stopped.

"Yes," I said. "Just to be informal, y'know."

"Don't. It's Detective Beadsworth." He pulled out his cellphone and dialed a number. "Excuse me for a minute." He went to the end of the hall and spoke for maybe two minutes. He came back and we moved to the elevators.

We went down.

"Where we going?" I asked.

"For a drive," he said.

Outside we walked to a blue GM station wagon.

"We can take my car," I said.

"When *you* drive we take your car."

We eased out of the parking lot and into the main road. I scanned the interior of the GM. The dashboard was covered with little colourful stickers. I looked down; my feet were stepping on a Winnie-the-Pooh mat. I looked up and a Mickey Mouse figurine hung from the rear-view mirror. I casually looked back and my mouth fell open. There was a baby seat.

"So, you got kids?" I said, turning to him.

"Excellent observation, officer," he said.

"How many?"

"Two."

"Wow, two kids," I said. "I have one myself."

"No, you don't," he said, turning the GM left and into another street.

"How do you know that?" I said, offended.

"I read your file."

"How come you get a file on me and I don't on you?"

"You're under me."

I blew my top. "I'm not under you. I'm your partner."

"You're my responsibility."

"I'm no one's responsibility," I said. "The last thing you want is to take responsibility for me. You could get into serious trouble for that. "

"Thank you for the information," he said.

"You're welcome."

The Lincoln was moving one hundred miles per hour on Highway 401 when Martin's phone rang.

"Yes," he said. He pulled out a pad from his briefcase and began making notes. As he wrote, he laughed harder and harder.

"What's so funny?" asked Ms. Zee.

He hung up. "The police are on to us."

She wasn't smiling.

"Your informant has told me that they've established a new unit to locate and stop us."

"What was so funny about that?" she said.

"They call this new force Operation Anti-R.A.C.E."

She didn't understand.

"They call us R.A.C.E. Radical Association of Criminal Ethnicities."

This made her laugh. "The police always need unusual acronyms to do their job."

"But that's not all. They've also made up a name for our product."

"A name?"

"Yes. Nex."

"Nex?"

"Yes, something to do with the stock market." He laughed.

"Nex." She thought about it. "I like it. Nex it is, then."

I stared out the window. After a short while the station wagon began to slow down and I realized where we were.

"Regent Park?" I said, turning to him.

"You've never been here?" he said.

"Um . . . of course I've been here. Many times. I live here, man. This is my 'hood." I lowered myself in my seat.

Regent Park is one of the poorest areas in the city and maybe in the province. Poverty equals crime and Regent Park is known for that. With narrow alleys and pathways leading in and out, it is designed for drug dealers. They consider it their territory. Shootings are common in this neighbourhood. What were we doing here?

Beadsworth circled and parked.

"Do you want to stay in the car?" he asked.

Stay out here? You nuts?

"I think it'll probably be safer if I cover your back," I said.

From the trunk, Beadsworth pulled out a plastic bag.

We walked up to a building. A group of teenagers looked across at us. This sent a shiver up my back. We went inside and up the stairs to the third floor.

Beadsworth knocked on a door. The door slowly inched open and a black boy peered through.

"How are you, Theo?" Beadsworth said.

Right away Theo opened the door. Beadsworth handed him the plastic bag. We went in.

"Who is it?" came another voice farther way. A man in his early twenties, wearing a white undershirt, black pants and no shoes appeared down the hall.

"Voshon, how are you doing?" Beadsworth said.

"Good," replied Voshon, smiling. "Come in."

We went down the hall and into the living room. There was a sofa in the middle, an old table to one side and an even older TV with knobs in the corner.

Theo came up behind me holding the empty plastic bag and a pair of Reebok shoes. His eyes were glowing.

"Voshon," he said. "Can I wear 'em?"

"Yeah, sure," replied his older brother. "But go watch the window."

Theo quickly laced up the shoes and went to the window.

Voshon leaned closer. "Thanks, he'd been asking for a pair for a long time."

"Don't mention it," said Beadsworth. "This is Officer Jon Rupret," he introduced me. I shook Voshon's hand.

"Can I get you anything?" Voshon asked.

"No," replied Beadsworth, looking in my direction. "We ate on our way here."

"Have a seat," he said, dusting whatever dirt might be on the sofa.

We sat down. Voshon grabbed a chair opposite us.

"How's college?" Beadsworth inquired.

"Good."

"And work?"

"Good. I do most of my reading after I make my rounds."

"Good," said Beadsworth. He paused and then spoke again, "Do you have any information for us?"

"There's this is one guy you can talk to," Voshon said. "I think his name is Max Vernon or Vernon Max but he goes by the name of DJ Krash, with a K."

"Where can we find this Mr. Krash?" Beadsworth asked.

"He's a DJ at the club House of Jam. He plays there on Fridays."

I then remembered the picture Garnett had put up in the front. The three guys were standing outside a club—was it the House of Jam?

"So you think he might be involved in this?" I said.

"I didn't say he was involved, only that he might have some information," Voshon said.

"How do you know?" I said.

"I worked some night shifts there and I heard some stuff, you know."

Beadsworth got up. "Thank you, Voshon. Anything you hear, you let me know."

"Sure."

We walked down the stairs and were out again. Beadsworth looked up and waved. Theo waved back and disappeared from the window.

"What was he doing?" I asked.

"Watching."

"Watching what?"

"The car."

"Why?"

"So nobody vandalizes it." He looked at me as if I were dumb and stupid.

I quietly got in the car.

When we were out of Regent Park I asked, "What's the story with Voshon?"

"A year ago we caught him stealing groceries from a variety store," Beadsworth said.

"Groceries?"

"Yes. He said his younger brother was hungry and he didn't have any money. Voshon's a good kid, just in a bad environment. So we acquired him a job as a security guard."

"A thief becomes a security guard. That's a first," I said.

"The security firm is owned and run by a retired police officer. Most of the people who work for him are young offenders looking for a second chance."

"So when Voshon said he worked night shifts at the club he meant security work?"

"Voshon's not into drugs. The only thing he cares about is his brother."

This Voshon guy wasn't all that bad. Come to think of it, Beadsworth didn't look like a bad guy, either.

"I think we got off on the wrong foot," I shrugged.

"Don't mention it, officer."

"But I do think I should be able get to know you, y'know. You already know a lot about me."

"What would you like to know?" he asked.

"Where you from?"

"England."

"That explains your accent. But I've watched a lot of British soap operas and you don't sound anything like them."

"I was born there. But I spent most of my adolescence in the United States."

"So you're married with kids?" I said.

"Yes." Beadsworth was about to say more when his cell phone rang. "Excuse me," he said. "Detective Phillip Beadsworth . . ." He listened. "Yes, Dear . . . where is he now . . . is he okay . . . I'll be right over."

He hung up and continued driving. I could tell he was thinking.

"Why don't you drop me off right here," I said.

He looked at me.

"Yeah," I said. "Headquarters is the other way. Don't worry. Drop me off and go, do whatever you have to do."

For the first time he looked at me as if there was more to me than met the eye.

"Are you certain?" he finally said.

"Yeah. Go. Don't worry. I'll call a taxi."

"When I'm done, I'll call you."

He dropped me off and drove away. I looked around; this was unfamiliar territory. I pulled out my cell phone, ready to dial for a cab when I saw one come to a halt across the street. I squinted. It was orange and navy green. The cab plate number looked familiar and the driver did too. I rushed over.

A guy was approaching the vehicle when I intercepted.

"Sorry, Sir," I said, catching my breath. "Police business." I waved my badge and got in.

"Police headquarters. Fast," I ordered the driver in a loud voice. He complied and put his foot on the pedal.

Once the guy was out of sight the driver slowed.

"You always do that," said the driver in a slight accent. "He called for the taxi."

"Hey, Mahmud," I said, shocked. "I didn't recognize you."

"Yeah, sure," replied Mahmud Hanif.

Mahmud always wore a Blue Jays baseball cap, even though he's not a baseball fan, and below that a plaid shirt and a sports jacket. He once tried to explain to me the similarities between baseball and cricket. Not sure what they were because I don't know anything about cricket or baseball, for that matter. He's from Pakistan and he came to our fine land almost three years ago with his wife and four children. Back in his country he was a qualified engineer, but once he arrived here, his experience and education were thrown out the window. He tried desperately to secure a job—any job—in his field, but it always came down to his zero Canadian experience. With a large family, going back to school was not an option. So he started driving a taxi to put roti, so to speak, on the table.

"Mahmud," I said. "How come I always end up meeting you?"

There are five million people in the Greater Toronto Area and somehow *I* always managed to run into people I knew.

Maybe it was my dashing good looks and sharp intellect—gravitating people toward me. Or maybe it was coincidences that only happened to me. That was the story of my life. Jon Rupret, man of infinite probabilities.

"So where *is* your car? Towed again?" Mahmud said smiling.

"I am ashamed, Mahmud, that you would say that," I leaned over to the front seat.

"It happened before. Many, many, many times," he said. "So what are you really doing with no car?" Mahmud asked.

"I'm glad you asked," I said. "I'm on a case. A covert operation."

"Covert?"

"Secret, top secret, to be precise. What I tell you must never leave this vehicle."

"Sure," he said, humouring me.

"I'm serious. I'm not supposed to tell anyone. Even some people I work with."

"Then why tell me?"

"You know they have doctor-and-patient relationship? Lawyer-and-client relationship?"

"Yes."

"You and I have passenger-and-taxi-driver relationship."

"Yes, that's very important."

"So with our special relationship I can trust you. I know what I tell you will never leave this taxi."

"You are correct."

"I'm on a mission between good and evil."

"Which side are you on?" he said. Then started to laugh.

"Very funny," I said, slightly hurt. "Keep driving. No more of those smart-ass remarks or else our special relationship ends."

“Sorry,” he said, still smiling.

“Like I was saying. There’s this new evil approaching our city and only *one man* can stop it—”

“—Sorry, I’m too busy driving taxi. Don’t have time.” Then he exploded.

“That’s it, Mahmud, our relationship ends right here.”

That didn’t bother him. He continued laughing.

“I’m warning you. I’ll find a new taxi driver. Someone who can appreciate our special relationship.”

“No, no. I’m sorry. Special relationship is very important.”

I sat back, crossing my arms. “Man, I was going to tell you everything. Now I’m not.” I pouted.

“No time. We are here,” he said looking at me through the rear-view mirror.

“So how much do I owe you?” I put my hand into my pocket.

“Forgot to turn on meter. Maybe next time,” he said.

Mahmud never charged me fare.

It happened eight months ago while I was driving through my usual route. I saw a taxi parked in front of a park with no driver in it. Parking around the park was not allowed. When I approached the vehicle, thinking I might get a tow, I heard a noise coming from the trunk. I pried it open and found the driver in bad shape. His was throat slashed, his palms bleeding, and he’d been stabbed in several places. I rushed Mahmud to the hospital. I guess I saved his life.

“You know you have to stop doing this,” I said.

“I forgot to turn on meter,” he repeated.

“I saved your life because it was my duty. If you keep doing this it could be seen as bribery; that’s illegal in this country, you know.”

“Next time I will turn on meter,” he smiled.

I patted him on the shoulder and smiled. "Thanks, Buddy," I said, and got out.

8

Ms. Zee came back to find Joey in one piece. "Good, Kong, you behaved yourself," she said, walking past him.

Kong didn't smile. His features stayed the same: empty and devoid of any emotion.

"Ms. Zee," said Martin. "We are still missing a chemist."

"I have already solved that problem."

"How?"

"Armand worked for Bantam Pharmaceuticals before he was fired, right? At Bantam, Armand worked in a team. He said there were others who influenced the design of the painkiller. Like him, some were also let go. We find these people and persuade them to continue our research."

Martin thought about this. If Ms. Zee had an idea she rarely went against it. "How do you suggest we do that?"

She turned to Kong. "With influence."

There was renewed energy in Kong's eyes.

After having retrieved my car from Central Command Headquarters I drove back to Parking Enforcement Headquarters. I found Sergeant Motley in his office.

He was glad to see me. "Jon, how did it go?"

"Good, I guess," I said. "Sir, I have an important question to ask you?"

“Yes, go ahead.”

“Can I still write parking tickets?”

“Um . . . No.”

“Not even part-time?”

“No.”

“On weekends?”

“No. Jon, what is really on your mind?” he said.

Motley could always sense when something was bothering me.

“Do you know Phillip Beadsworth?”

“No, I can’t say I do. Why?”

“He’s my new partner.”

“You have a partner?” he asked, shocked.

“I’m not too proud of it. I don’t tell many people.”

“Of course not,” he said.

“How about Andrew Aldrich?” I asked.

Motley’s brow furrowed. “I met him once at a charity event. Good man. Believes in authority. He doesn’t like those who disobey him. There was something about him and the drug squad but I can’t remember what that was all about. How are you two getting along?”

“Great,” I said. “I’m like a son to him.”

Motley didn’t believe me.

“What about Ronald Garnett?” I then asked.

“That name sounds familiar,” Motley said searching. Then his eyes lit up and his face went pale. “Jon, of course. I’m so sorry.”

I raised my hand up. “That’s all right. He and I will work something out.” It was more like he’d work me into a pulp.

“Who’s taken over my shift?” I asked.

“Calvert.”

"George Calvert?" I exhaled. "That man is no good. He'll mess up all my clientele."

The telephone rang and Motley looked at me.

"Have you heard of a group called R.A.C.E.?" I asked.

He shook his head.

I thanked him and let him answer the phone.

I didn't know what else to do, so I went home. I turned on the TV and flopped on the couch. I flipped through the channels. Flip. Soap opera. Flip. Crappy show. Flip. Soap opera. Flip. Soap opera. Flip. Weather channel: chance of everything. Flip. Flip. Flip. Shopping channel: a butt sculpture was on sale. I made a mental note of the item number. Flip. Reruns. Flip. Soap opera. Flip. Sports: nothing good on, only figure skating. Flip. Cartoons: seen this episode but will watch it again.

In the middle of the episode where the anvil was falling on the helpless coyote I fell asleep.

My cell phone rang.

I opened my eyes and checked the time. It was after 6:30 p.m. "Jon Rupret," I answered.

"Officer Rupret." It was Beadsworth. "Am I disturbing you?"

I lowered the volume. "No, driving my car."

"I thought I heard the television."

"No. I'm in my car. It's probably noise from outside. Let me roll up my windows." I paused. "Yeah, now that's better. Everything okay?"

"Noel, my son, broke his arm during a soccer game. He'll be all right. Thank you."

"Good." I was actually glad to hear from him.

"Where are you right now?"

"Um . . . sorry?"

"What part of the city are you in right now?" He meant where I was driving.

"I'm almost near my house." That was roughly the truth.

"You live on Gerrard Street. Correct?"

"Yes . . ."

"I'll be there in a short time."

"Where you coming from?" I asked.

"Forest Hill." He hung up.

Forest Hill? *Didn't the rich live there?*

I shook my head and quickly washed up.

The doorbell rang and I rushed down to the main floor. I took Beadsworth upstairs to my apartment.

"Hi, Mike," I said, passing Michael Jordan, but then stopped.

Beadsworth looked at me oddly.

"It's a family tradition," I began. "Never mind."

I offered him something to drink but he declined.

"Do you live alone?" he asked.

"For now," I said, as if I was in a serious relationship.

Beadsworth didn't take a seat. "On my way I made a search of Max Vernon and Vernon Max through CPIC and it came up empty."

The Canadian Police Information Centre is a database used by the police, corrections and immigration officials, and the Royal Canadian Mounted Police, to track dangerous criminals. As a PEO, I had used CPIC to track stolen vehicles. The problem with CPIC is that it does not record summary offences—minor crimes that range from fines to six months in jail, crimes that do not require fingerprinting or mug shots.

"This guy is clean," I said.

"Not quite," Beadsworth said. "I then did a search on the Criminal Information Processing System, alternating between the two sets of names. I managed a hit. Max Vernon had a collision on Highway 427 in 1999. From there I was able to acquire his address."

"So we go and pay him a visit," I said.

"Tomorrow. Right now we have to meet Detective Nemdharry and Constable Terries."

We were rushing down the stairs when my landlady popped her head out her door.

I stopped and introduced her to my new partner. Living alone and having no alarm system, she was my only security. If an unknown person ever came into our building I had instructed her to call the police. She was my first and last line of defence against would-be thieves and robbers. My partner gave a small courteous bow. She smiled back.

We drove to Scarborough and parked in the back of a coffee shop. We found Nemdharry and Terries sitting near the front windows.

Nemdharry spoke first. "Thanks for coming," he said.

We sat opposite them.

Terries smiled—at me—and I smiled back.

"Phil," Nemdharry started. "I think we're on to something."

Nemdharry's grayish hair was gelled back, and his light brown skin was smooth and without a blemish. He looked much younger than his age, around Beadsworth's.

He looked out the window. There was a huge white building across from the coffee shop. It had a wide sign that read: OFFICE SPACE FOR LEASE.

“I think there’s something going on in there,” Nemdharry said. “A tip from our informant gave this address. The owner of the coffee shop says he’s seen some peculiar people come in. Not too friendly. Couple of days ago he saw a moving van in front of the building. I spoke to the company that manages the building and they say it’s an export company.”

“What do they export?” Beadsworth asked.

“Clothes.”

“To where?”

“Southeast Asia,” Nemdharry said.

“What’s the name of the company?”

“LLPM Imports & Exports.”

“What does LLPM stand for?”

“Don’t know.”

I caught Terries staring at me. Her cheeks flushed. I turned back to Nemdharry as if it happened all the time.

“You think it could be R.A.C.E.?” Beadsworth asked.

Terries spoke. “I paid the company a visit,” she said. “I told them I was looking for some cheap space to rent. I was willing to share space with someone, maybe a quarter of the portion. The receptionist was very polite but said they needed all the space.” As Terries spoke I realized I was staring at her. Her long hair slid down her back, her tiny nose moved up and down while she spoke, her eyes, full of excitement . . . I blinked and then blinked again . . . *focus, Jon* . . . She was saying, “The floor space is huge—about two thousand square feet. But there’s a large divider in the middle.”

“How do they operate?” Beadsworth said.

“They purchase used clothes in bulk from places like the Goodwill and the Salvation Army and they sell it to countries like Bangladesh, Sri Lanka, and Indonesia.”

That didn't make sense so I interrupted. "Don't we import clothes from these countries because it's cheaper to produce there?"

"That's what doesn't make sense," she said with admiration.

I felt smart.

"What could be behind the divider?" Beadsworth asked.

Terries replied, "It could be a production lab for Nex."

We all thought about it.

"Can't be a clandestine lab," Nemdharry said. "Too risky."

"Too many people," Beadsworth concurred.

"Should we go in?" Nemdharry said.

Beadsworth shook his head, "Let's not jump the gun. It could be something or it could be nothing."

He walked out of Mount Sinai Hospital with a heavy bandage wrapped around his head. He was well over six-feet-four and close to three hundred pounds. He made his way to the parking lot. With his fat fingers he rummaged through his pockets searching for the keys. He pulled out the set, but being on medication he was unsteady and uncoordinated. The keys fell to the ground.

He cursed.

Huffing and puffing, he knelt down on one knee and retrieved them.

"Mr. Burrows," said a voice from behind.

He turned.

A man in a nice suit stood holding a briefcase. "My name is Martin. My last name is not important, but I am a representative and business advisor to someone who is interested in you."

Ed Burrows was not interested in anyone right now. He was getting a massive headache and he wanted to go home and sleep. "Buzz off," he said.

"Sir, if you hear me out I promise you'll be interested in what I have to say."

"I said buzz off." Burrows was on his feet now. He was gigantic but that didn't bother Martin. Someone sitting in a car not far away was much bigger and more menacing than Burrows.

"You used to work for Bantam Pharmaceuticals."

"Those rat bastards," Burrows cursed.

"You were working on a painkiller, model P147, until your unfortunate departure."

"I got fired. Plain as that."

"Yes, we're interested in what you know about this painkiller."

"It was months ago," he said, finding the right key. "Whatever I worked on, Bantam owns it."

"We have the design."

He stopped. "You're . . ." His eyes narrowed. "You're not supposed to have that."

"We do and we need you to work on it."

"You're not from Bantam, are you?"

"No."

"Then what you want me to do is illegal?" Burrows scratched the growth of hair under his chin.

"That's right."

"No, thank you. I've got my own troubles."

"Yes, we know. What do you say to ten thousand?"

"Dollars?"

"Yes. That would clear up your immediate troubles, no?"

Burrows touched the heavy bandage above his eye. "You know?"

"Of course. You do what we say and don't ask any questions and we assist you in alleviating your troubles."

Burrows looked around the parking lot. It was empty. "Is this some kind of prank? Am I on some reality TV show?"

"Not quite."

He eyed Martin hard. "You said I won't have any more problems?"

"None whatsoever, If you do as we say."

Burrows nodded. "Okay. I'm not doing anything anyways."

Martin gave a signal and a white Lincoln drove up with Hause at the wheel. Kong and Suraj emerged from the vehicle.

"What about my car?" Burrows asked.

"We'll park it at your home."

Burrows reluctantly handed over the keys to Suraj who immediately went to work. "Mr. Burrows, get in. You've got a lot to do."

9

Burrows sifted through the pile of paper—reading and glancing at the writing, scribbles and notations. Finally he said, "This is changed a bit from what we were working on at Bantam."

Ms. Zee, sitting across and watching his every move, said, "The chemist made some modifications. Some of the ingredients in our product are . . . not officially permitted."

"Who designed this?" he asked.

"That is not important, only that the product is made."

"It can be made, but I need some time."

"A few days are all we can give."

"About my ten thousand . . ."

"Consider your problem solved. Your debts are no more."

He nodded and went back to the notes. "It is supposed to cause relaxation and numbness. From what I can tell there were several variations of the painkiller made. But . . ." he paused. "Why so many variations when the first painkiller does take effect?"

"It wasn't effective enough," Ms. Zee answered.

"What results are you looking for?"

"Overwhelming."

I convinced Beadsworth to take my car. Compared to his it was not in the best of shape, but it was my turn to drive, so I didn't care.

Beadsworth instructed me to drive to a condominium in the west end called Palace Pier. I had never heard of the place but it sounded pricey.

Palace Pier looked like a five-star hotel. "Are you sure we're at the right place?" I said, getting out of the car.

"I believe so," he said.

"You sure he's a DJ?" I said as we walked up to the main doors.

Everything looked rich and elegant. The carpet I was walking on was worth more than all of my assets combined.

As we moved to the elevators, the security guard eyed us suspiciously. He knew everyone at the building. He didn't stop us and I think it had more to do with Beadsworth than me. Beadsworth was decked out in a fine suit while I was wearing what had smelled cleanest that the morning.

We waited for the elevators. I was still admiring the luxuries of the place.

"Drug money," I whispered to Beadsworth.

Beadsworth said nothing but I could tell he was suspicious too.

We went up to the fourth floor and knocked on the addressed door.

No answer.

We knocked harder.

No answer.

I banged on the door with my fists. "Yo! Grilled fish delivery. Open up."

Beadsworth shot me a look, "Grilled fish?"

I shrugged. "I'm making it up."

"Hold on!" we heard a voice from behind the door.

"See," I said to Beadsworth.

Two seconds later the door eased open.

DJ Krash, or someone we thought was DJ Krash, was short and skinny, wearing a Nike t-shirt, shorts, and socks. He looked tired, as if someone had just interrupted his sleep.

"I didn't order any grilled fish," he said, but before we could answer, he said, "Oh, you guys must be from the magazine. Am I late?"

We both looked at each other.

Seeing the confused look on our faces, he said, "You're not from *Lyrics & Beat* for my interview?"

Beadsworth flashed his badge and said, "No. Are you Max Vernon?"

"Yeah. What's this all about?" he said.

"You're not in any trouble, Mr. Vernon, at least, not yet. Can we come in?"

"I guess so."

The condominium was spacious, to say the least. Lush carpet, fine leather sofa, a plasma high-definition TV; this place was loaded.

Max Vernon didn't offer us a seat, but we sat.

"We just need some information on a group that we believe frequents the clubs you play in," Beadsworth said.

"I play in many clubs."

"The House of Jam, in particular."

He sat across from us and rubbed his eyes. "Sorry," he said. "I was doing a gig last night. So what do you want to know exactly?"

"Anything and everything."

"I might have heard something or nothing," Vernon said. He was reading us to see what we were after.

"Do you know who owns House of Jam?" Beadsworth asked.

"Sure. My brother-in-law."

"His name?"

Vernon paused. "We're not into anything, if that's what you mean."

"Maybe your brother-in-law is," I said, seeing how defensive he was.

"Hey, Cal has a family," he snapped. Then he lowered his voice. "Listen, he's got two beautiful children. He's not into . . . into . . ."

"Drugs," I said.

"Yeah." Vernon looked away. Then he sighed and said, "Okay. Okay. Cal told me some people came by and they said they are working on this new drug that's going to be the next big thing."

"Next big thing?" I asked.

"Bigger than Ecstasy."

"What did they call this new thing?" Beadsworth said.

"Cal didn't mention a name. He said they wanted to open shop at House of Jam and they were willing to give him a twenty per cent cut."

"Did Cal agree?" I said, testing him.

"No, of course not," he turned to me. "We don't do drugs, man. We make enough money doing our own stuff."

"It's hard to believe that someone would just throw away that kind of money?" Beadsworth said, trying to get more out of him.

"Don't believe me. I don't care. But let me tell you, drugs are bad for business. You have no idea how much business we lose because of Ecstasy. The police always showing up at the club, parents afraid to let their kids go there, fights breaking out, you name it—it happens because of drugs. It's just not worth it. All we want to do is make music and earn some money. That's it."

Some money? I glanced around the condo.

Beadsworth said, "Why didn't Cal call the police?"

"You know, I hate to say it, but drugs and music go hand-in-hand. You expect these types of things. Cal is a smart guy. You don't want a police cruiser parked in the front every time you open your doors, you know what I mean?"

"Did Cal describe these people?"

"Not really, but one of them scared the shit out of him." He leaned over and whispered. "I'll show you something."

He disappeared and came back holding several clear plastic sandwich bags. He placed them on the coffee table. We leaned closer. Each contained different coloured tablets.

"Those guys came down several times. They left these samples with Cal,"Vernon said.

I picked one bag and examined the tablet. There was nothing unusual about it. No distinguishing marks, symbols, or signs on it. To me it looked like a prescription drug your pharmacist would give you.

"The orange ones were the first sample they brought. The green second, and then the brown,"Vernon said.

"When did they bring the brown one?" I said.

"Last week. They said their drug was still in process."

"Why leave samples with your brother-in-law?" Beadsworth inquired.

"They wanted to prove that they had a genuine product, I guess. They were refining it. I think they wanted it to be more addictive."

"Have you tried it?" I asked.

"No way!" he spat. "You crazy? This stuff could be anything."

"Why do you have it?" I asked.

"Cal didn't want to keep it. What if he got raided or something? If the cops found it they'd shut down his business."

"Why didn't *you* get rid of it?"

"Cal wanted me to hold on to the stuff so that if he ever got in trouble I would give it to the cops."

"Have they given samples to owners of other clubs?" Beadsworth asked.

"Probably. But they keep coming back to the House of Jam."

"Why is that?" I said.

He looked at me as if I had just crawled out of a hole. "You've never been to the House of Jam?"

I shrugged no. I looked at Beadsworth, hoping he hadn't either.

"House of Jam is *the* hottest place in Toronto," Vernon said. "Everyone goes there."

I didn't. Should I tell him I don't get out much?

"Celebrities, athletes, business executives, everyone goes there, man. It's the best place to build a diverse clientele." Vernon leaned closer. "Drugs are part of the music biz. It's the one place where people are more open to try new things."

"We're going to take these samples," Beadsworth said, not asking.

"Yeah, sure. Whatever."

"We would also like to visit the club," Beadsworth said.

"Hey, man, no cops," he stood up. "We don't want to be part of this."

"You're already part of it," Beadsworth said. I was amazed at how calm he always was. Is that a British thing?

Vernon scratched his head and made a twisted face.

"If this thing gets into the market, you better believe your business is going to suffer," Beadsworth insisted.

Vernon nodded. "Come down Friday night. I'm playing there," he said. "You can meet Cal there also."

"What's his full name?" Beadsworth asked.

"Calvert Murray."

We got up to leave.

"One more question," I said. Beadsworth looked at me oddly. "How can you afford a place like this?" I asked.

"You mean as a DJ?"

I nodded. "Nice place. Expensive, though."

“I’ll show you something,” he said and disappeared.

Alone, Beadsworth said, “Why did you bring that up?”

“Come on. You wanted to know, too,” I replied.

Vernon came back holding an album. He placed it on the coffee table and began taking out newspaper articles. There were articles from different countries in different languages. “I’m the best DJ in Toronto and Canada for that matter,” Vernon beamed. “I’m also the second best DJ in the world.” He pulled out one article, which was in a language I couldn’t identify. “In the Frankfurt Hip Hop Festival I came in second. I think it was rigged. They wanted the Swedish guy to win from the beginning. His beats weren’t *crisp* enough, you know what I mean?”

I nodded absentmindedly.

“But those German fans were wild. I had a blast.”

“Second best,” I said. “So you can make good money doing this?”

“Yeah, sure. But you gotta first find a new beat. Your unique style, you know. Each time you gotta take it a step further, elevate the music so that no one can do it except you. Master it, you know what I mean?”

I nodded. I had no idea what the man was talking about.

“There are so many freestyle competitions around the world where you can make serious money.”

“Serious money.” I turned to Beadsworth. “That’s what I want to do. Make serious money.”

“You into music?” Vernon asked. “What kind?”

I stumbled. “Um, all kinds. You know, techno, jazz . . . opera.”

“Diverse.” Vernon nodded to himself. “You could probably do it,” he said. “Just come up with a cool name. Experiment and find your own style, man. That’s all.”

"Cool name, eh?" I said. I thought about it. "How about DJ Crimefighter," I turned to Beadsworth and gave a thumbs up.

"How about DJ Bigmouth," he shot back.

"Not bad," Vernon said.

"We have to go," Beadsworth said. "Tell your brother-in-law we'll meet him on Friday."

Back in the elevator, I said, "DJ Bigmouth? I can't believe you would say that. I was serious."

"So was I," he replied.

10

After dropping off the samples at the Toronto Drug Analysis Service Laboratory, or DAS, for short, we drove back to Scarborough where Nemdharry and Terries were observing the export company. We met a block away. Nemdharry was drinking coffee and Terries was in the unmarked cruiser. She stepped out once she saw us.

"Anything?" Beadsworth asked.

"The building contains eight units." Nemdharry read from a small piece of paper. "Two dental offices, one used-parts wholesaler, two clothing wholesalers, our export company, and two vacancies. But the management said one unit might be leased by the end of the week."

"Doesn't seem like the best place to start a clandestine laboratory," Beadsworth said.

"No, it doesn't. In the morning a white U-Haul truck came and went around the back. It left forty-five minutes later."

"Do you know where?'

"No idea. We're timing the schedule. Hopefully we'll make out a pattern. What's surprising is that when I was talking to the manager of the building, I happened to walk past that unit and there was no smell. No chemicals burning in the back."

"What does the front look like?" Beadsworth asked.

Terries spoke, "It has nothing except for a sign that says LLPM Imports & Exports, and a receptionist. No chairs, and the back area is entirely sealed off."

"Then why have a receptionist?" I said.

Terries answered, "I think it's just to show they are a legitimate company. While I was there the receptionist didn't get a single call."

Beadsworth wiped something off his coat and then said, "We believe we have a sample."

"Nex?" Terries said.

"We're not sure. It could be anything."

"What does it look like?" she asked.

"Like Ecstasy."

"Shit," Nemdharry said. "Where is it?"

"We dropped it off at DAS. We'll find what's in it. I would like to talk to the owner of this coffee shop."

"Yeah, sure," Nemdharry said.

They left Terries and I at the car and walked down the street.

We were alone.

There was silence.

I looked at my feet and she was looking away.

I had to say something. "So you like the job?" I asked.

"It's not bad. A good learning experience," she said, smiling.

Silence again.

"How about you?" she said.

"Yes, good learning experience." I couldn't think of anything clever to say. My mind was frozen. I tried to stay cool, calm, and collected. I leaned on the car and looked across to the many shops lining the street.

There was a laundromat, a drycleaners, and a convenience store at the corner. Beside the convenience store there were a couple of guys trying to place a sign above the window. The sign read: BUBBLE T SHOP.

"Have you ever tried bubble tea?" I turned to Terries.

"Not really."

"Neither have I. Maybe someday we could try it together." I stopped. *I couldn't believe I had just said that.* I looked away, not wanting to hear what she was going to say next.

She smiled. "Maybe some day."

I was relieved.

Nemdharry and Beadsworth came back.

It was a long, slow day.

Next morning, we drove to DAS and inside found our analyst. She was a short round woman who wore black-rimmed glasses. She also wore the traditional long white coat. Her name was Eileen Mathers.

"What is it?" asked Beadsworth.

"I'm not sure," she said. "Come with me." She scanned a white card, the door beeped, and then we heard the sound of unlocking. She took us inside to the laboratory. There were many analysts wearing similar white coats, hovering over microscopes, looking through charts, staring at monitors, and examining liquids in test tubes.

It reminded me of my grade-nine science class.

“From the information you provided,” Eileen said. “It’s supposed to blow up inside the human body?”

“Yes,” Beadsworth said.

“Are you sure you don’t mean it dissolves in the body?”

Beadsworth looked at me and I at him.

“No. From what I’ve been briefed it is supposed to blow up.”

“I don’t think that’s possible. Pills and tablets don’t blow up. They dissolve. Capsules *do* dissolve faster than tablets because their outer layer is made of soft gelatin shells.”

“I think it is supposed to work instantly,” I said.

“For it to take instant effect it is better if it were taken intravenously, or even inhaled or snorted. Tablets take time to break down. Come, I’ll show you something.”

She took us to the corner where there were three glasses filled with liquid propped on top of a table. The glasses were labeled with yellow stickers. The first glass: Exhibit A—Orange, the second glass, Exhibit B—Green, and the third, Exhibit C—Brown.

She pointed to the glasses. “These are the samples you submitted. I cut a small piece from each tablet and placed them in water at precisely the same time. Exhibit A was the earliest sample. Look closer.”

The water had turned white with visible chunks of what used to be the orange tablet resting at the bottom.

“You can see,” Eileen began. “The tablet did not dissolve entirely. Just as it made contact with the water the tablet broke up into pieces and then fell to the bottom.” She pointed to the small clumps. “I have not stirred so most of the tablet dissolved on its own.”

We moved to Exhibit B. The glass was completely clear.

"It's translucent. This sample has dissolved entirely but it took a good half-hour to do so. "

We moved onto the last glass—Exhibit C. The tablet was completely dissolved but you could still see tiny white particles floating at the top.

"Once the sample touched water it immediately fizzled and shrank. But there is still this white residue and a white film at the top of the glass."

She turned to us. "What we are seeing is the evolution of the sample. Whoever is trying to manufacture this is trying to produce the effect you mentioned. But from my experience it is not possible. I'm not saying it is impossible. With the technology these days I wouldn't be surprised."

"What's in it?" Beadsworth asked.

"I'll show you."

Being inside the small room, filled with all sorts of equipment: beakers, test tubes, and other science equipment, I was getting claustrophobic. If I were forced to work in here I'd end up drinking one of those green or brown liquids just to escape.

We went to another table and the analyst fixed a bright light on a ceramic plate.

"I've scraped a bit off from each tablet," she said. With a tiny scoop she placed a small amount of white powder onto the plate. "This scraping is from the orange pill—the earliest sample."

From a cool storage she pulled out a small glass bottle, "This is a Marquis reagent consisting of sulphuric acid and formaldehyde. I first saw it in Amsterdam. Now it's widely used everywhere."

She tilted the bottle and discharged two drops of fluid onto the scraping.

We waited.

"No reaction," said Eileen. "Good."

She pulled out another small bottle, this one not from the cool storage. "This is a Mandelin reagent." She did the same as before by placing two drops on the scraping.

This time the reagents rapidly turned dirty orangey-brown.

"Just as I thought," Eileen said. "This is Ketamine."

Beadsworth nodded. He understood.

"What's Ketamine?" I said, looking around. I didn't want to sound stupid but I had to ask.

She said, "Ketamine is an anaesthetic used primarily by veterinarians. It's a central nervous system depressant. Taken in higher doses Ketamine causes hallucinations and delirium. Numbness in the extremities is also common. So when you said the drug is supposed to numb, right away I thought of Ketamine, but I wasn't sure. In liquid form it can be injected into the muscle and the effect can usually be felt within four minutes. If swallowed, the effects come from ten to twenty minutes, but only in higher concentrations. So it would be more viable to keep it in liquid form. Let's look at the second tablet."

She placed more scrapings on a clean ceramic tile and again discharged two drops of the Marquis reagent. The reaction was green.

She looked at us with one raised eyebrow. "The colour dyes of the tablets are an indicator of what's in them. This contains caffeine and Ketamine. Caffeine being the prominent substance in the tablet."

"Caffeine?" I said. "The stuff in coffee?"

"Yes," she answered. "Caffeine is a stimulant."

"I get it," I said, as if I had just discovered the cure for cancer. "Ketamine knocks you out and caffeine brings you back in."

"In simple terms, yes."

I smiled at Beadsworth. *Now look who's smart.*

Eileen said, "Now for the last tablet. I can already tell you what's in it." She performed the same procedure using the Marquis and the reaction was blackish brown. "This tablet contains many substances, with Ketamine being the primary. My guess, the secondary substances would be caffeine and methamphetamines. These tests that I have performed only indicate the most prominent substance in the tablets. The Marquis test was made specifically for Ecstasy. So if there *are* any other substances, the fluid might not change colour or react. Also, these tests don't indicate how pure the substance is or how much of it is in the tablet, but it is a fine primary indicator. What I'm trying to say is that I wouldn't be surprised if it contained cocaine, speed, or acetaminophen." She paused. "I'll have to do a gas chromatograph mass spectrometer analysis."

"Uh?" I said.

"The most accurate drug testing method available. It will tell us what substances are in the tablets and how much."

Beadsworth touched his beard as if in deep thought. "What I don't understand is, this isn't something new or innovative."

"That's what I thought too. We've had hundreds of capsules or tablets that contain these kinds of ingredients. I've even had pills brought in that are sold as Ecstasy with just caffeine, sugar, and flu medications in them."

"A perfect cure for the common cold," I laughed. But neither of them laughed back.

“The only way it could be unique is if the delivery is as fast as it states,” she said.

“But you said that is not possible,” Beadsworth said.

“That’s right.” She pulled out the form Beadsworth had submitted. She adjusted her glasses and then glanced over it, reading it again. “I can’t see this doing what it says. It’s like any other tablet out there.”

Beadsworth nodded and his eyes narrowed in contemplation.

Eileen said, “I’ll provide you with a Certificate of Analyst when I thoroughly process the tablets.”

We thanked her and left.

The sign, BUBBLE T SHOP, had just been placed out in the front. From inside Martin stared out to the street. He had leased the shop for six months. The plan was to set up several Nex labs all over Toronto. Instead of one large manufacturing plant, they would have several mini labs.

The costs were large, of course, but the logic was that if one lab got raided the others would keep up production. With a product like Nex the costs were nothing compared to the profits. All that was needed was demand. Once demand was established, supply was no problem.

Martin was on the phone now. The cops standing across the street had made him a little edgy. Many things made him edgy.

For one, he was now unsure if the desired Nex could actually be produced. He was, in fact, becoming unsure of the whole scheme. There were too many factors he could not avoid. One: how potent Nex could be. Two: whether they could be the sole providers of Nex when it came out. Others would make generic versions of it. Three: whether Ms. Zee could handle such a massive operation. But how could he complain, with the kind of money he was being offered? Lawyers are a dime a dozen and this was good money.

He shut the phone and closed his eyes. He had been arguing with Ms. Zee about moving the store elsewhere. The cops were too close. Their focus was on the building across the way, but in the end it'd divert to them. He'd advised they relocate as soon as possible. But Ms. Zee thought otherwise. The cops would not look under their noses. They were expecting Nex to be produced in a large building, not underneath a retail store.

Then Martin thought of their informant in the police force.

Driving back from DAS I was excited. This was just another regular, made-in-the-basement type of drug. Aldrich was getting all worked up about nothing. I turned to Beadsworth but saw that he didn't share my enthusiasm.

"Cheer up," I said. "This isn't as bad as we thought, is it?"

Beadsworth didn't answer.

I tapped the steering wheel with my fingers. "We can cruise through this investigation," I said. I was looking forward to wrapping this case up. I was also looking forward to Aldrich's commitment that once we had completed this investigation I would be transferred to the intelligence unit. I would fit in nicely in the intelligence unit.

I smiled, the widest smile possible.

"This isn't right," I heard Beadsworth say.

His comments snapped me out of my happy thoughts. "How is it not right?" I said.

"This could mean many things," he started. "One, this is a decoy. Provide us with different versions of the drug, hoping that we will get off track. Two, the desired drug has already been produced."

I thought about it and it kind of made sense.

I hadn't known Beadsworth very long, but now I could count on him to ruin my happiness.

11

Next morning I was ready to leave the house when I got a call from Ronald Garnett.

"Rupert, I'm going to tag along with you," he said. This wasn't a request, it was an order. "Pick me up from headquarters."

I was ready to make some excuse, like I was taking the subway, but thought against it.

"Yes, Sir," was all I could say.

The drive to headquarters was painful. I had to pick up Garnett there, who, in my opinion, was waiting to bite my head off, then drive to Scarborough and meet up with Nemdharry and Terries. Beadsworth would join us later.

The lonely ride with Garnett was not going to be pleasant. What would we talk about? *So Ronny, can I call you Ronny? Buddy, how's it going? Sorry I screwed up your investigation. What's one investigation when crime is everywhere? What's four months? Maybe the next one will be quick; you might even wrap it up in one month.*

I found Garnett standing in front of the main entrance. He opened the passenger door with a bewildered look over his face. He tried, to the best of his abilities, to get into the car. Ronald Garnett is enormous. He is massive. He could be someone's bodyguard or even a bouncer at a club.

"You're late," he growled.

"I had to stop at the red lights," I said.

He didn't find my comment amusing.

I told him we were meeting Beadsworth in Scarborough. He made no comment, which was good. I didn't want any small talk either.

While I drove, I found my body gravitated toward him. In fact, the entire car seemed lopsided. Wait a minute. Garnett's side seemed lower. *Great, there go my shocks.*

"Can't this toy go any faster?" Garnett said. It was ninety kilometres per hour on this highway. My car was barely going over eighty.

I wanted to say, *Get out of my car. You're too damn heavy. Stop eating entire cows for lunch.*

I pressed harder on the accelerator. The car jerked and I saw the hand on the speedometer quiver and touch ninety.

Happy? This vehicle will fall apart any minute. This is an economy class vehicle. It's not a truck. It can't handle your weight.

"I don't like you," Garnett said. He turned to me. "I don't have to like you." He looked like a deranged bulldog.

"I don't like you either," I said, but then all the data started bombarding my head: stuck in car with Garnett, driving fast on highway, no possible chance of escape. I then wished I hadn't said that.

"I don't know why Sergeant Aldrich chose you but I think it was a mistake."

I thought it was a mistake too, but you wouldn't hear me mention it to everyone.

"You're not even fit to give parking tickets," he said.

I think he was trying to provoke me. He wanted me to say something so Aldrich would dismiss me from the team. I wasn't going to let him win so I just smiled.

"What're you smiling at?" he said.

The smile on my face vanished. But inside, I was still smiling.

"Just stay out of my way," he finally said.

Sure, I nodded. I had no desire to get pulverized.

If ever I was in trouble I couldn't see Garnett saving my ass. I couldn't see him saving anyone else's either.

I don't know how, but we reached Scarborough.

Once Nemdharry saw our car approach he got out of his. He was surprised to see Garnett.

"Morning, Ron," he said. "Didn't know you'd be joining us."

Garnett smiled and said, "Sergeant Aldrich wanted me to assist you guys in any way I can."

"How's tight-ass doing anyways?"

Tight-ass?

I thought Garnett would lose his top but he replied, "Cut him some slack. He's under a lot of pressure."

"I bet he is," Nemdharry said.

"It's not his fault what happened."

"I don't like working under him. Wouldn't have minded if you were heading the operation."

Garnett shrugged.

"I don't like his decisions," Nemdharry said.

Garnett looked in my direction. "Neither do I."

Subtlety wasn't Garnett's strong quality.

"Anything?" Garnett asked.

Nemdharry looked over at the building across and said, "I checked to see what LLPM stood for and came up empty. But the company was registered two months ago."

Garnett said, "You said something about a white truck?"

"Oh, yeah. We were able to get a better view this morning. They brought in empty cardboard boxes—"

"How'd you know they were empty?" Garnett asked.

"They were flat sheets, you know. Later they were assembled, I guess. We did clearly see them load the truck with the boxes afterwards. Forty-five minutes later they were gone."

"Are they shipping Nex in those boxes?" I said.

"Can't say," Nemdharry answered. "If a dealer could set up shop in the middle of city hall and not be caught he would do it. It's all about finding that one way of getting away with it." He scratched his clean-shaven cheek. "I wouldn't open a clan lab here. No. There are too many people around. It's too risky. But you can't underestimate these guys. Hell. They might be thinking we won't come looking for them here."

"How many people work in there?" Garnett asked.

"I can't say exactly. But last night a green minivan with tinted windows drove up, dropped a few passengers off, picked some up and left."

"Where'd they take them?"

"To Kennedy Station."

"They could just be giving their employees a ride," Garnett said.

"Yeah, but there are several bus stops around here. They couldn't walk up to the bus stops?"

There was silence. We were all thinking. Something was definitely fishy.

A GM station wagon drove up and in it was Beadsworth. He got out and came over to us.

"How's your kid?" Garnett asked Beadsworth.

"He's doing much better."

"Phil, what're the results from DAS?" Nemdharry asked.

"The samples contained some part of Ketamine."

"Special K," Garnett answered.

"K-hole," Nemdharry shook his head.

"Sorry?" I said.

"Ketamine," Nemdharry started. "The high, or K-hole, as it is called, can make you do weird shit. I remember," he said laughing, "I had just started in the force and they put me on foot patrol. I got a call one night that some guy was committing suicide off a tower on Wellington. So I rushed over. When I got up, I saw this guy, hands on his knees, on the ledge, looking forty stories down. The guy looked respectable, nice suit and haircut and all. So I thought, maybe a stockbroker, probably lost all his client's money. So I started talking to him, telling him life is worth living and that his family would miss him if he were dead. After five minutes of me talking he looked up and his face had this confused look. He smiled and pointed below. So I went over to the edge and looked down. All I saw were tiny cars and ant-like people. I told him what I saw. He got angry and shook his head. No. Look carefully. I did and I still didn't see anything special. He smiled and said all his friends were down there. I looked again. Maybe this whole stunt was to prove something to his friends? He said thousands of his friends were waiting for him down below and they were not from this planet. They wanted him to jump so that they could catch him. The guy was flipped. So I talked to him about his friends hoping to buy some time. Close to an hour later the guy comes to his senses.

"Earlier he had gone into a club and snorted Ketamine. He remembered feeling like his mind had left his body and then a voice told him to go up to the tower and jump. He clearly saw green men with arms extended waiting for his dive." Nemdharry's eyes widened. "Weird, eh?"

I nodded.

Garnett spoke, "So what else is in it?" He was speaking to Beadsworth.

"Caffeine. We'll find out the rest after the chromatography tests are done."

Ed Burrows paced the room, sweating from the exertion. "There are pages missing," he cried.

"What?" Ms. Zee said.

"I've gone through the designs three times and sections are missing."

Ms. Zee was not amused.

"The previous chemist was playing with pills and capsules, knowing full well that they would not provide the *bust* you require. At Bantam I heard they had invented this innovative delivery process . . ."

"What is it?" she demanded.

"I didn't work on that aspect of the drug." He shook his head. "I worked on how each ingredient reacted to the other. That is how I know that the previous chemist's formula works. His notes were very good. He had a clear model in his head."

"Get to the point," Ms. Zee said.

"But for some reason his last formula was different, as if he were going in another direction—or—altering the drug entirely."

It was more like he was sabotaging their operation, Ms. Zee thought.

"With his initial designs and process in hand, replication would be no problem. But without the missing pages we can't do that."

Even in death Armand had screwed them, Ms. Zee thought.

"I think I know a man who could solve that for us."

"Where is this man?" she asked.

"I'll find out where he is."

12

I was still thinking about Nemdharry's story when Garnett said, "Let's go get some coffee."

I was looking forward to getting something to drink.

"Not you," Garnett said, stopping me. "Someone has to watch over the building."

I shrugged. Fine. I didn't want their company anyways.

"I'll get you a cup," Beadsworth said.

They left.

I was alone.

Across, I saw people enter and leave the building. I wanted desperately to walk over and knock at the door of this LLPM Company. What would I find? Mad scientists hunched over their instruments making Nex? Or maybe nothing. But whatever it was, it was inside that building.

A black pickup truck entered from the side. I moved to the right trying to get the license plate of the vehicle. From this distance I couldn't make out anything—not a single number or letter. I should have brought my binoculars.

I needed to get closer. Without thinking I began to cross the street. It was a busy road, where cars zoomed passed me.

I looked up and the truck had disappeared around the back. It was now or never. I dashed across, narrowly missing the bumpers of several cars.

I entered the side pathway and ran towards the back. As I was halfway, the same pickup emerged from around the corner. I stopped instantly, and retreated.

I could feel the pickup move closer. I didn't look back; I just continued walking. The pickup stopped beside me and then the windows came down.

A woman with dark sunglasses was sitting behind the wheel.

"Can you tell me which way is Eglinton Avenue?" she said.

She was lost!

I sighed and gave her the directions.

I went back to my car, soaking wet from perspiration.

Not two minutes later Beadsworth, Nemdharry and Garnett came back. Beadsworth was holding my cup of coffee.

"You're sweating," Beadsworth said handing me the cup.

"I was jogging," I said. "I try to stay in shape."

Garnett and Nemdharry looked at each other.

"We're heading down to headquarters," Beadsworth said. "Constable Barnes and Detective Herrera will be joining you."

"Sure," I said taking a sip of the hot coffee. Right now all I wanted was a cold glass of water.

Eight minutes later a car drove up and parked in an empty spot. Herrera and Barnes came over.

"Carlos Herrera," said a short man with a blotchy face, but a genial smile. "I don't think we were properly introduced." He extended his hand. I took it. "You weren't at our little lunch."

"Yeah." I shrugged. "Jon Rupret. R before E."

"Michael Barnes," said a good-looking white kid. He had curly hair and he was about my age. I shook his hand, too.

"So where's the action?" Herrera said.

"Across the street." I pointed to the building.

"So what are we doing here?" he said.

"We're supposed to wait," I replied.

"Wait," Barnes said. "Sure, we could do that. All we've been doing is waiting."

Herrera nodded.

"So, what're you guys working on?" I asked.

Barnes said, "Sergeant Aldrich told us to search for Armand Dempiers."

"Who?" I said.

Herrera answered, "He used to work for Bantam Pharmaceuticals at Danforth and Victoria Park. We went over there and they told us he was let go almost six months ago. They gave us his home address. We found the place empty. The property owner said he'd moved out months ago. Then we got a hold of his ex-wife. She said she hadn't talked to him for over a month. The last time she'd spoken to him he sounded nervous but told her he was working on something big."

"Nex?" I said.

"We think so; his ex was really upset. She said when the money from his severance ran out he stopped paying child support; that was two months ago. He promised he was going to pay everything in a lump sum. But she hasn't heard from him." Herrera glanced at the building and then said, "What did you guys find?"

"We know what's in Nex. It's Ketamine," I said.

They both had a confused look on their faces.

I then took the time to educate them about Ketamine. I ended by telling them the story—where, as a parking enforcement officer, I received a call that some guy was ready to jump off a building on Wellington. "Ketamine is a powerful hallucinogen," I ended off.

Both Herrera and Barnes looked amazed.

I said, "We also met some DJ from the House of Jam."

"You mean, DJ Krash?" Barnes asked. "He's the second—"

"—Best DJ. Yes, I know," I said.

"Have you ever been to the House of Jam?" Barnes asked.

I shook my head.

"In my opinion, it is *the* best place to be in Toronto. But it's so hard to get in. I would love to go again."

Herrera was feeling left out, so he said, "What's the story over there?" He jerked his head in the direction of the building. "Detective Beadsworth never detailed me."

"We believe it's possible that Nex is being produced in there," I said.

"Okay, great." Herrera rubbed his hands with pleasure. "Then let's go."

"Um, I think we should wait," I said, scratching the back of my head. I didn't like saying this but I might have to take command. "If we see anything suspicious then we go in, only after we get approval from Detective Garnett or Sergeant Aldrich." I couldn't believe it. I was sounding like Beadsworth.

"Yes, of course," Herrera said. He placed his hands in his pockets and squinted. "Something doesn't make sense."

"What?" I said.

"Wouldn't you be suspicious if you saw three guys standing across the road looking at you?"

I nodded. It would be suspicious, even though the road dividing us was very wide.

"If you were making a product like Nex wouldn't you have more safeguards?"

"Probably," I said.

"Maybe," Barnes said. "They're trying not to be suspicious and that is why they'd put their lab in a place like this."

I was trying very hard to understand their point.

"Maybe Nex is not being produced there but somewhere else." Barnes moved his head in all directions. "Maybe it is being produced inside one of those stores."

What? That made absolutely no sense.

"It could be inside that textile store," he pointed. "Or that barber shop. Or that convenience store, or that pizza parlour or that bubble-tea shop. Maybe we're purposely being diverted."

"That was what I was thinking." Herrera agreed.

Okay.

"I like your theory," I said, narrowing my eyes. "Why . . . don't . . . you guys go and scope out the area. Find out what you can. I'll watch the building."

"What?" said Martin, flabbergasted. "Nex is not going to be in tablet form?"

"We're not sure," Ms. Zee answered.

Martin took a deep breath and adjusted his tie. He laughed. "Ms. Zee, this is bad business. We have been marketing Nex in tablet form. We've even distributed samples."

"We need to get them back."

"All of them?"

"Kong has already retrieved some, while others have guaranteed on their lives that the samples were destroyed. Only one left. Cal Murray has it."

"Isn't that the owner of the House of Jam?"

"Yes, Kong and I will pay him a visit tonight."

Alone again, I rubbed my temples. Something was bothering me but I couldn't put my finger on what. I felt like I was supposed to remember something—a date, a number, something. Did I have some unfinished business? Was I supposed to meet someone? *Think, Jon. Think.*

There was enough money in the bank for the rent, so that wasn't it. The car insurance was paid last week, so that wasn't it either. Cable bill. Check. Telephone bill. Check. Returned old library materials. Check.

I was supposed to go somewhere, but where?

My cell phone rang.

"Hello," I said.

"Hello, big shot," said the familiar voice. It was Roberta Collecci, from PEU. "Since your promotion you've forgotten about us," she said.

"Us?" I said. "Who is this?"

She went silent. "Jon, it's Roberta from parking enforcement."

"Roberta? I remember. One of those little people who give out tickets," I said snobbishly.

"Little people?" She snapped.

I started to laugh.

"Jon, I'm glad you haven't changed. You're still obnoxious."

"Thank you."

"So, how's everything?"

"I'm on a stake-out." I lowered my voice. "The ultimate drug is being produced in the building across from me. I have my gun ready." I began whispering. "Any moment when signaled I will run across and break the door down."

That didn't affect her. "You're standing around, aren't you?"

"Yes," I said like a child who's been told he's fibbing. "So what's up?"

"I just called to see if you were still alive. No one at the drug squad gave you a hard time?

"Nah, they knew I'm not the type of guy they could mess with."

"Sure, Jon," she said. "Are you with the drug squad indefinitely?"

"No. Just for another twenty years."

She didn't laugh.

Roberta missed me. I felt guilty. With everything happening around me I hadn't thought twice about her.

"You miss giving parking tickets?" she said.

"Yeah, sometimes," I said. "I did enjoy my daily routine."

"It's not the same without you," she said. "No one around to tell stories."

"Hey," I said in a defensive tone. "Those things actually happened to me."

"What about the time you said you saw ghosts outside your window."

"That was true. They wanted to borrow money."

"Why would they need money?"

"Hey, I don't know. These modern ghosts don't care about scaring people any more. All they want is someone to spot them a twenty."

"What about the time you said you scored fifty-two points in a basketball game."

"Is that what you heard? Let me clarify. I said my team scored fifty-two points. I didn't even get to touch the ball."

She didn't laugh but I knew she was smiling.

"Roberta, something is bothering me and I don't know what it is. Am I supposed to do something soon?"

There was silence. "Yes, but I'm not going to tell you. We had a deal you were not going to depend on me."

"But this is seriously bothering me. This could jeopardize my new position."

"No way."

"Just this once."

"Nope."

"Is it someone I know?"

"Not saying a single word."

"Is it a date I'm supposed to remember?"

"Not going to get pressured."

"Yes, I've got it," I said in a fake British accent. "It's our meeting anniversary."

"Meeting anniversary? What is that?"

"It's when we met the first time."

"Get help, Jon. You're hopeless."

"Yes, and you know it and you still persist in behaving like this."

"Jon, I just called to see how you were doing. Not to get badgered about things you can't remember."

Herrera and Barnes strolled toward me in the distance. "Roberta, can I call you later? I've got to go."

"You take care of yourself."

"Will do."

"Anything?" I said, hanging up.

"Nothing out of the ordinary," replied Herrera. "The owner of one of the convenience stores said that in this area stores come and go. One week you see a new restaurant and four weeks later that same restaurant will be out of business."

There was silence.

"Anything happen while we were investigating?" Barnes said.

I shook my head. "Nothing unusual."

Silence again.

"You're ringing, Dude," I heard Barnes say.

"What?" I said.

"Your cell phone is ringing."

I pulled out my cell and said, "Hello."

It was Beadsworth. "Leave Herrera and Barnes and meet me at the House of Jam. You know where it is?"

"Sure I do."

"Good." He hung up.

I turned to Barnes, "Where is the House of Jam, anyways?"

"On Queen Street West, near Simcoe Street," he answered. "Why?"

"I have to go there."

"We keep an eye out?" asked Herrera.

"Yeah, I guess until you hear from Garnett or Aldrich."

13

I drove along Queen Street West searching desperately for the House of Jam. I asked several passers-by if they knew where it was but they shook their heads. Most of them were middle-aged, so I guessed they were not into that stuff. A young kid, wearing the Canadian flag as a bandana, told me it was around the corner, but he said it had no signs or markings in front of it. Great, that was going to help me a great deal.

I parked at the corner of Queen and Simcoe with a full view of the street. From here I was hoping to see Beadsworth.

I'm not much of a club hopper. In fact, this was my first time being inside a club. My mother never allowed me to get involved in music. She considered music the path to lawlessness. She couldn't stand those who drove around blaring loud music from their speakers.

I waited for Beadsworth's station wagon. The GM swerved around and parked a few cars away.

"Why are we here?" I asked.

"Cal Murray is willing to meet us," Beadsworth said. "He'll be out in a minute."

"Where is this House of Jam?" I asked, looking around.

"You're standing in front of it," he replied.

I turned to a heavy black door. "You've got to be kidding me." I moved back to get a full view of the place. The building, from the outside, looked like an abandoned storehouse. There was graffiti sprayed everywhere.

A few minutes later a man appeared at the door. He had gray hair and he was sporting a goatee. He smiled and extended his hand, "I'm Cal Murray."

We shook hands and introduced ourselves. "Come," he said.

We went past the door and up a long flight of stairs. "We have four entrances and exits to the building," Cal started. "Plus two more exits in case of emergencies." We were in a narrow hall. "This is one of the emergency exits. But it leads straight to my office and it's away from the public." He unlocked a door and motioned us to enter. Opposite this door was another door.

The office was small, confined. The only objects inside were a brown leather sofa with a desk and chair opposite it. Behind the desk and chair the wall was covered with photographs of Cal with celebrities and other important people. Most of them I didn't recognize. A fourteen-inch television was perched on a platform higher up.

Cal sat behind the desk. Beadsworth sat upright on the sofa while I sprawled.

"Max told me why you wanted to meet me," Cal said. His face was serious. "First, we don't do drugs. We don't deal in that shit. We clear on that?"

"Of course," replied Beadsworth.

"Sure," I said, relaxed on the sofa. All my tensions were draining out. I moved my hand over the hand rest. The leather was soft and smooth. I was ready to go to sleep.

"These people came to me a while back," continued Cal. "They said they have the next best thing and that if I let them open shop they'd give me a cut."

"They told you about Nex?" asked Beadsworth.

"What's Nex?" he replied.

"The drug. It's the name."

"I don't know," he waved his hands. "They might call it that now. Names come and go. All I said to them was no thank you."

My eyes were closing.

"But they came back?" Beadsworth said.

Cal looked down at the desk, "Yes. They are very persuasive. You know, it took me three years to get this club on the map." Through my bleary eyes I could tell Cal was now into promotional mode. "We get the latest bands launching their CDs. We have parties for film premieres. We even host fundraisers for the Hospital for Sick Children. If you're in Toronto, this is the place to be."

"Do they keep coming back because they think you're interested?" inquired Beadsworth. I knew Beadsworth was onto something, but in my state of happiness I didn't care.

"Yeah, a little," I heard Cal say. "You have to understand. Drugs are hard to control. Ecstasy is everywhere. Deals take place behind your back. At least with this new product I could have some control over it. So, yeah, I thought about it. If I knew who was selling and who was buying I could maybe keep it away from the most vulnerable."

"Children?" Beadsworth said.

From half-open eyelids I saw Cal nod.

"What do they look like?" Beadsworth asked.

Cal thought about it, "Their leader is a woman. She has . . ."

Maybe I was snoring. Maybe four or five minutes had passed when Beadsworth nudged me and I sat up straight. "Tell us more," I said, crossing my leg.

Cal continued. "Then, finally, there is this big Asian guy. Mean looking." Beadsworth was making notes on a small pad.

Beadsworth said, "His name?"

"I heard them call him Kong."

"When did they bring you the samples?"

"A little over a month ago. The second one two weeks after that and the most recent early last week."

Last week. We were getting close.

Cal said, "I gave the samples to Max. I think you guys have them now. So what more do you want from me? You have the evidence, go nail them."

My eyes were half-closed. I tried to fight it. I really did. But then I fell back into darkness.

Beadsworth turned to me and said, "Officer Rupret will tell you."

That woke me up.

Cal looked at me attentively.

I shot Beadsworth a look. "Um, yes," I said trying to get out of my haze. "This sofa. It is real leather?"

"Yes," replied Cal, slowly.

"Good. We would like a tour. We want to know why R.A.C.E. wants to do business here." I had no idea what I was saying.

"Who is this R.A.C.E.?" said Cal turning to Beadsworth.

Before he could answer I got up and pointed to the sofa, "Whenever you decide to throw it away you give me a call." I slid a card with my phone number on his desk.

Cal was confused but he nodded and said, "Yes, I can give you a tour." He got up. "But you still haven't answered my question. Why don't you guys arrest these people?"

"He'll answer that," I pointed to Beadsworth. "I've talked enough." I rubbed my eyes.

"We need to know if they have the drug," Beadsworth replied. "The samples we have aren't the final product. That is where you come in. We need you to get it from them. So far we have something that sounds dangerous, but is it? We need to be certain."

"You want me to do business with them?" he said.

"Yes, we believe they are still processing the drug. Once they have it they will be eager to push it and before they do we have to stop them." Beadsworth handed Cal his card. "If and when they contact you, you give us a call."

"Come, I'll show you the place," Cal said. We were now in the narrow hall again.

"What's in that room?" I pointed.

"If any of our special guests or performers want to chill out, we let them use it. Mostly, DJs use it to get a break. Max is our resident DJ, so he uses it. You want to see it?"

I shook my head. "That's all right."

He led us out through another door, this one heavy, and onto the mezzanine level. It was low-lit and a girl, wearing a t-shirt and jeans, was wiping the tables.

Cal said, "On the left of this floor we have the VIP lounge with ultra-comfortable couches."

"Even better than the one in your office?" I asked.

"I suppose," he said, not realizing my love for his sofa. "Beside it we have two pool tables. In the middle we have the soda bar. From here you can see there are two stairs going down to the dance floor."

We moved to the railings. From this vantage point I could see the stage across.

"We'll go to the main floor in a minute," Cal said.

Beadsworth had his arms crossed behind his back and was strolling through the tour. His face had the expression of someone who didn't care much for these things.

"On the right, beside the soda bar, we have the washrooms with attendants." Cal smiled.

“Attendants?” Beadsworth said.

“Yes, so nothing illegal or improper happens.”

Something caught my eye. It looked like an arcade machine with a screen and a joystick.

Cal saw my interest and said, “That’s what we call a Find-a-Friend. You see that black semi-oval ball atop the soda bar?”

“Yes,” I said.

“That’s a camera. When turned on, using the stick you can control the camera. You can zoom in and out. We have two more downstairs. Here is where we have the private lounge. These sliding doors give you privacy. We keep this area for the celebrities or other important people.”

He slid the door and we peeked in. I saw those ultra-comfortable couches lining the wall with a coffee table in the middle. A thirty-inch television was set up facing the couches.

We went down the stairs and on to the middle of the dance floor. From here I could see how big the place actually was.

“Eight thousand square feet,” Cal beamed.

A disco ball hung from the middle. A curved stage was planted facing the mezzanine with, I guess, all the DJ equipment. There were two large video screens on both sides of the stage.

“There are cameras on either side of the mezzanine,” Cal said. “They are aimed at the stage.”

“You have a lot of cameras,” Beadsworth commented.

“It’s an attraction for the public. For us, it’s security. On the left of the stage we have the back entrance and exit for the performers. There is a decent size room for the bands to change or set up or leave their equipment. We never keep this entrance open. This also leads to an exit in the back. On the right we have another emergency exit. There are lots of building codes that need to be followed.”

"What are those?" I said looking at these small booths behind the chairs.

"Those are our main attractions. We have one on either side of the floor. They are referred to as interactive zones." We went to the right side of the floor.

"This is called the Beam Breaker," he said.

I saw a round elevated platform that could maybe hold four people.

"There are parallel light beams that come down above the participants' heads. When someone breaks the beams the light sensors detect it and this triggers four to sixteen musical keynotes." He looked at his watch and then turned as if to say the tour was over.

"Can you show us the other interactive zone?" I asked. Beadsworth gave me a *Let's go* look. I shrugged.

We headed to the left side of the club. "This is the Infrared zone."

The platform was elevated but square. It could also hold four people. There was a camera pointing to the platform and a large white blank screen at the back.

Cal said, "It's an infrared video camera. It registers the participant's body heat and projects the infrared image on to the large screen. The unspoken rule is that if you're not hot enough, you're not dancing hard enough. Lots of fun." He turned to us. "This is the House of Jam. The best entertainment experience in the city."

"I would like to experience it, too," I said.

"Doors open at eight," he replied.

"I'll come tonight."

"Come to the back door and I'll let you in," Cal said. "Call me first, okay?"

14

They were all in the Lincoln—Ms. Zee, Kong, Joey and Suraj—heading to the House of Jam. Suraj was behind the wheel and he was nervous. He found the Lincoln too big to handle. He would rather be in his Sundance. But there was no way Ms. Zee would allow that. She only went anywhere in the Lincoln.

Ms. Zee was not in a good mood. It was embarrassing to have to go to your clients and retrieve the samples. Joey yawned beside her. His head was facing the other direction. She was sick of babysitting him.

Joey yawned again, this one longer and louder. Kong fidgeted on the front passenger seat. At first Ms. Zee had refused to bring Joey along but he begged her. It had been a while since he'd been outside the lab. He needed some time to relax. So did she. But this was business.

When I was all dressed up, I looked in the mirror. I was decked out in shiny black boots, brown khakis, a green silk shirt and a smooth artificial leather jacket. I was ready to have fun.

Barnes was going to pick me up and together we were going to check out the best entertainment experience in town. Beadsworth thought he'd stick out at the House of Jam, or maybe he didn't like clubs, so he opted to not go. Whatever the reason, I was glad I was going with Barnes. At least I didn't have to follow someone around. I was the boss. I thought maybe, given the way I was behaving earlier, Barnes would consider me his superior.

As I was touching up my hair there was a honk.

I rushed out the door and was halfway down the steps when I stopped. I went back up, unlocked, and said, "Goodbye, Mike." Michael Jordan smiled back at me. He approved of me having fun. He always did.

When I turned the handle of the main door my landlady peered out. "Jon," she said, "You're very busy?"

"Yeah," I smiled.

"You're eating well?"

"Yes, great."

"Come and have dinner with us tomorrow."

"No," I said. "I don't have time."

"I'm not going to argue with you. Come. I'll make your favourite dish."

"Mechado?" I said, slowly.

"Yes, mechado." She smiled.

When I was first introduced to mechado, a Filipino beef stew, I immediately fell in love with it. Now, whenever I hear the word mechado my taste buds start to water.

"I will not come for you, but for mechado. Okay?"

She knew I was joking. "Okay."

There was another honk.

"Gotta go," I said. "See you tomorrow."

Barnes was behind the wheel, grinning. "I can't believe we'll be going to the House of Jam. Y'know, you've gotta be important to get into that place. I tried going the second time. They wouldn't let me in. I even tried bribing them, but nope, it didn't work. Can you believe DJ Krash will be playing today? This is awesome."

“We’re still on duty,” I said.

“What if I get lucky?” he smiled devilishly.

“Your luck will run out if Aldrich hears about this. We’re not authorized to be there. Beadsworth persuaded Garnett to let us go, in the hope we find something.”

He put the car in gear.

“Also, don’t get hammered. This is work. And you don’t want to show up the next day with a hangover.”

“All right, sure,” he said, a little disappointed. “We go in and we scope the place out.”

“That’s it.” I smiled. “If somehow, out of the blue, we see someone nice, we just get their number. That’s it.”

“That’s it.” He nodded.

It was well past eight in the evening and there was a huge line up outside the House of Jam.

“There must be a couple of hundred people,” Barnes said as we drove past the waiting people. We went down the block searching for a parking spot. It is all but impossible to find parking in downtown Toronto. I should know; I used to give tickets to those who parked illegally. I was afraid we would have to park in front of a fire hydrant or something.

It took us twenty minutes but we did find a spot four blocks away from the club.

“It’ll take us forever to get in with this long line,” Barnes said, concerned.

I dialed Cal Murray’s number and after a few minutes hung up. “We’re going through the back.”

When we got there Cal was waiting for us. I introduced Barnes and we went up the stairs.

“You guys have fun,” said Cal. “If you need me, I’ll be here.”

We went through the narrow hall and into the club. I was blown away by the sheer energy of the place. The noise was immense. It had done a three-sixty transformation from the quiet place it was this morning. It was already bustling with people.

Barnes said something inaudible.

"What?" I yelled.

He leaned closer. "This is what I'm talking about."

"How 'bout we split up. You stay up here and I'll go down. If you see anything you ring me." I was yelling hard.

"Sure," he yelled back.

I moved forward and made my way to the railing of the mezzanine. Below there was a good crowd on the dance floor. On the stage DJ Krash was mixing feverishly. He was wearing a white cap and a black t-shirt. A pair of headphones was around his neck. The crowd was into the music. I think it was retro or contemporary—but what the hell did I know. Different coloured lights beamed down on to the dancers.

I was getting into the music too. Involuntarily, my head started bopping to the beat. I made my way down the right side stairs. There were a lot of people and a lot of girls. Now I knew why Barnes wanted to come here.

A few people had taken spots on the Beam Breaker.

I danced—if you call shaking your body in different directions dancing—my way to the stage. DJ Krash was focused on mixing records on the turntables. For a split second he looked up and when he saw me he smiled.

I felt important. I knew the DJ.

The Lincoln turned off Queen Street West and headed south. It turned into a dark alley and parked in a lot that could hold eight to ten cars. It was the parking lot of the House of Jam: reserved for the owners and its guests.

Ms. Zee dialed a number and Cal answered.

"We're coming to see you, Cal," she said.

"But . . . but . . ." Cal started.

"Only for a few minutes," she said.

"No. Come back later," he said firmly.

"We're outside your door," she said.

Defeated, Cal said, "I'll be down in a minute."

The back door swung open. Cal was not happy to see them, but he managed a smile.

All four of them followed Cal to his office. Suraj and Joey headed out to the club.

"What can I do for you?" said Cal, getting behind his desk.

"We want the samples back," Ms. Zee said. Kong was with her in the room.

"What samples?"

"The samples of the drug."

"Um . . ." Cal put his fingers to his lips. "I disposed of them right after you left."

"I don't believe you," Ms. Zee answered.

"Don't, but it wouldn't do me any good to keep them. What if the cops found the drugs? They'd shut the place down." Cal leaned forward. "Why do you want it back anyways?"

"The samples are not to our liking."

"And why is that?"

"We have our reasons," Ms. Zee said.

Not satisfied, Cal said, "Let me ask you this and tell me honestly. Will you have the drug or not?"

"We will," she said.

I went to the bar and ordered a ginger ale. I nearly choked when the bartender told me it was three dollars. *It was ginger ale, not imported wine*. Disgruntled, I headed for the chairs lined around the dance floor. This would be a good spot to scope out the place. It had an indescribable energy. I could see why this was *the* club to be at. The Beam Breaker already had a lineup. They all wanted to try it out.

I already had a personal tour.

A girl walked up to me. She smiled and said, "Buy you a drink?"

"No thanks, already bought one," I said, raising my ginger ale.

Her face turned sour and she left.

I took a sip and then realized what a dope I was. The girl was interested in me and I turned her down. I looked around, hoping to find her again.

I forgot my glass and headed in the direction she'd gone. There were too many people and searching for her was like trying to find a toothpick in a stack of toothpicks. I thought of the Find-a-Friend. I went to the machine but changed my mind when I saw two huge guys with cut-off tank tops, which by the way revealed well-muscled arms, standing in front of the machine having a good time. I didn't want to disturb them. That wouldn't be polite. I went back to my chair.

As I got near I saw a white kid with shaggy hair sitting on my chair.

"That's my glass," I said pointing to a half-empty glass perched on the rail.

"Sorry," the kid apologized. "I didn't know someone was sitting here."

"That's okay." I leaned over to retrieve my drink.

The guy next to us suddenly got up and left. I think DJ Krash was playing his music. I took the empty seat and turned to the kid.

"Hey, I'm Jeff," the kid said, offering his hand.

“If what you’re saying is true,” Cal said. “Then this new drug will be huge.”

“Very,” Ms. Zee reiterated.

“Then I would like a piece of the profit.”

Ms. Zee was taken back a little. In their previous meetings he was ardently against them opening shop in his establishment. “Why the sudden change of heart?”

“I cannot completely stop drugs from entering my club. If I join you I can control exactly what gets in and what gets out.” This sounded like perfect business. “On top of that, I can make some money.”

Ms. Zee seemed pleased. “How much are we talking about?”

“Fifty-fifty,” Cal said.

“No,” Ms. Zee was a good negotiator. “Thirty-seventy.”

“Fifty-fifty. House of Jam is *the* place to be in Toronto—fifty-fifty it is.”

“Thirty-five-sixty-five.”

“No. In my place you’ll have more returning clients than anywhere else.”

“Forty-sixty.”

“Also,” Cal leaned in for his final kill. “If I get raided I’ll lose everything.”

“All right. Fifty-fifty,” she said. House of Jam was *the* place to start a venture. It was also good business, considering she did not have the drug yet.

“I’m Jon Rupret,” I shook Jeff’s hand. “R before E.”

He thought about it, “Not Rupert but Rupret. Interesting.” He moved his head up and down.

“You got it.” I took a sip of my drink.

"Hey, wait a minute." He narrowed his eyes as if he was trying to locate something in his head. "Aren't you the guy who messed up the drug squad investigation last year?"

I couldn't believe he recognized me.

"Yeah, you are that guy," he concluded.

I hung my head and took another sip.

"Don't worry," he said. "I would have done the same thing. You did your job."

"I did," I said. "So you come here often?" I asked.

"Naw, whenever I get the chance. How about you?"

"First time."

"Wow, you don't get out much."

"Working."

"You still in the police force?"

"Yep, they couldn't get rid of me that easily."

"In parking?"

"Nope. Got transferred." I took a sip. "What do you do?"

"I just graduated."

"In what?"

"Pharmaceutical chemistry."

"We'll return with the drug," said Ms. Zee. She turned to Kong. "Get Suraj and Joey. We're leaving."

Kong went through the narrow hall and into the club. The music was loud and it hit him hard. He winced. There were too many people—moving, talking, laughing, yelling—it was all too much for him. He grunted.

Kong pushed through the throng of people—actually, they moved away as he passed them. He was too big and no one wanted to mess with him. He bumped into a guy holding two glasses filled with coloured liquid that spilled onto the guy's nice shirt. The guy apologized and quietly walked away.

Kong found Suraj standing at the bottom of the left staircase. Suraj looked bored and annoyed. He would rather be anywhere but here.

Suraj looked up and they made eye contact. Suraj understood.

Barnes was chatting up a couple of girls in the mezzanine lounge when he squinted and moved his head to get a better view. Through the group of pool players he saw someone he recognized. Or thought he recognized. This guy had just come out of the narrow hall. His bald head was clearly visible, but from this angle Barnes could not see his face.

Barnes dialed a number and waited. "Come on," Barnes said. "Come on." A few more rings later Rupret answered.

"Come upstairs. I think I see someone," Barnes yelled into the phone.

"What?" Barnes heard Rupret say.

"Come upstairs, now," Barnes repeated.

"You have to speak louder. I can't make you out," Rupret said. "Why don't I come upstairs?"

Barnes looked and the bald-headed man had disappeared. Barnes hung up and went in the direction where he had last seen the man.

"Wow, pharmaceutical chemistry," I repeated. "What do you learn to do? Make drugs?" I laughed.

He laughed too. "Yeah, drugs."

My cell phone vibrated.

"Excuse me," I said. "Hello."

It was Barnes.

"Come . . . (inaudible) . . . I think . . . (inaudible) . . . someone . . ." I couldn't clearly make out what he was saying. I even had one finger shoved in my other ear. I guess I was too close to the stage.

"What?" I said.

"Come . . . (inaudible) . . . now."

"You have to speak louder. I can't make you out," I said. I was not going to understand him through the cell phone. "Why don't I come upstairs?" He hung up.

I turned to Jeff, "I gotta go, man."

"Me, too," he said, looking at his pager.

"Nice talking to you," I said.

"See you around," I heard him say as I hurried up the flight of stairs.

Barnes moved past the bar and was standing in the middle of the floor. Where did the guy go? He looked around. Was he dreaming? He wasn't sure what, but there was something familiar about this man. He just couldn't put a finger on what.

He spotted the bald-headed man at the corner of the left staircase. Still he couldn't see his face. Barnes pushed and shoved past several patrons and made his way to the stairs. The man was not there. He looked down. He was not on the ground floor either. Barnes knew the bald-headed man could not be on the mezzanine level. He could only have gone down.

Barnes rushed down, skipping several steps. There were too many people. The lights were low and only when the strobes of beams dropped down onto the dancers could Barnes make out faces.

He decided to push forward. Go to the front of the club, near the stage.

On the mezzanine level I searched around. Barnes was not at the lounge. I moved further, scanning each face. No Barnes. There was no way I could ask someone if they'd seen Barnes. How would I describe him? He's tall, young and white. *Right.* That would narrow it.

I passed the soda bar and went to the left side of the floor. No sign of him. The Find-a-Friend machine was vacant. I hurried and grabbed the joystick.

My excitement fell as I realized this machine was just for the mezzanine level. I had already searched that level.

I pulled out my cell and dialed his number again.

Barnes passed a line of people who were eagerly waiting to dance on the mini stage. It was one of those interactive zones that he'd seen on TV. This one had the dancer's body heat projected onto the screen.

Barnes went forward and something caught his eye. A door to the left was a little ajar. A stream of light appeared from the opening. Something inside him said to check it out. It would be impossible to search through the entire dance floor. So there was no harm in this.

Barnes didn't have a gun. He didn't need a gun. He was only there to check the place out.

He pushed the heavy door slightly and peered inside. There was a dark hallway with a door to the right. There was another door at the end of the hall. Barnes entered and, feeling along the wall for guidance, moved down the hall toward that door. He stopped when he realized there was a figure standing in front of that door.

The hallway was very dark and Barnes tried hard, with no success, to make out this figure. When his eyes adjusted he immediately recognized the bald-headed man, holding the door open.

Something hit Barnes hard on the back of the head. There was a subdued clunk, like metal hitting flesh. Barnes fell forward and saw darkness.

Suraj stood above Barnes, holding a metal pipe. He had been hiding behind the door. There was a noise. The noise was coming from Barnes. Suraj looked at Kong. The noise sounded like the ringing of a cell phone. Suraj dropped the pipe and both he and Kong ran out of the House of Jam.

No answer. I hung up. This was not good. I decided to go down. I knew the place well now.

Downstairs was even worse. There were way too many people.

My heart started beating faster. The longer it took to find Barnes the more nervous I became. Barnes would never have called me unless it was an emergency.

I took a deep breath. I would find him.

My eyes caught the door on the left of the stage.

I remembered Cal saying, *We never keep this entrance open.*

I rushed to the door and pulled it open. The hallway was dark but I could make out something on the floor. I slowly advanced into the hall.

There was a body flat on the ground and I instantly knew it was Constable Michael Barnes.

My knees became weak and I was ready to fall.

15

"What the hell were you doing there?" Aldrich yelled.

It was the next morning and Beadsworth and I were in Aldrich's temporary office. The police department had given him this office for the duration of the investigation. It had your standard: desk, chairs, lamp, cabinet, bookcase, and a few other items.

Aldrich was pacing back and forth.

"Will someone tell me what the hell you were doing at a club?"

He was talking to me.

"Scoping the place out," I said.

"I beg your pardon?"

"Checking the place out, Sir," I said.

"Who authorized you to check this place out?" he demanded. He was now leaning across the desk.

I glanced at Beadsworth.

"I did, Sir," Beadworth said.

Aldrich looked disappointed. "I expected more from you, Detective."

"I'm sorry, Sir," said Beadsworth.

"It was my fault," I said.

"Of course it was your fault," Aldrich shot back. "Who else's fault would it be?"

I'd been hoping Aldrich would say it was no one's fault.

"I have an injured officer." He shook his head. "The drug squad is already going through so much. We don't need this.

You know how hard it was to keep it out of the papers. If anyone questions us we have to say the officer was off duty. We would have to lie. You know why?"

Beadsworth and I didn't answer.

"It would have jeopardized our mission." He stood up. Adjusted his coat. "You were only supposed to observe and not get involved. What were you hoping to find?"

"R.A.C.E.," I said, but then realized I should have kept my mouth shut.

"R.A.C.E.?" he blasted. "What if you had seen R.A.C.E., what would you have done? Do you remember our mission?"

I did not open my mouth.

"Our mission is to find where Nex is being produced and distributed. If you had intercepted they would have realized how close we were. They would have become cautious. We DO NOT want them to be cautious."

"How is Barnes?" Beadsworth finally asked.

"He's at Toronto East General, recovering. He took a hard hit on the head and his memory is questionable," Aldrich answered. "We were lucky to get him out of that place without anyone knowing."

"Can we—" I started.

"No. You will continue with the investigation." He paused. "We are fortunate Constable Barnes' injuries weren't more severe. Detective Herrera is with him; he will rejoin the operation in due time."

Aldrich blew air through his nose. He was staring out the window. "We need a break. We need a lead. We need anything." He turned to Beadsworth. "What about this import and export company?"

"We're monitoring it," Beadsworth said.

“If you feel there is a cause for intervention I will authorize it,” he said.

“Yes, Sir.”

“What about the surveillance cameras at the club? Did they catch anything?”

“We have not viewed the tapes yet . . . but . . .”

“But what?”

“One tape is missing.”

Aldrich looked like he was going to lose his head. “A tape missing?”

“Yes.”

“Did you question the owner of the dance club?”

“Yes. He said he left his office for a minute and perhaps at that time someone took the tape.”

“Where are the other tapes?”

“At the Video Services Unit.”

Aldrich nodded as if he was thinking. “Dismissed,” he said.

We got up, but before we could leave, Aldrich said, “Not you, Officer Rupret. I’d like to have a word with you.”

I looked at Beadsworth who refused to make eye contact.

“Officer Rupret,” started Aldrich when we were alone. He was looking straight at me. “You were with Constable Barnes when this unfortunate event happened. Is there anything you would like to tell me that you—didn’t or forgot to tell—Detective Garnett?”

Last night Garnett had driven me home. The ride was not pleasant. Garnett was not pleasant. But it wasn’t just him. It was the fact that Barnes got hurt—and got hurt while with me. Garnett drilled me on every point: what time I got there, what did I do? Whom did I talk to?

Beadsworth had instructed me to keep my answers vague, which I did. I told Garnett about the girl who wanted to buy me a drink and the chemistry kid, Jeff, but nothing specific.

"Who was this Jeff?" asked Aldrich.

"Some guy."

Aldrich sensed I was hiding something.

"What did he look like?" Aldrich asked.

"He was short, black, wore funky clothes," I lied. I had a feeling if I told Aldrich the truth he would start investigating the kid's background. I didn't want the kid involved in this mess. He was at the House of Jam to have a good time. He had just graduated.

"Officer Rupret, remember what I said when we first met?"

I thought hard. "I was . . . young . . . creative . . . good looking . . . and imaginative." I stopped, hoping that was it.

"No." Aldrich shook his head. "That there would be a lot demanded of you and I hoped you were prepared for it."

I remembered now.

"I'm afraid I was wrong. You are *not* prepared for it."

I didn't know what to say.

"You're not fit for this unit and you're most certainly not fit for intelligence. After we are through I will have you sent back to parking enforcement."

My blood was boiling. My middle finger was twitching rapidly. *Introduce me. Please introduce me. Just once.*

I held back.

I was cut deep with Barnes getting hurt. This was salt rubbed on those cuts.

"Remember what I said to you, Sir?" I said.

He listened.

"I'll quit the force."

"Are you resigning, Officer Rupret?"

"No. Not until the task is completed."

He paused and then waved me off, "Dismissed."

Ms. Zee slammed her hand on the table. Suraj took a step back, while Kong stood his ground. "He was a police officer," she yelled. "What if we were discovered? Do you know our plans would have been destroyed? Do you know how much I've invested in this? Both of you placed our operation in jeopardy. If he was killed, the entire force would be after you two."

Joey and Hause were also in the room.

Ms. Zee turned to Joey, "Did you talk to anyone?"

"No. I would never do that."

Her stare pierced into his heart.

"All I did was get a drink and maybe dance a little, that's it," he pleaded.

She believed him. He had no reason to talk to anyone.

Martin entered. He didn't look too happy. Ms. Zee couldn't handle any more trouble.

"What is it?" she said.

"Can we talk alone?" he said.

She dismissed all of them with a wave of her hand.

"Four of the five businesses are up and running," he said.

"Then what is the problem?"

"The start-up costs have been huge; from registering the businesses to hiring the employees. With no immediate revenues we won't be able to run these businesses forever."

"Call Burrows," she said. "Let's have a word with him."

A few minutes later, Ed Burrows entered the room, looking weak and tired. He'd spent all his waking hours trying different combinations of the drug, but nothing so far that could get the results they wanted.

"Mr. Burrows," Ms. Zee said. "Do you have any news for us?"

He thought hard about his answer.

She rephrased her question, "Will we ever be able to produce Nex?"

Ed Burrows didn't have an answer.

We drove to DAS to meet our analyst, Eileen Mathers. She motioned us to follow her. We went inside the lab and to a corner.

"What have you found?" Beadsworth asked.

"What we already knew," she said. She was holding several sheets of print-outs. She pulled out the first sheet. It showed two graphs. The graph resembled the display of a sound synthesizer or a heartbeat monitor with steady lines, but sudden abrupt peaks.

"As you can see—" she started.

I interrupted her, "Can you explain how this gas photography machine works?"

"Gas chromatography," she corrected me.

"That's what I mean," I said. I was curious. Also, I needed something to divert my mind from the conversation with Aldrich.

"Gas chromatography is an analytical method used to separate mixtures. It indicates, based on the component's volatility, solubility and absorption of the relative quantity of each component."

I stared at her blankly.

She tried again. "Gas chromatography separates the different components in the sample. The mass spectrometer identifies the atomic composition of each of the components. This data is then compared by a computer to a database of hundreds of known drugs and other compounds to see if there are any matches."

"Interesting," I said, nodding. I had no idea what she was talking about.

She was not talking to an intelligent adult; she was in fact talking to an eight-year-old as far as science was concerned, who was more interested in looking at comic books than reading a textbook.

"How does that work exactly?" I asked.

"First we dissolve the solid with a solvent, and then, using an injector, pass it through a long tubular column with a stream of helium gas. It separates the liquids on the basis of their boiling points. As they exit the columns, the mass spectrum detector records the drugs. Then you have this." She held up the graphs again.

"Yes," I said, not understanding. "The graphs."

"Each peak represents a single component. If we have several components in a drug then we'll have several peaks. The first graph shows the amount of each component, the other the time it took to emerge from the drug."

She pointed to the one peak. "This is the analysis of the first sample—the orange tablet. From the Mandelin test we already knew it contained Ketamine but this further verifies it. Ketamine is the sole component in the tablet."

She pulled out the second print. This one had two peaks.

"This is for the green tablet. Earlier, through the Marquis test, we verified it contained Ketamine and caffeine, but we did not know how much. If you look at the graph, caffeine has a higher peak, almost five times as large as Ketamine."

She pulled out the third graph. This one looked like it had gone berserk. It had many peaks.

"This is a mixture of many components. The largest being Ketamine—just by looking at the peak you'll agree. Then caffeine, then MDMA—"

"What?" I said.

"Ecstasy."

"Thank you."

"Then pseudo ephedrine." Before I could say something she said, "If taken in large quantity it has the same effect as speed. You'll find it in Sudafed."

I looked satisfied so she continued.

"Then DXM, found in Vicks formula. Finally, methamphetamine, more potent than amphetamine."

"That's a lot of components in one drug," Beadsworth said.

"Yes, but not uncommon. That is why it is so dangerous. This particular tablet contains components that give you the speedy effect with ephedrine, caffeine, and methamphetamine. The relaxation effect with DXM. And the altered state of consciousness effect with Ketamine."

"So it *can* numb you, relax you, and then pop you back out?" I asked.

She thought about it and then said, "Yes."

Beadsworth and I looked at each other.

"But, it will not take immediate effect," she said.

We both blew a sigh of relief.

"Is there any way for it to take immediate effect?" Beadsworth asked.

"Intravenously. That's the only way I can think of."

She handed Beadsworth a brown envelope: The Certificate of Analyst.

Beadsworth didn't look inside; he just nodded and thanked her.

16

The ride through downtown was tough. I was upset. No matter how hard I tried I couldn't get myself in a good mood. I kept seeing Barnes' face—bloodied on the floor. I couldn't shake off the fact that it could have been me.

I shook my head.

That was too much to think about.

As we drove by I saw people sitting outside on benches eating and chatting away. I wished I were outside eating on one of those benches. I wished I worked in one of those big financial buildings. All I would do is get up in the morning, dress, and go to work. Work eight-to-four, or my favourite, nine-to-five. Not ever having to worry about your co-worker getting hurt.

I hate to admit it.

My mother was right.

She's always right.

On my sixteenth birthday my mom got me a year's subscription to *Business Weekly* magazine. She hoped by reading these I would somehow be enticed to enter the world of commerce. I remember now what a lousy birthday that was. I was hoping for the latest Nike Air Jordans. I can truly say my heart was broken.

It suddenly struck me.

"Shit," I yelled. "Tomorrow is—"

"Is everything okay?" Beadsworth said.

"Yeah, great," I said. "Just thinking."

"You want to talk about it," said Beadsworth.

"Talk about what?"

"What happened at the House of Jam. You've been unusually quiet."

"No. I'm fine."

"Yes, of course," he said and abruptly shut up.

We drove in silence, passing more of Toronto's magnificent buildings. "Can you drop me off here?" I said.

He stopped the car. He didn't say anything.

I said, "I just need some time to myself."

He nodded and drove off.

I walked down Yonge Street. I saw a store and entered. The place smelled nice. A girl behind the counter smiled as I walked up.

"I'm looking for a perfume," I said.

It was obvious. This was a perfume shop.

"For someone special?" she asked.

"Very." I smiled.

"Do you know what she likes?"

"Perfumes. That's all I know."

"That's not a problem," she said, and began showing me different brands from the display counter. She handed me a strip of hard paper and sprayed one of the brands on it. I smelled it. Nice.

She sprayed another. Nice too.

Then another.

And another.

By the fourth one my nose had had enough. After that, all of the brands smelled the same.

"Any you think she might like?" the girl behind the counter said.

"I'll take that one," I said pointing to the first brand, not because I thought it was better but because it was the one that registered most accurately in my nose.

I thanked her, paid, and left the perfume shop with a bag containing Elizabeth Taylor's Black Pearl.

With the bag of perfume under my arm I strolled out onto the street. There were too many things on my mind. What was I doing in Operation Anti-R.A.C.E.?

I was walking along the sidewalk when I felt something—on the road—follow me. I could feel a presence, as if a car was right behind me, moving at my pace.

I stopped. I sensed that it stopped, too.

This was bullshit. I turned.

A familiar orange and navy green taxi had come to an abrupt halt. The driver instantly looked away as if he was sight-seeing.

I shook my head.

I went over and knocked on the window. The driver rolled down and innocently looked at me.

"Sir," I said in my police-like tone. "Are you following me?"

"No, Sir," he said.

"Then you're stalking me. That's illegal in this country."

"No, I was not stalking." He shook his head.

"Then what were you doing?" I demanded.

He paused and then said, "I was waiting to run taxi over you."

I laughed.

Mahmud Hanif laughed back.

I got into the back.

"Where do you want to go?" he asked.

"Nowhere special," I said, stretching in the back, but then suddenly I went upright. "Did you turn on the meter?"

"It's not working," he said. He tapped the meter.

"Yeah, right," I said. "Let me see." I leaned over and began poking into the small machine.

"No," he protested. "It will break."

"I thought it was broken," I said.

"Yes, but it will break more."

"Turn it on." I was now serious.

He hesitated.

"Now."

He complied.

"Good," I said falling onto the back seat.

"Something wrong?" he said. "You don't look good."

". . . Just that one of my co-workers was brutally beaten and of course I'm the one to blame. Also, I'm going nowhere in the force. In fact, I might just quit the force all together. Apart from that, everything is great. How 'bout you?"

He narrowed his eyes and through the rear-view mirror looked at me hard. "You're making jokes, yes? You call it sarkasim."

"Sarcasm," I corrected him. "And no, I'm not joking. Mahmud, I don't know what's going on."

"Your covert operation not going good?" he asked.

"Not exactly."

"You're not beating evil people?"

"No. It looks like they're beating us."

"You know what you need?"

"What?"

"Chai."

"What?"

"Indian tea. That's what you need. Hot cup of chai."

I shrugged. I wasn't a tea drinker.

"Come, I'll take you to a place where they make the best chai."

"Maybe later. I need time to collect myself."

"Collect?" he said.

"Time to think."

"Yes."

I leaned back and closed my eyes. One camera tape from the House of Jam was missing. My gut told me it was the very tape that had recorded the attack on Barnes. My gut also said that something was happening behind my back. Something that I was not supposed to know. What could it be?

Why was I brought into Operation Anti-R.A.C.E. when I was the very person who had ruined another drug investigation? Also, I was not even a constable. There must be more qualified officers than me. Of course, there *are* more qualified officers than me.

Maybe, just maybe, I was brought in because I was an outsider: a civilian officer. Aldrich had said *There would be a lot demanded of me and that he hoped I was prepared for it.* What did he mean? Prepared for what? Did Aldrich have plans for me? If so, what plans? If I was brought in from outside, there must be something for me to uncover.

"There is an old saying," Mahmud said, snapping me out of my thoughts. "We dug out a mountain but discovered only a small mouse."

I thought about it. I had no idea what that meant.

"Your big problem may only need a simple solution."

I nodded. "I hope so." I gave Mahmud an address in Scarborough.

I told him to park a block away. He parked and said, "That will be twenty-two dollars and seventy-five cents."

I shoved my hand into my pocket and could just manage thirteen dollars. "Do you know what IOUs are?" I said, embarrassed. Here I was forcing him to turn on the meter and I didn't have enough money to pay him.

"Don't worry," he said. "If you don't pay next time I will follow you and *for real* run you over." He smiled.

"Thanks, Buddy." I patted him on the shoulder. "You're now officially my best friend."

I found Beadsworth sitting in the car. I tapped on the passenger-side window. He unlocked and I got in. He was going over some papers that looked like a child had written on them.

"My son's homework," he said, realizing I was staring. "Just making sure it's correct."

"Sure," I said.

I stared out to the building across while he continued double-checking the papers. I kind of admired him for that. He seemed like a devoted family man.

"One boy and one girl?" I asked.

He looked up from the sheet of paper. "Two boys."

"Which one got hurt?" I asked.

He thought about it and then realized what I was talking about. "Noel—the oldest—broke his arm. He's a goalie in his school's soccer team. Then there's baby Liam."

"How old is Liam?"

"Five months."

I moved my head up and down, not knowing what to say.

After a few seconds of silence he went back to the papers.

I glanced at the building across and all looked normal.

"Where's Nemdharry and Terries?" I asked.

"Every morning a U-Haul truck drives into the back of the building and leaves shortly after. Today, Constable Terries followed it to Hamilton. Detective Nemdharry just went to meet her. We're waiting to hear from them."

There was a loud tap at the window.

I started.

I looked over at Beadsworth, who was rolling down the glass. A man was leaning down, smiling.

"I saw you working behind the wheel," the man said. "Just thought I'd give you a surprise."

The man had smooth light brown skin and a long ponytail.

"You got my message, David?" Beadsworth said.

"Sure did," the man answered.

Beadsworth introduced me. "This is Officer Jon Rupret. This is Detective David Longfoot."

The man leaned in, extended past Beadsworth, and shook my hand. Suddenly, his smile faded. "Aren't you—"

"—David, we have a lot to talk about," Beadsworth interjected. "Officer Rupret, why don't you go for a walk?"

"A walk?" I said, confused.

"Yes, check out the area. Familiarize yourself with the surroundings." Beadsworth had a broad smile.

"Yeah, sure," I said, and got out.

17

There was definitely something happening behind my back.

I should have protested. I was on duty. I had every right to not go for a walk. Whatever they had to discuss they could do so with me. But I decided against it. I was now infamous for ruining the drug-squad investigation and I sensed Detective Longfoot had recognized me.

I walked east, not knowing where else to go.

Scarborough is very multicultural. There are a lot of ethnic stores. I passed by a Sri Lankan clothing store. A barber shop—with Chinese barbers. An electronic shop . . . looked like owned by East Indians. A bubble-tea store, probably owned . . . hey, it was the same one I wanted to try out with Detective Terries.

I leaned on the window and took a peek. The interior looked cozy.

Martin was in the basement of the Bubble T Shop. The heavy metal door to the entrance of the basement was secured and locked. Only he and Ms. Zee had keys.

Martin was not happy. The pill-making machines were sitting idle. After a lengthy meeting with Ms. Zee it was decided capsules were the direction they would go.

According to the initial plan they would have been producing thousands of pills each and every hour.

He circled the machines, scooping the dust with his finger. So many hidden meetings, so many bribes, so many lies went into acquiring these machines. Now, they sat with no use. Maybe he could sell them, but to whom?

Martin found a chair and sat down.

He adjusted his tie. He had come to the conclusion that Ms. Zee would never have Nex.

She was paying him well, and she trusted him, but that wouldn't last very long. Once the money ran out she'd turn on him—just like she did on Armand. *That fool!*

They were all fools for believing him.

Martin sighed. He had also believed Armand. His shoulders slumped. He had to find a way out. This bubble-tea venture was his idea. It was only to serve as a disguise for the production of Nex. Several others would be up and running in a matter of weeks.

Once money ran out, Kong would have his head.

I entered the shop. The place was dim. Tables and chairs lined the middle with couches and other seating to the side. There were a few people sitting and talking. Music piped from the corners of the walls. A friendly and welcoming atmosphere, if I may say so.

I headed straight toward an Asian girl.

"Hi, welcome to Bubble T Shop. My name is Susan. How may I help you?" she said with a pierced tongue.

"Um, yes," I smiled, looking intently at the menu on the wall behind her. There were so many names I didn't recognize.

"What would you like?" she said.

"No clue."

"First time at a bubble-tea café?"

"Yes, what is bubble tea anyways?" I inquired.

"It's simply tea mixed with tapioca pearls. We have it in several flavors: passion fruit, strawberry, mango, taro, honeydew, kiwi."

"I'll take strawberry, please," I said, not wanting her to recite the entire menu.

"Okay."

I went and sat in the corner facing the doors.

A few minutes later the girl placed a tall glass with a straw on the table. I looked at it. It was sort of pinkish. I took a sip and waited. Then took another sip.

Martin gently shut and locked the metal door and went upstairs. He moved past Susan and stopped. Sitting in the corner was someone he recognized, sipping a strawberry tea. Yes. He was a police officer.

John Rupert or something along that line was his name. Their informant in the police force had provided names and photos of the members of Operation Anti-R.A.C.E. What was Rupret doing here? Inspecting the premises, perhaps.

There must have been a leak. Someone must have tipped the police. They were after him. No. Stop. He controlled his composure. It was just a coincidence this officer was here.

Martin took a deep breath. This was absurd. He shouldn't be acting like this. He was a lawyer, a reputable business advisor. Not a criminal.

Martin relaxed, but tensed up again when, in the distance, he saw Kong get out of his car and approach the shop.

He knew the police had a picture of Kong. If this police officer saw Kong, their cover might be blown.

He had to do something, but what?

This tea wasn't half bad. I sipped. I was glad I had come here. I could finally relax and chill out.

There were a few more customers in the place now. A man in a suit stood behind the counter, staring at me.

Once he realized I saw him, he smiled and began walking toward me. I turned around but there was a wall behind me. I was cornered.

"Hi," he said.

"Hello," I replied.

"Is this your first time at the Bubble T Shop?" he said.

"Um . . . yes," I said.

"Oh, forgive my rudeness, I'm the owner of this shop," the man said. He was standing very close. "How do you like our establishment?" He had a wide smile.

"Nice. Good tea," I held the half glass of strawberry tea in the air.

"We want all our customers to be fully satisfied. If there is anything you don't find to your liking you just let us know and we'll do everything to have it corrected."

"Thank you," I said. *It's good that these days businesses aim to please their customers.*

"What do you think of the wallpaper?" he pointed behind me.

I wasn't sure what he wanted but I turned. "Very nice."

"Do you think the colour is pleasing?"

It was brown.

"Um . . . I think so."

"Have a closer look."

He was very keen on my answer. "Yes . . . now that I have . . . um . . . a better look, I think it's good. But it could be a little . . . darker."

"Darker? Oh, dear." He looked heartbroken.

"No-no, just a little. Overall it still gives the place a cozy . . . touchy . . . feely . . ." I was searching for more words. "Touchy, friendly feeling."

"I'm glad," he said, wiping at his forehead. "This is my first venture and I want it to be a success."

"I understand," I said, raising my hand in protest. "I'm more than happy to provide my insight."

"Thank you," he said, looking around, more relieved.

I'm always glad to help those in need.

"The next time you come," the man said. "Anything you like will be complimentary—on the house."

"Hey, thanks. Sure, I'll come back. Many times."

At that moment my phone went off. It was Beadsworth.

I thanked the owner and left.

Martin's shoulders sagged when the officer was out of the premises. He adjusted his tie. During the entire ordeal he had been sweating profusely. He felt wet and sticky.

He barged to the back and confronted Kong, who was standing with his huge arms folded.

"What are you doing here?" Martin snapped.

Kong did not answer.

"That was a police officer. We could have been shut down. For all we know there could be a surveillance van waiting outside recording our every move—*recording you entering here.*"

There was no reaction. Kong stared back.

Martin adjusted his tie once more and smoothed his coat. It was useless talking to him. If he wanted anything done he would have to talk to Ms. Zee.

Beadsworth was sitting alone when I got into the passenger seat.

"Done with your private conversation?" I said.

He didn't answer.

"Come on," I snapped. "I see what's going on."

He turned to me. "What *is* going on?" he said.

"Stuff . . . secret stuff. Stuff you don't want me to know."

"Officer Rupret, let me just say, things were happening before you arrived. These things may continue to happen even after you leave."

"I have no idea what you just said."

"Precisely, and I prefer it be kept that way."

I was ready to say something when he said, "Constable Terries and Detective Nemdharry are in Niagara Falls."

"Niagara Falls?"

"The U-Haul briefly stopped in Hamilton and moved on to Niagara Falls."

Something occurred to me. "Could Nex be made there," I pointed to the building across. "And then distributed in Niagara Falls?"

"Maybe."

Something else occurred to me. "From Niagara Falls it might then be passed through the border and into the States."

He thought about it and his face went grave.

I was going to say more when another car drove up and parked right beside us.

"We're being relieved," Beadsworth said.

I entered my house and headed straight for my apartment. I was halfway up when the ground-floor door opened and my landlady popped her head out.

"Jonny?" she said.

"Yes," I said, then realized I was supposed to have dinner with her. "Am I too late?"

She had a gentle smile. She handed me a white container. "I left some mechado for you. I know you're very busy."

I thanked her and went upstairs.

I opened my door, walked down the hall, and placed the container in the microwave. I walked back and stopped, "Sorry, Mike. I missed you, too." I'm proud to say that Michael Jordan never got angry with me.

I pulled out Elizabeth Taylor's Black Pearls and wrapped it in a flowered wrapping paper.

I leaned back on the sofa with the container of mechado in my hand and began watching the fourth quarter of the basketball game.

18

Early in the morning I showered, shaved and made breakfast. From the closet I pulled out a suit, pressed shirt, drycleaned pants, a tie that had belonged to my father, and recently shined shoes. I dressed as if I was going to a high profile business meeting.

With the package under my arm I waited outside. When Beadsworth's GM pulled up I got in the passenger side.

The car did not move. Beadsworth was staring at me.

"Something wrong?" I said.

He was wearing his three-piece brown suit, which was what I wanted for this occasion.

He did not speak. He just kept staring.

"What?" I said.

"I'm sorry, did someone die?" he asked.

"No, no. Is that what you think?"

He shrugged slowly. "You don't normally . . . dress."

"Today is different."

He waited.

"Today is my mom's birthday," I beamed. "You and I are going to meet her."

"Where?"

"Guelph."

"I don't think we are authorized to go there," he said.

"I know," I said.

"Sergeant Aldrich would not be too pleased . . ."

"I don't care. I am going to meet my mom. Either you come with me or I'm going there by myself, which means you won't be able to watch over me." I hoped the last part would get him.

He thought about it. "All right."

Guelph is an hour's drive from Toronto. Beadsworth did not say a word during the ride. Every so often he would flip an occasional glance in my direction. I don't think he believed what he was seeing.

He parked on the side of the street like I instructed.

He was ready to get out when my hand stopped him. "Before we go in, there are a few things I would like to tell you."

He waited.

I considered my words very carefully. "We were a close family when I was young, very close . . . but . . . after my father left us . . . well . . . my mom became very protective."

Beadsworth nodded.

"So." I paused. "My mother is a little sensitive when it comes to law enforcement. So let's not mention any of the . . . complications that are happening in our case."

He listened. "Yes, of course. The incident at the House of Jam."

"Um . . . yes. That incident. Definitely. In fact, let's not talk about the police force in general."

He thought about it and then nodded.

"Good," I said.

We got out and went up to an old brick house.

I hid the package behind my back and pressed the doorbell. I was really excited to see my mother. I spoke to her occasionally but not as often as I used to.

The door opened.

My mother, whom I consider the most beautiful person in the world, was wearing a light green dress and an apron.

"Jonny," she said with a big smile.

"Mom," I said, and gave her a tight hug.

"You look weak," she said. "Have you been eating right? You look skinny as a cat."

Mothers, aren't they great?

I pulled out the package. "Happy birthday."

"Oh, I bet I'm going like it."

She was not going to open the present in front of me. She never did. But she always praised it. She always praised me.

"Oh, who's your friend?" she asked.

"This is Phillip Beadsworth."

Beadsworth smiled. "How do you do?"

"Nice to meet you," she said. "Come in. Come in."

The house was the same as the day I left. The same furniture, same decorations, same carpet—a little cleaner, though.

"Did you have it washed?" I said, pointing to it.

“I got it shampooed.”

“You got rid of that stain I made? You know, it took me a long time to get that on the carpet.”

“Have a seat,” she said to Beadsworth. She then disappeared into the kitchen. I knew she would return with something to eat. Some people never change.

“I’ll go help her,” I said.

I found her behind the counter quickly arranging snacks on a plate. Aesthetics were very important to my mom. Biscuits must be arranged in a pleasing way; so should the croissants and the cake.

“Mom,” I said. “It’s okay. You don’t have to do all this. It’s your birthday.”

“You should have told me you were bringing a guest,” she said, arranging the plate. “Lucky I had these things to serve.”

My mom’s the perfect host.

“Now, take this outside,” she handed me the plate. “What does your friend like? Coffee or tea?”

Beadsworth was kind of British, so I said, “Tea.”

I took the plate and went to the living room.

I placed the plate on the coffee table.

I sat down near Beadsworth.

“Have something,” I said, pointing to the plate.

“No, thank you. I’m quite fine.”

“No. Really. Have something. My mother would be insulted.”

He immediately leaned over and picked a biscuit.

My mother returned holding a tray with three cups.

Once we had all sipped our tea, my mother leaned back and spoke, “What do you do, Mr. Beadsworth?”

I interrupted. "He works with me."

"Oh, you're also a broker?" she said, smiling.

Beadsworth looked at me. I smiled back with pleading eyes. "Ah . . . yes," he answered.

"Are you married?" she asked.

"Yes. I have two children."

"How wonderful. Children are a joy. We were only able to have one."

I turned to Beadsworth. *That's me.*

"But trouble equivalent to two," she said.

That's definitely me.

"How long have you worked with Jonny?" she asked.

Beadsworth turned to me. "Just recently," I said.

"Forgive me for asking so many questions?" she said. "It's not every day that Jonny brings a friend over. I think . . . this is probably the first time."

"First time for everything, Mom," I said.

Beadsworth took a slow sip.

"Have they promoted you?" she said to me.

"You could say that," I answered. I didn't want to tell her I had just moved from parking enforcement to drugs and narcotics.

"A promotion. Really?" she said with excitement.

"Yes . . . but a lot of travel," I said, feeling swamped with work.

"You see, Mr. Beadsworth, Jonny won't help in my investments. You would think working at Nesbitt Burns he would help his mother."

"Nesbitt Burns?" Beadsworth whispered.

I beamed like a proud son. Yes. Nesbitt Burns.

"Maybe you can talk some sense into him," she continued. She turned to me, "You know everyone at work would love to have you look into their finances. They are always asking about you and all I can say is that Jonny is too busy."

"But Mom," I protested. "Mr. Chiklist is doing a good job."

"Yes, but you could do a better job."

"Mr. Chiklist's been watching over our finances since I was a kid. He helped us pay off this house."

"I have nothing against Mr. Chiklist. He's wonderful. But when you have a son working in the industry—and working in a place like Toronto, you can't help but think differently."

I was about to say something when the phone rang.

"I'll take it in the kitchen," she said, "excuse me."

"Nesbitt Burns?" Beadsworth looked at me. "What do you know about Nesbitt Burns?"

"Not much in the beginning. I thought they made cookies. Now I can differentiate between the bull and the bear market."

My mother returned. "It was an old friend congratulating me," she sat back down.

Beadsworth spoke, "May I use your washroom?"

"Yes, of course, it's on the second floor to the right."

When we were alone, I said, "Mom, I won't be staying long." I let the words trail off. Every birthday, my mom and I, go out for dinner. But I didn't think Aldrich would be too happy with us being in Guelph.

"Why not?" she said softly.

"We have to go . . . to . . . this meeting, you know, to meet new clients. That's how we make money, by getting new investors."

"I understand," she said. She paused. "I was hoping you wouldn't come alone this time."

"See, I didn't," I said. "I brought a friend."

"No, it's not that. I mean a lady friend."

"Come on, Mom. Let's not start with that."

"Jonny, when am I going to see grandchildren? I'm getting old and I don't know . . ."

"Mom, please."

She leaned over and motherly rubbed my hand. "Find a nice girl and settle down. You already have a good job."

I scratched my head.

"Jonny, you're everything I've got."

"I know."

We heard Beadsworth's footsteps coming down. I got up.

"Happy birthday, Mom," I whispered and hugged her.

"We'll be leaving," I said to Beadsworth.

"Thank you for the tea, Mrs. Rupret," Beadsworth said and headed for the door.

In the hallway I stopped and said, "Mom, right now I've got a lot of things going on . . . I'm in a new position." This *was* true. I was no longer a PEO.

"I understand, Jonny," she said.

"I'm sorry that I can't stay."

"Sorry for what?" she said cheering up. "This means I'm free to go see Tom Jones."

"What?" I piped. "You got tickets to Tom Jones?"

"Yeah, Patty has to two tickets."

"Patty McNicoll? She still teaching grade six?" Mrs. McNicoll was my teacher when I was in grade six.

"No, she's retired and at home. That's why she got the two tickets, so we ladies can get out."

"You know what?" I said. "I'm not going back to Toronto. I don't need the money."

"Is that right?" my mom said, putting her hands on her hips.

"As the man of the house I demand I get Tom Jones tickets, too."

My mother laughed. She was the most beautiful woman in the world.

She hugged and kissed me.

When we were out of Guelph, Beadsworth spoke. I knew what he was going to say and I was ready.

"Your mother doesn't know you're a police officer?" he asked.

"Not exactly," I answered. He waited for more. "My mother doesn't feel law enforcement is a safe profession."

"She is correct."

"I just can't get the courage to tell her."

"My apologies, it's none of my business."

"I'm going to tell her. I'm definitely going to tell her. One day. Soon." I was talking more to myself.

19

The Lincoln jetted down the Gardiner at speeds well over one hundred kilometres an hour. Hause was behind the wheel.

"Slow down," Ms. Zee ordered from behind. This was no time to be pulled over.

Ms. Zee had asked Martin to accompany them. He had been acting different these days. She didn't need her business advisor getting any ideas. She was going to pay close attention to him. That was why she had sent Kong to pay him a visit at the Bubble T Shop. The close encounter with the black officer had made Martin even more . . . difficult. He was constantly asking about Nex, suggesting, not in exact words, that they pull out of the operation.

They drove to an address near Bathurst and Dupont Streets and parked in front of a semi-detached house.

"Your friend lives here?" Martin asked.

Burrows didn't answer. He was too busy trying to get out of the car.

"Hause, stay here," Ms. Zee ordered. "Keep your eyes open."

Burrows led the way from the side of the house to the back. They passed through a gate and went to the basement.

Burrows knocked. "Frank, open up. It's Ed," Burrows demanded.

The door opened and a short man wearing a Limp Bizkit t-shirt stood facing them. "Come in," he said.

The basement didn't smell too welcoming. Martin took out a handkerchief and covered his mouth. Pigs lived better than this man, Martin thought.

"Did you bring the money?" Frank said to Ed Burrows.

"First show us what we want," Ms. Zee said.

Frank looked in the direction of Ms. Zee but didn't make eye contact. He went to a room and came back holding a plastic bottle. There was a small table with styrofoam boxes scattered on it. With the back of his hand he cleared it; the boxes fell to the floor.

He dropped a couple of white tablets on top of the table and stood back. "That's what you want," he said, still refusing to make eye contact with anyone.

They didn't understand.

"What is it?" Ms. Zee said.

"Rapidly disintegrating tablets," he responded, looking at the ground. "They will dissolve in the mouth within two to three seconds."

"Three seconds?" Ms. Zee said. "Is that possible?"

"Yeah. Two to three seconds."

Burrows brow furrowed and he made no comment.

"Try it," Frank said.

Ms. Zee looked at Burrows, who shook his head. She didn't even bother turning to Martin, who was still holding the handkerchief over his mouth.

"All right," Frank said. "I'll try it." He picked one tablet and placed it on the back of his tongue and closed his mouth. Hardly a second later, he opened and his tongue was empty of the tablet. "It's safe. It's just a placebo."

Seeing this, Burrows had to satisfy his scientific curiosity. He gingerly picked one tablet and placed it in his mouth. The tablet disappeared on his tongue. He smiled at Ms. Zee. "Yes, it's possible."

She picked one tablet and tried it. It was true. She turned to Martin.

Martin wasn't interested, but her stare pushed him. He didn't like the tablets lying exposed to the filth on the table. He carefully picked one up and immediately shoved it into his mouth. His eyes widened. Nex could actually be produced.

"It dissolves with the saliva," Frank said. "And goes straight into the blood stream—"

"—Having an immediate effect," Burrows completed the sentence.

There was a brief silence.

"Satisfied?" Frank said, as if he was talking to someone else in the room.

"Yes, but how?" asked Ms. Zee.

"Do you have my money?" he said.

"First. How?"

"No, no, no. I showed you, now my money."

Ms. Zee nodded to Martin, who removed a folded manila envelope and placed it on the table. Frank snatched it and disappeared into another room.

Burrows plucked another tablet off the table and crushed it between his two fingers. "It's powder."

"Yes, of course it's powder," Frank said coming back.

"Now will you tell us how?" Ms. Zee said. "That is why we paid you."

"It's freeze-dried. It's a precise process—but once done will give you that result."

"What does it contain?" Burrows said, looking at the powder on his fingertips.

"Gelatin, mannitol, glycine, sodium lauryl sulphate, and sodium hydroxide, and some sweeteners for elegance."

Ms. Zee didn't understand, but she hoped Burrows did.

Burrows responded, "Those are polymers, permeation enhancers and flavour and sweeteners: the usual excipients you find in any tablets."

"Yes, the key is the process."

He disappeared into the same room and reappeared with a stack of paper bound at the corners. "Everything you want to know is in here. The steps must be meticulously followed to ensure a functional product."

Ms. Zee picked the stack and, without looking, handed it to Burrows. He immediately began digesting the pages.

"I never gave that to you," Frank said.

Ms. Zee understood. Patents and copyrights were not his problem.

"Everything is in here," Burrows said with a glimmer of hope. "It *is* possible to have that result."

Back in the car, Martin asked, "How did you know about Frank?"

"Frank works for Bantam. Once I realized what the drug needed I contacted him. He refused at first; he didn't want to lose his job. But when I told him how Bantam had screwed me and so many others and that one day they'd likely screw him, too, he agreed to provide Bantam's secret delivery process designs. For a large sum, of course."

Ms. Zee didn't care for the reason, just that she finally had the manufacturing process in her hands.

We were in Scarborough and Beadsworth had just gotten off the phone with Aldrich. We were good to go. Tonight we were going to raid the building across.

Shortly before, Nemdharry had notified us that the white U-Haul had made a stop at a large warehouse in Niagara Falls.

We were waiting for sunset. We were waiting for darkness. It was only a few hours away. I was getting anxious. This was my first raid.

"Have you ever used a gun?" I heard Beadsworth say.

"Yeah, of course," I replied.

I had trained, of course, but had never used a gun in real life.

He leaned over and from the glove compartment pulled out a Glock. How do I know it was a Glock? I watch a lot of movies.

"This is more for intimidation than enforcement," he said.

It was heavy and black. I felt powerful and scared—all at the same time.

"Would I have to shoot anyone?" I asked Beadsworth. He was sketching a diagram of the building. Earlier he had circled the building from a distance.

"If necessary, yes," he answered.

"Have you shot anyone?"

He paused and thought about it. "Do you mean have I fired at anyone?"

"Same thing."

"Not quite. I *have* fired my gun at someone but I have never hit anyone."

I thought about it. "What if I have to shoot someone?" I asked.

"If you have to."

"What if I can't?"

"Then they will shoot you."

What if I did shoot someone and they died? I didn't know if I could live with that. Or worse, what if I got hit? I might die. This lingered in my mind.

A Toyota drove up and parked a few cars away. Garnett and Herrera emerged. Garnett had the usual *I'm-gonna-rip-your-head-off* look. Herrera looked different. He didn't have the cheerful look any more. He had the *Let's-get-down-and-nail-these-guys* look. I would look like that too if my partner had gotten hurt.

"Finally, we do something practical," Garnett said.

Herrera nodded. He looked anxious, and fidgeted.

Garnett had given authority over this raid to Beadsworth. Like us, he was looking forward to ending this.

Another car approached. Two plainclothes officers emerged from inside. They were introduced as Officer Ross and Officer Moro. They were both in their early thirties and looked like they knew what they were doing.

"Now that we are all here," Beadsworth said, spreading the paper with the design of the building on top of the car hood. We all circled around. "From my observations the building has one main entrance and several exits in the back. There is a main loading dock. There are two emergency exits on either side. Beside these exits there are two additional fire exits going through each level."

Beadsworth paused, looking over the paper. "Around eight-thirty a white U-Haul truck will park behind the building. Management has confirmed that the loading dock is shut down after eight o'clock. Meaning if there is any movement of goods it occurs through the emergency exits.

"Detective Garnett and Detective Herrera will move in from the front. Officer Ross and Officer Moro will take the fire exits and Officer Rupret and I will go up the emergency exits. Do you all have protection?"

Protection? I looked around.

Both Ross and Moro tapped their chests.

"Officer Rupret will need one," Beadsworth said.

Garnett went over to his vehicle and pulled a blue Kevlar vest from the trunk and handed it to me. It was heavy. "Do I get a helmet?" I asked.

"What?" he snorted.

"What if I got shot in the head?"

"That might not be such a loss," he said, and walked away.

I put on the Kevlar and then my jacket. I tapped my jacket pocket for the Glock. I then returned to the group.

"How's Barnes doing?" Moro asked Herrera. In the force only a handful knew what had happened to Barnes.

"He's recovering," said Herrera, not wanting to talk about it.

There was silence. I was getting anxious. My palms were sweating. My stomach was churning. My heart was beating. I had to calm myself. I looked around. I spotted the Bubble T Shop. That would relax me—a cup of bubble tea. Strawberry. But I couldn't just leave. Could I?

"We still got time," I said as casually as possible. "You guys want something? Coffee? Bubble tea?"

Except for Beadsworth, they all gave me their orders.

I walked in the direction of the shop. I took deep breaths. I needed to relax. I entered the shop and found Susan behind the counter. She smiled, recognizing me.

"Welcome back," she said.

"Hello," I said.

"Let me guess," she smiled. "Strawberry bubble tea. Right?"

"Yes, one please," I responded.

"On the house," said a voice from behind the girl. It was the owner.

"But I need other stuff too. For my colleagues."

"Everything is complimentary," he said. He looked very happy.

"Thank you. You know, I'll come back here often."

He went silent.

"Next time I would like to pay, though," I said.

"Of course, of course."

I leaned closer. "You know what?" He also leaned closer. "I'm in the police force."

"Really?" he said, looking tense.

"And you know what?"

"What?" he said.

"I'm going tell everyone about you guys—"

He looked a little pale now.

"—Because you guys know how to treat your customers."

"Thank you," he said with a smile.

"After I'm through, this place will be packed. You know how cops are, always eating doughnuts and drinking coffee. You'll have more business than ever."

"Thank you," he said again.

I really didn't mind helping good, decent, hard-working people. All they ever want is to make an honest living.

Susan handed me my order and I left.

"This is good," said Ross. He was drinking a kiwi bubble tea.

"Yep, the best," I said sipping my strawberry. "You sure you don't want any?" I said to Beadsworth, who shrugged me off.

"Not bad," Garnett grunted.

Nemdharry and Terries and a team were waiting outside the warehouse for us. When we went in, they'd go right after us. The raid had to be at exactly the same time. No chance for R.A.C.E. to warn anyone.

Half an hour later a white truck drove up and eased into the back of the building. We were sitting in our cars. Beadsworth speed-dialed and said something on his cell. He then signaled the two other vehicles.

The car with Ross and Moro sped out first, followed by the car with Garnett and Herrera. We were the last to leave the parking lot.

As we entered the front of the building we saw Garnett and Herrera swerve left and park at the main doors. We drove past them and straight through the side lane that led to the back parking lot. Up ahead we saw Ross and Moro's vehicle park vertically so as to block the entrance and exit to the back.

We stopped behind them and got out. This all took less than thirty seconds.

I raced around the corner to the back, sweating profusely underneath the vest. My heart was thumping and my knees felt like they would give at any minute. The back lot was dark and empty, except for one vehicle—the white truck. It was parked in front of a wide-open emergency door and it was still running. Ross stood beside it. He shook his head; no one was in it.

Beadsworth signaled me to take the other emergency door. I nodded and headed in that direction. I heard metal clangs and looked up to see Moro racing up the fire escape. I reached the door and found it had no handle.

Of course it had no handle. It was an emergency door, only to be opened from inside.

What should I do now?

Go back?

I had seen Beadsworth go through the open emergency door. I should go help him.

I was about to turn back when the metal door swung open and hit me straight in the face. I fell back, my head spinning and my eyes watery. A man stood beside the door holding a carton. When he saw me, he immediately dropped the box and retreated up the stairs.

I felt something roll through my nostril and onto my upper lip, but I didn't have time to check it out. I started after the man.

At the top of the stairs he turned right.

Skipping steps, I made it to the top. He turned again. I kept after him.

When I turned right for the third time, he was still climbing the stairs ahead of me.

"Stop!" I said, but he kept moving. I pulled out my gun. At the top he passed another man who was holding a large box.

The man froze. I was halfway up the stairs when he threw the box at me. I tried avoiding it, but it hit me like a brick. I lost my balance and tumbled down the stairs. My head hit something hard and I went blank.

20

They were in Regent Park, inside the laundry room, waiting for Marcus. Ms. Zee, along with Kong and Martin, waited patiently. Ms. Zee didn't care how long he took. Now she had the upper hand.

Martin was in a good mood. He had been in a good mood ever since they had received the manufacturing process. He moved from one washing machine to another, trying to find the best spot to lean on. He also continued tapping his coat pocket, checking, double-checking, as if the contents inside might disappear.

Kong stood beside her with his arms crossed over his chest. Kong was probably happy to be out of his confinement, but no one could really tell.

The door swung open and Marcus, in his fur coat, appeared. His bodyguard closed the door.

"I hope you have good news," Marcus said, dropping his coat to the bodyguard behind him. "I'm getting tired of these meetings."

Ms. Zee said nothing. She stood staring at him.

"*Yes*, can we get down to business?" Marcus sounded annoyed.

She still said nothing. Martin moved beside her.

"Okay," Marcus said. He snapped his fingers and the bodyguard immediately placed the fur coat over his shoulders.

"If you leave this meeting," Ms. Zee said. "I guarantee you'll regret it."

"Hey, Lady," Marcus snapped. "Don't ever threaten me." His face was getting red.

She smiled. "We have the product."

The redness faded and he said, "You do?"

She turned to Martin, who walked across and placed two white tablets on top of the lid of a washing machine.

"What is this?" Marcus said.

"Try it."

"I'm not trying none of your shit," he said.

"Fine. Then you'll never know." She turned to Martin.

"Okay, okay. Slow down," he said. She could tell he was eager. "I just don't want my man to get sick, you know." He sounded more polite now.

"There are no active ingredients in those. It's just a placebo."

"Then you don't have the drug?" he said.

"We will soon."

He nodded to his bodyguard, who picked up a tablet and placed it in his mouth. The bodyguard waited but did not swallow. He quietly went back to Marcus and whispered in his ear.

Marcus smiled.

"You don't want to try it?" Ms. Zee asked.

"I trust my man," he replied. "Now let's talk business."

I lay sideways on the sofa with my eyes open. The back of my head was sore and this position was more comfortable. I slept this way the entire night and suspected I might sleep this way for many more nights.

My nostrils were stuffed with bandages. My nose was not broken, only bruised. It hurt when I touched it. So I avoided doing that.

The time on my VCR was after ten in the morning. I was not to report to work until I had recovered fully and that could take days. I was up early and had managed to walk from the bed to the sofa.

Now I lay staring at the blank television and the digital clock on the VCR.

I remembered last night.

I remembered falling down the steps and hitting my head on the floor. I remembered being woken up by the paramedics. My head throbbed and ached but I was able to walk to the ambulance, yes, I did remember that. That's where they bandaged me up. I was told that when my head hit the floor I fell unconscious. They insisted I go into overnight observation but I protested. They relented after determining there was no serious damage and gave me some painkillers and told me to rest.

I also remembered being driven home by Beadsworth. I remember asking him if we had stopped R.A.C.E. At first he would not answer my question, but after much persistence he told me.

We did not find R.A.C.E. in the building. But that didn't mean there were no illegal activities transpiring inside.

LLPM Imports & Exports were not acquiring used clothing from the Goodwill and Salvation Army and sending them to third-world countries; they were pirating DVDs. At their location in Scarborough they were copying thousands of titles and shipping them to a warehouse in Niagara Falls before sending them across the border into the United States.

We were on a wrong trail from the beginning.

Yes, we had suspicions about the late night deliveries. Yes, we did stop an illegal operation, but we were nowhere closer to R.A.C.E.

This made my head hurt even more.

I tried changing positions but even that became difficult. My head was throbbing. I forced myself up, took one aspirin, and was back on the sofa.

The process was in motion. Things were happening fast. Orders were sent out for liquid nitrogen freezing tunnels, blister packs, refrigerated cabinets, and freeze-dryers.

Money was switching hands quickly, but Ms. Zee didn't care.

Burrows entered the room. "How long before we're set?" he asked. He was eager to begin.

"In a day or two," Ms. Zee said. "It will take time to acquire the equipment from our sources."

She was surprised at how well Burrows had adapted into the organization.

Joey walked into the room. He scratched his shaggy hair and slumped down on a chair.

Ms. Zee dismissed Burrows and said, "Is something wrong?"

"Yeah, I guess so." He didn't look at her directly. "I was thinking . . ." he let his words trail off.

She waited.

"After you have Nex . . . I . . . I want to leave."

"Of course," she said.

"I mean . . . I don't want any trouble. I just want to do my job and leave and get on with my life."

"Of course."

"I also need some money."

"How much?"

"Three thousand," he said, swallowing.

"Of course."

He nodded and got up. "I'll go see if Ed needs help or something."

She said nothing.

Joey closed the door and paused. He didn't really think Ms. Zee would let him walk away. That was not how it worked. Once Nex was complete his life would be in danger. He hadn't thought that when he had first started. But his mind changed when Armand disappeared. Joey was sure Armand had been killed.

Ever since Burrows arrived, Joey could sense his worth declining. Burrows liked to work alone. He rarely asked Joey for his opinions. Even if Joey had opinions, Burrows shrugged them off. Armand had not been like that. Armand hadn't liked him, but at least he let him do his job.

Joey had to get away and he had to get some place safe.

There was a knock at the door.

My eyes opened. I was still on the sofa. The VCR clock blinked 11:05 a.m.

More knocking.

I forced myself up and dragged myself to the door. I opened it. It was Beadsworth.

"It's early," I said.

Without saying a word he entered.

I went back to the sofa. My head hurt worse. The noise from the door had given me a migraine. "Pass me the aspirins," I said, lying down.

Beadsworth went into the kitchen and returned with my order. I took another pill.

He sat down. "I was going to bring you flowers but . . ."

"But you didn't," I said.

He nodded.

"Good. I'm not dying and I don't care."

He unbuttoned his coat, sat down, and crossed his legs.

"So what's up?" I said.

"I just returned from the meeting and Aldrich has halted the operation."

"What? He can't do that."

"He can and he did."

"We did stop an illegal operation."

"The Chief was not happy with our progress. Valuable resources are being wasted, she said. The investigation into the drug squad is already in the media and the Chief doesn't want any more publicity."

"This is bullshit, you know?"

"Yes, it is."

"Then how are we supposed to do our job?"

"We are not," he said with a hint of a smile.

"What?"

He said, "I spoke to Detective Herrera and he told me Constable Barnes is doing much better. He doesn't remember much from that night but he's slowly recovering."

"That's good to hear." I closed my eyes and then opened them. "You know," I started. "I've been meaning to ask, was there really money missing from the fink fund?"

"Yes," he replied.

"I read in the papers it was like over twenty thousand."

"More like forty."

"Wow," I said. "I guess those drug-squad guys do deserve the heat they are getting."

"Why would you say that?" he said.

I sensed Beadsworth was defensive.

"I—I mean how can you lose forty grand?" I said.

"Simple," he answered.

I waited.

He crossed his other leg and said, "Let me explain, this is how it is supposed to work and I hope you see a flaw in this. An officer receives information from an informant and decides what this information is worth. To pay this informant the officer gets approval from his supervisor, then goes to the cashier's office and collects the money. The officer then gets the informant to sign his *real* name for the money, which at the time is witnessed by a second officer."

I didn't see a flaw. It sounded reasonable.

"This is how it works in the real world: the cashier's office is open only during normal business hours, but the officer needs the cash during off hours. Also, the informant has the information but will not, under any circumstance, sign his real name. Remember, most informants only offer information when they need money and most of them have lengthy criminal records, which means they are not very trustworthy. Officers must rely on their judgement when dealing with these people.

"In order to further the investigation, the officer will pay the informant from his own pocket. Under certain situations the officer may credit payments to one informant but in fact be paying another, as the real informant refuses to sign for it.

Also, if an officer is working under cover and is alone, it is very difficult to have another officer as a witness. Don't you agree?"

I nodded. That made more sense.

We both fell silent.

"What do we do now?" I said, wiggling my attractive toes.

"We wait, I suppose," he replied.

"What about me?"

"You will rest and after . . ." he paused.

"After what?"

"You go back to parking enforcement."

I didn't protest. All this was taking a toll—physically and emotionally. It would be nice to go back. Sergeant Motley would welcome me with open arms.

I really missed giving out parking tickets. Except for the occasional irate driver, the job was primarily safe. I never had to see a co-worker get hurt, or see myself get hurt, for that matter.

"When can I go back?"

"You're very eager?"

"Yes . . . and . . . like I said before, I don't know why I'm on this team in the first place."

"I think I know why," he said. But before I could say something he stood up, "I read your file and it said you worked in the Guelph Police Services and particularly in the drugs and intelligence unit. Is this correct?"

I was ready to say yes but then thought about it. I was already being punished by the powers-that-be. No point in prolonging it. "I did work briefly for the Guelph police," I said. "But not in that unit."

"May I ask in what capacity, then?"

"Keying and filing."

Beadsworth did a double-take. "I beg your pardon?"

"I was an assistant to the records and data manager." I turned my head away. "I entered criminal records into the computer and filed them away."

I heard him say, "hmm."

I felt ashamed.

He then said, "I must go."

"Where to?" I turned back to him.

"Back to 23 Division."

Ms. Zee stared at the small clear container that held the white tablets. Nex would give her the power to control Toronto.

And they *would* expand.

She was determined to make it an empire. A business empire.

Nex was for lawyers, judges, doctors, politicians; yes, people with power would use Nex. Make people with influence dependent on Nex and you would control the city.

Her mind drifted to another thought. Joey.

She was going to miss him. She had given Kong the green light to get rid of him. Kong was pleased. Hause would dump the body in the Scarborough Bluffs.

Many mistakes had been made in the beginning. Trusting Armand, hiring Joey, these were crucial mistakes. Now she was going to have none.

The door flew open.

Hause entered, huffing and puffing.

"What's wrong?" she demanded, infuriated at being disturbed.

"He's gone," he said.

"Who's gone?'"

"Joey."

"Gone where?"

"I don't know."

"Did you search everywhere?"

"I checked the entire building. Kong is doing another sweep."

Joey never ventured out of the building alone. Never. He knew the consequences if he did.

Kong returned, displeased.

"What now?" Hause said.

"He may have gone to his parents' house," Ms. Zee said. "Go check."

21

I lay still, silently staring up at the ceiling. It had been more than an hour since Beadsworth had left. I was thinking about nothing in particular. My mind was shifting from one thought to another. There was so much I wanted to understand.

Operation Anti-R.A.C.E. had been set up too quickly. The team needed members with experience in catching criminals like R.A.C.E.

Now the team was being disbanded just like . . . the drug squad.

There was a loud bang.

I listened.

Bang, bang, bang came in rapid succession.

I got up and went to the door.

I opened it.

"Hey, Jeff!" I started. "What're you doing here?"

The shaggy-haired kid looked nervous.

"Hey, man," he said. "I'm glad you recognized me."

"How did you get up here?" I asked, thinking about my ultra-protective-security, my landlady.

Jeff said, "There was an old woman outside cleaning up stuff and I told her I was your friend."

"And she let you in?" I said. I must have a word with her.

"Can I come in?" he said.

I glanced back at the apartment and then said, "Sure. Come in."

He entered but leaped back, almost hitting the wall, when he saw Michael Jordan. "Oh, it's only cardboard," he said, laughing.

"Yeah, sorry about that," I said.

I led him to the sofa, where he sat down.

I offered him a drink but he declined.

I sat opposite him.

"What happened to you?" he said.

I touched my stuffed nose, "Long story."

He rubbed his hands nervously and seemed to be shaking.

I said, "I don't remember giving you my address at the club."

"I looked you up in the phone directory," he replied.

"Right, right," I said, nodding. "What can I do for you?"

"You're a cop, right?"

I nodded, slowly. "You could say that."

He seemed relieved. "Good, then I'm safe."

"Safe from what?" I said.

"Do these walls have ears," he said.

"Um . . . I don't think so. But if you talk loud enough my landlady downstairs will hear you."

"Then I'll talk quietly," he said, lowering his voice. "I'm in serious trouble."

I listened.

"I can't say right now from who but if I get protection, like those victim protection programs, then I'll tell you everything."

"Jeff, you have to first tell me why you are in trouble."

He lowered his head and stared at his fingers. "My name is not Jeff. It's Joseph Lenard."

"Okay, Joseph."

"Joey."

"Okay, Joey," I said. "Why are you in trouble?"

"There is . . ." he searched for the right words. "This group that is very dangerous."

I listened.

"They are trying to make—no, they are in the process of completing this drug."

"R.A.C.E.," I blurted.

"Who?"

"R.A.C.E.," I said. "I mean, Radical Association of Criminal Ethnicities."

"No," he shook his head. "I think you're confusing it with something else. But this group is working on this drug—"

"Nex?" I said.

His eyes widened and he said, "Yes. You do know?"

I immediately picked up the phone.

"No, don't," he said grabbing at it. "Please listen to me first."

His hand was on top of mine.

"There is a mole inside the force," he said.

"A mole?"

"Yes, someone was feeding information to us."

"Do you know who it is?"

"No."

"Don't worry, I'm calling my partner," I said.

"Can you trust him?"

I thought about it. I hadn't known Beadsworth long, but he was the only one I could call right now.

"Yes."

Joey released my hand and I called Beadsworth.

Beadsworth was in my apartment in less than half an hour. He eyed Joey suspiciously. Joey stared at his fingers. Beadsworth sat across from him and unbuttoned his jacket.

I said to Joey, "Tell him what you told me."

Joey coughed. "I need protection," he said, not looking up.

"From whom?" Beadsworth said.

"I can't say that right now. I need a guarantee first that I will be protected. The people I was working for are making a drug that's bigger than anything . . . it's going to be bigger than Ecstasy."

"Nex," Beadsworth said.

"Yes," Joey said.

"Do they have the drug?"

"Yes."

Beadsworth went silent. He was mulling over something in his mind. "Where can we find these people you worked for?"

"Not so fast," Joey said, waving his hands in the air. "First, my protection."

"I can't give you that," Beadsworth said.

Joey and I both looked at him.

"Why not?" I said.

"But I know someone who can."

"Who?"

"Sergeant Aldrich."

"You've got to be kidding," I said.

"Can you trust him?" Joey asked.

"Yeah, can *we* trust him?" I said. "There's a mole inside the force."

Beadsworth's face went pale. "Do you know who it is?"

Joey shook his head.

Beadsworth said slowly, "Sergeant Aldrich is in charge and our superior. It is our duty to inform him of this situation."

Joey nodded, understanding.

"Why are you helping us?" Beadsworth inquired.

"My life is in danger. I'm no longer needed. If I stayed they would kill me."

"All right," Beadsworth said. "Let me see if I can arrange something." He got up and headed for the door. I followed.

"Watch over him," he said.

With that he left.

With Beadsworth gone I was left with Joey. He massaged his hands while examining the interior of my apartment. There wasn't much to look at. The walls were adorned with old picture frames that I'd picked up from yard sales. They looked antique so I bought them. The previous tenant had left behind the sofa. After much shampooing it looked almost brand new. Almost.

The floor was hardwood, so no carpet was needed, and no vacuuming either. My landlady donated the dining table after she saw me eating on my sofa. She had bought a new one and was going to give it away anyway. My mother paid for the bedroom set, which was my moving away gift.

The television was probably the one thing that was new and the most expensive in the apartment. It was a Sony fifty-two-inch flat screen high definition with built-in stereo surround sound. It was my pride and joy. It made me want to come home every night.

"Nice television," said Joey.

"Thanks," I beamed like a proud father. "It's a Sony."

He relaxed.

"You want a drink?" I asked.

"Yeah, sure."

I brought him a can of Fruitopia.

After taking a sip he passed his hand through his thick hair. He leaned back and stared at the ceiling. I looked up at the ceiling too, but I couldn't find anything particularly interesting up there. I concluded he was tired.

Hause returned, shaking his head. Joey was not at his parents' house. Ms. Zee was worried. Where could he have gone?

Kong appeared behind the door. He didn't look her in the eye. She knew he was angry for not being allowed to kill Joey earlier. Maybe, she should have let him. It would not have caused this problem now.

The phone rang and she picked it up. She listened to the voice on the other end and hung up with a smile.

"We know where he is," she said.

"Do you have a computer?" Joey suddenly said.

"It's old," I answered.

"Does it have internet?"

"Yes."

"Can I use it?"

"Yeah, sure, it's in the bedroom."

He jumped up and then disappeared.

A long while later he emerged looking distressed.

"You find what you were looking for?" I asked.

"Kind of," he said. "One of my friends from college lives outside Toronto. I called him before I came to you but his number had changed. I did have his e-mail address so I just sent him a message. Hopefully he'll e-mail back."

"Your parents still alive?" I asked.

"Yeah, sure. Why?"

"I mean, why don't you go to them?"

"You crazy, these people know where my parents live. I bet you they checked to see if I was there. I can't go to them."

I nodded. He didn't want his parents involved. Smart kid.

I ordered Chinese food.

We sat on the dining table sucking down noodles and munching chicken wings.

It was getting dark when a Sundance parked at the corner of Gerrard and Greenwood. Two figures occupied the red vehicle. Suraj was behind the wheel with Hause in the passenger seat.

They had their orders and it was simple. Go into the house and finish the job. Hause pulled a sawed-off shotgun from under the seat and got out. Suraj cocked his pistol and concealed it in his pocket. They were halfway across the street when they stopped.

A blue Volvo turned onto Greenwood and parked in front of the house. Two men got out and headed for the door.

Hause and Suraj looked at each other and then doubled back.

I had a piece of chicken stuck between my teeth when there was a knock at the door.

Joey dropped his chicken and looked at me.

"Don't worry," I said, trying desperately to remove the intruder from my teeth with my tongue. "It's probably Beadsworth."

I went to the door and peeked through the eyehole. "I think we have trouble."

I unlocked and found Aldrich standing with his hands folded at his back. Behind him was his guard dog, Garnett.

"May we come in, Officer Rupret," Aldrich said drily.

No. You may not. In fact, get your blonde ass out of my home. And take your mutt with you.

"Of course, Sir," I said politely.

They both moved by me, with Garnett taking loud steps. They went into the living room.

"Where is he?" Aldrich asked.

I looked around and the living room was empty. So was the kitchen. "I'll get him."

I found Joey hiding in my bedroom closest.

"What are you doing?" I whispered.

"Who's outside?" he asked.

"The guys I work for."

"I thought it might be the guys *I* worked for."

We came out and Aldrich immediately sized Joey up. The kid held his ground. He looked Aldrich directly in the eyes.

"I want protection," Joey said.

"Your name?"

"Joseph Lenard."

"First, Mr. Lenard, tell us what we need to know and then we give you your protection."

"Okay, okay," Joey said. "I don't know any R.A.C.E. you keep mentioning. I do know that they are close to making a new drug."

"Nex," Aldrich said.

Joey shook his head. "Yes, Nex or whatever. That's what I heard them call it, too. In a couple of days they will have it and it will be all over the city."

Aldrich said, "You mentioned there was a mole in our organization. Do you know who it is?"

"No."

Aldrich listened. He then nodded as if he knew and understood everything. "You will accompany us and be placed in my custody."

"That won't be necessary," said a voice from behind. We all turned to see Beadsworth at the door.

"Excuse me?" Aldrich demanded.

"Sir," Beadsworth said walking up. "It would be better if he stays under Officer Rupret's protection."

"Detective Beadsworth, do explain," Aldrich said.

"A mole is working inside the department. Until we find out who it is we must not expose the witness."

Joey said, "I'm not a witness yet. First my protection."

They ignored him.

"It would be better," Beadsworth continued, "For the witness to be allowed to stay with Officer Rupret, who is outside the department and is on medical leave and would therefore be able to watch the witness at all times."

It felt like Joey and I were two little children whose fates were being decided by strangers.

There was a pause and then Aldrich said, "Detective Beadsworth, I respect your opinion. It may be better if the witness stays with Officer Rupret."

"Thank you, Sir," Beadsworth said with a slight nod.

Aldrich turned to Joey, "Give us something to begin our investigation."

Joey thought about it; his eyes searched for what information to divulge. "At the Scarborough Bluffs you will find the body of Armand Dempiers. He created the drug."

This caused a reaction. Aldrich spun around and was out the door, followed by Garnett who was dialing on the phone.

Beadsworth turned to me and whispered, "Do not let him out of your sight." With that, he disappeared around the door.

The chicken wings were cold and shriveled up. Joey shrugged and said, "I'm full."

Everything was packed and in the process of being moved. They could no longer use the current location. If Joey spoke, the police would be paying them a visit very soon.

Ms. Zee had taken certain precautions just in case something like this ever happened. Everything in their small headquarters was portable, from the furniture to the pharmaceutical equipment.

There was another problem that she had to resolve. The new technology required that they produce in one location. It was not financially feasible to purchase several freeze-dryers and other expensive equipment.

They needed a good location, not only for the production of Nex, but also for the distribution of it. Martin had been dispatched to search for one.

Her cell rang and she knew who it was. She listened and then hung up.

She already knew Joey was at the home of an officer named Jonathan Rupret. But this officer was not to be harmed under any circumstances. One officer had already been assaulted and injuring another would place more attention on them. She was not happy with this information.

She would have to find a way of getting to Joey without harming the officer. She couldn't rely on anyone in the group. Kong would snap the officer's neck at the first chance he got. Hause and Suraj weren't known for their smarts. She would have to do something on her own.

22

It was the next morning and Hause dropped Ms. Zee off a block away from Greenwood Avenue. She was wearing a beige skirt and a white blouse. Her auburn hair was untied and flowed freely to her shoulders.

Hause waited in the car for her signal. She walked in the direction of the officer's home but stopped at the corner of Gerrard and Greenwood. The plan was to get the officer out of the house, giving Hause enough time to go in and finish Joey. How she was going to do this she had no idea.

She looked across to the house and tried to think. Should she walk up to the door and say that she was lost? No, that didn't make any sense. She could ask anyone on the street for help. What if she went up to him and said she had just been robbed? No, then she would have to go to the police department to report it.

She put her hand through her hair, thinking of a plan.

I woke up and found Joey sleeping peacefully on the sofa. The coffee maker was brewing so I went to the bathroom. After I was done, I filled my cup and went to the balcony. The air was semi-fresh but the sun was shining brightly. I leaned on the metal railing and took a sip. The coffee needed a little more sugar.

I spotted a woman standing at the corner of the street. She looked distressed. She looked up at me. I smiled.

She looked around. I suddenly understood. I motioned her to wait and I went back inside.

Ms. Zee saw the officer come out onto the balcony and then smile at her. He then waved and disappeared. What was he doing? She didn't have any time to think when the front door swung open and the officer, still in his pajamas, came out running toward her. His nose was covered in a bandage.

"Has your car been towed?" he said.

"Sorry?" she said.

"Your car was towed, right?" he pointed to a spot beside the sidewalk. "You parked it here last night and this morning it was gone."

"Uh . . . yes," she understood. "How did you know?"

"I just do," I said. I wasn't going to tell her my car had been towed several times from the very same spot.

She said, "I don't know what I was thinking. I parked here, but this morning it's gone."

"From seven-to-nine it's a tow-away zone," I said.

"I didn't know that," she said.

"Did you just move down here?"

"My sister lives over there," she said pointing to a street adjacent to us. "What am I going to do?" she said.

She had amazing green eyes and even more amazing long red hair.

I said, "It's towed to Joe's Towing." I read her the address. "Just tell Joe Coultier I sent you."

"I didn't get your name," she said, smiling.

She had a great smile.

I don't know why but my face flushed. Maybe it was the way she looked at me. "It's Jonny *Rupert.*"

NO!

My face burned. "Rupret. R before the E," I said, collecting myself.

"Rupret," she said, repeating it to herself. "R before the E. Different but unique."

Now my knees were getting weak. Maybe it was the pajamas.

She said, "If it isn't too much trouble can you take me to Joe's Towing?"

"Sure," I said.

She smiled even more.

Suddenly I remembered. Joey. "Um . . . I can't."

Her smile faded.

"I've got . . . to . . . go somewhere."

"It'll be a quick drive," she said. "You can just drop me off and come back."

"I'm sorry, I can't." I hated doing this. I really did. But I couldn't leave Joey alone. Our investigation was relying on him. "I really cannot." I gave her the directions again.

She was disappointed, but she still smiled. She thanked me and headed in the direction of the streetcar.

Ms. Zee waited until the officer was out of sight and then went to the car. She entered the Lincoln and shook her head. Hause was ready and waiting with the shotgun. Without saying a word he started the car and they were gone.

As I got to the door I realized I hadn't asked her name. Damn, what an idiot I was. Going up the stairs I cursed myself for being so stupid.

I heard the toilet flush and a few seconds later Joey emerged from the bathroom.

"There's coffee if you like," I said.

He nodded and filled a cup.

"I'm going to go check my e-mail," he said, and with that he disappeared into my room.

Martin found a perfect spot, located in the warehouse of an industrial site along the waterfront of Lake Ontario.

The new technology demanded an area with enough room for the heavy equipment. The open interior of the warehouse was ideal for this type of manufacturing.

This would confine them to one location, but they had no choice. Too much money had already been wasted and now it was time to earn some back. Once Nex was produced and distributed they would find another location, but for now this would have to do.

Martin saw three U-Hauls enter the warehouse. He was determined to have Nex ready in the next couple of days. Ms. Zee was not available, so everything had to be done by him. She was busy trying to get rid of Joey.

I lay on the sofa with my eyes closed. It was close to afternoon and Joey was still in the bedroom. I didn't want to bother him. In fact, I didn't want him to bother me. I was not his babysitter. I was doing my job, while resting at home.

I tossed over. I was restless. I was upset at myself for not getting her name. She was friendly. A real damsel in distress and I couldn't help her. Maybe I could go to her home. What home? I didn't know where she lived. She pointed to a street but I didn't know the exact house. Maybe I could go and knock on each door and ask for someone I didn't know the name of. I tossed once more and decided to watch TV.

There was a knock on the door and grudgingly I opened it. It was Beadsworth. He entered without saying a word. I went back and flopped onto the sofa.

"Where's Joey?" he asked.

"In the bedroom," I answered.

He seemed relieved.

"So, what can I do for you?" I said.

"We found the body of Mr. Armand Dempiers. He used to be an employee of Bantam Pharmaceuticals Limited."

"Barnes and Herrera already briefed me on him," I said.

Beadsworth took a seat and then leaned over towards the bedroom.

"He's on the computer," I said.

Beadsworth fixed his tie. "They'll be performing an autopsy on Mr. Dempiers." Beadsworth looked nervous. I had never seen him nervous. "Um . . . we're waiting for the results . . . has anyone from the force visited Joey?"

"No, why?" I said.

"Sergeant Aldrich was upset that I requested Joey be put under your supervision."

“He was? Good. It’s about time the man grows some white hair. I don’t like him.”

“Can I have a word with Joey?” Beadsworth asked.

“Go ahead.”

Beadsworth got up to go over to the room when there was a knock on the door. Beadsworth answered.

Aldrich came in, but no Garnett.

I got up.

I sensed tension between Beadsworth and Aldrich. They exchanged welcomes, which I felt were contrived.

“Officer Rupret,” Aldrich said, with a nod.

I knew he wasn’t here for me so I called out for Joey. He came out of the room looking red-eyed. He’d been staring at the monitor for hours.

Aldrich got right to the point, “We’ve found the body that you mentioned. You were correct. It is why you must tell us more. Time is running out.” He shoved a stack of paper at Joey. “Sign it and you’ll have your protection.”

Joey looked at the bundle. He scanned it and then scribbled his signature. He then gave them an address. “You can find them there.”

“I will have Detective Garnett pick you up tomorrow,” Aldrich said.

Joey shrugged an okay.

Both Aldrich and Beadsworth left.

I lay back on the sofa and Joey sat on the opposite chair.

The ringing of the telephone broke the awkward silence, and I was glad it did.

“Hello,” I answered it.

“Hi, is this Jon Rupret?” said a female voice.

I recognized the voice. It was the woman with the red hair. I immediately felt energized.

"Yes, speaking," I said, calming myself.

"Hi, we met outside your house . . ."

"Yes, yes, of course. Did you get your vehicle?"

"Exactly where you said it would be," she laughed.

I laughed.

Joey quietly picked up a magazine and began flipping the pages.

"How did you get my number?" I asked.

"The phone book."

Ah, the good old white pages.

"I didn't get your name?"

"It's Laura," she paused. "Um . . . I didn't mention it earlier, but I'm here visiting my sister. She lives around the block from your house and . . . I'll be leaving for the U.S."

My heart sank. "You're leaving?"

"Yes, tomorrow. I was hoping we could meet . . . maybe over dinner."

"I don't know . . ." I looked across at Joey. "I'm sorry, I can't."

"You can't even spare an hour?"

I squirmed. I wanted to go. I really did.

"Okay," I said, caving in.

23

Ed Burrows found Martin in the makeshift office. Martin didn't look up; he was busy talking on the phone. Burrows walked back to the door and waited. He looked across to the middle of the warehouse, and saw two people unloading heavy barrels of gelatin from the U-Haul.

A tank of water had already been delivered, along with a truck filled with glycine and sodium hydroxide. Metal containers of dextroamphetamine were going to be delivered later in the day. Caffeine was the easiest component to get, so he wasn't too worried about it.

Martin was off the phone now.

Burrows walked up to him.

Martin had the *What-can-I-do-for-you-now* look.

"We still don't have sodium lauryl sulphate," Burrows said.

"What do we need that for?" Martin said.

Burrows said, "It helps to absorb the drug transmucosally into the mouth, throat and esophagus. Without it the drug is useless."

Martin went silent, and then said, "I don't have unlimited resources. I can't just call a company and say ship me a ton of this and a ton of that. Alarms would go off."

Burrows said nothing.

"All right," Martin said, waving his hands in the air. "I'll make some calls."

It was getting dark when I came out of the bathroom. I had showered and shaved and applied some heavy-duty deodorant. Joey was in the living room watching an old movie. I went into my room and changed into a nice silk shirt, unwrinkled pants, and a dark jacket. I checked myself in the mirror and except for the exposed little bruise on my nose I looked mighty fine.

Joey saw me and said, "You get dressed up to buy groceries?"

I had lied to Joey about meeting Laura. No need to tell him.

"I'm going to drop by a friend," I said. "He's not feeling well and all . . . but I'll be back in an hour." I checked my pocket for my cell phone. "You got my number?"

"Yeah," he got up.

"Don't open the door or answer the telephone. As far as anyone is concerned you are not here."

"What if it's your partner?" he asked.

"Don't. If no one opens the door he'll call my cell and I'll tell him I'm out doing grocery shopping."

Joey followed me to the door.

I hurried down the stairs, hoping my landlady wouldn't stop me. I got into the car and drove off.

Joey locked and bolted the door. He turned and leaped back startled. The life-size cutout of Michael Jordan smiled back at him. Joey started to laugh. This was the second time he had been unnerved by it.

He picked up the giant cutout and placed it somewhere away from him. He was already nervous and he didn't want something over six-and-a-half feet tall silently staring at him. It reminded him too much of Kong.

He then went back to his movie.

We had decided to meet at Sona Mahal—an Indian restaurant not far from my home. I found her sitting at a table near the window. She smiled when she saw me. She was wearing a full black dress and some jewelry around her neck.

"I hope you haven't been waiting long?" I said, taking a seat.

"A few minutes," she answered. She looked beautiful.

We placed our orders, when I said, "How long have you been staying here in Toronto?"

"Only a few months," she said. "I work for a consulting firm and one of our clients was interested in establishing a business in Toronto. I came here to see if that was financially viable. We have another client who is interested in expanding his business to Connecticut . . ." She paused. "So I have to go down there for a while."

I moved my head up and down.

"What do you do?" she asked.

"I'm in law enforcement," I said, then thinking I shouldn't have.

"I like a man in uniform," she said.

Yes. I still had my parking enforcement uniform.

Outside it was nightfall, but the lights from the restaurants illuminated the street.

Our orders came and we started to eat. I had chana masala, a dish of basmati rice with chickpeas, onion, garlic, and Indian spices, while she had a butter chicken entrée of basmati rice with chicken pieces in a rich sauce of tomatoes, cream, butter, garlic, ginger and tandoori spices. *Who ever said I couldn't recite menus?*

She swallowed a spoonful of rice and said, "Oh, before I forget, can you excuse me? I just have to make a call." With that she went outside.

The Sundance sat parked a block away from Greenwood and Gerrard. Suraj was behind the wheel, and Hause in the passenger side. They had seen the black officer come out of the house and drive away.

They were waiting for the signal. Ms. Zee was going to let them know when they should make their move. The cell phone rang and Hause answered it. He hung up and nodded to Suraj, who immediately put the car in gear and drove toward the house. Suddenly he pressed hard on the brakes, causing Hause to nearly hit the dashboard.

"What the hell is wrong with you?" Hause cursed.

Suraj said, "Look."

An old woman came out of the house and began sweeping leaves.

"Shit," Hause said.

Suraj pulled out his pistol

"No. Go back," Hause said.

"Why?"

"Go back. Now."

Suraj reversed the car back to its original position.

"Why can't we just shoot the old woman?" Suraj asked.

"We shoot her and then what?" Hause said. "What if there are more inside? We can't shoot everyone to get upstairs. We have to do it quietly."

"How?"

"Let me think."

Through the window I saw her say something on the phone, shut it, and come back in.

"Who were you calling?" I asked as she sat down.

"My sister. I had to tell her I'd be a little late."

We went back to eating our dinner.

"Rupret?" she said. "That's an interesting name."

I don't know why, maybe to just talk to her, I told her. "I might have not mentioned it, but I'm from Nigeria. I was born there. Before my father was born, my grandfather worked for a British mining company. He wanted to fit in and get promoted so he decided to change his name. He chose the name William Rupert, but the clerk who was filling out the required forms typed his name incorrectly as William Rupret. My grandfather didn't care if it was Rupert or Rupret, only that it sounded British." I looked down at my plate. "My father never corrected it out of respect for his father, and I never changed it out of respect for him."

"That's so sweet," she said.

I was staring at the plate, thinking of my father.

"Are you okay?" she said, concerned.

I nodded. "You haven't told me your full name."

She laughed, "Laura Spencer."

"Laura Spencer," I repeated. "Interesting."

"Not as interesting as yours."

"Do you have to leave tomorrow?" I asked.

"Yes, or we'll lose our client."

"You could get another client."

"He's worth millions."

"Maybe you could get someone who's worth billions." I wanted her to stay. I wanted to get to know her.

Hause and Suraj were debating what to do when suddenly the second floor bedroom lights came on. Through the window drapes they could make out someon's shadow. Joey was inside. But they couldn't do anything. The old woman was still sweeping away the leaves.

"We shoot her?" Suraj pleaded.

Hause said nothing.

"We shoot and shoot and leave. That's it."

Hause understood, two shots: one for the woman and one for Joey.

"No," Hause said. "There has to be another way."

Suraj's eyes suddenly lit up. "I'll show you."

He got out of the car and went to the trunk. He pulled out a bag and opened it. Inside, four Molotov cocktail bottles lay side-by-side.

"You made them?" Hause asked.

Suraj moved his head up and down. "We drive up, throw these and drive away," he said.

Hause thought about it and then agreed. They were wasting too much time. Suraj grabbed two bottles and shut the trunk. That's when they realized the woman was no longer there. She must have gone inside.

They went back inside the car and waited. When it looked like the street was empty, Suraj put the car in gear and sped toward the house.

The Sundance screeched to a halt right in front of the entrance. Suraj lit one of the Molotov cocktails and got out. Hause fired two shots at the silhouetted figure on the second floor, who fell upon impact. Suraj hurled the Molotov into the window and they were off.

It was done in less than ten seconds.

We were laughing hysterically; I was telling her jokes, well, not really jokes but my stories with comical twists. The waiter took our empty plates and brought us dessert, custard mixed with cake and assorted fruits.

"This place is great," she said.

"I discovered it," I said modestly.

That got a small laugh out of her. I liked her smile. Those perfect teeth.

I said, "When will you be coming back to Toronto?"

"I won't be," she said.

My face dropped, my chin nearly hitting the table. "Why not?"

"After this contract I might get another elsewhere."

"So you're always traveling," I said, trying hard to conceal my disappointment.

"Yeah." Her eyes dropped to her dessert. "It doesn't leave much time for a relationship."

I nodded.

My cell phone rang. I apologized and answered it. It was my landlady. She was beyond hysterical.

"Slow down . . . what . . . fire . . . where . . . my house . . ." So many questions roared through my head. "I'll be there." I hung up. I thought about Joey. This was a mistake. I shouldn't have left him alone. Oh, shit. I had a feeling in my belly that something terrible had happened.

"Is everything okay?" I heard Laura say.

My head was spinning. My landlady sounded frightened. She never called me. Never.

"I have to go," I said and got up.

"Do you want me to come?" Laura said.

"No—no."

She kissed me on the cheek and I left her in the restaurant and headed for home.

I drove to my house to find it in a blaze. Fire trucks, police vehicles, ambulances, the whole emergency unit was there. I thought about Joey. My stomach turned and something moved up my throat. I threw up right there on the sidewalk.

I was inside Beadsworth's car on our way to his house. I remembered seeing my landlady, comforted by her son, crying. I remembered seeing the firefighters trying to subdue the flames. I remembered meeting Beadsworth, Aldrich and Garnett. I remembered Beadsworth asking about Joey. Joey was inside the house, I remembered saying.

I remembered vomiting again.

I remembered Garnett saying, "It should have been *you*."

I wished it were me.

24

I woke up. The sun streamed through the window and hit my face. I rolled over to shield myself. The room was bare. Beige, with nothing but a bed and a dresser.

I was wearing the clothes I'd worn to dinner the night before. I saw my jacket hung in the open closet and my socks on the floor.

I got up. I moved the blinds and found myself staring down into the back yard. There was a huge pool on the left and a children's playground, with swings and slides, on the right.

I left the room and walked along a nicely carpeted hall. I went down a spiral staircase to the main floor. I heard noises coming from the living room. I leaned in and saw a woman holding and talking to a baby. She caught me peeking and smiled.

"I hope we didn't wake you?" she said with a heavy English accent.

I shook my head. "No, I like getting up early." But then I realized it was well past ten.

"I'm Amy."

"Jon Rupret, R before E."

"Yes, Phillip told me." She smiled. "He'll be in later. What would you like for breakfast? I'm not much of a cook, but I can put something together."

"Anything is good."

"Toast and scrambled eggs, then?"

She was a little heavy, with brownish cropped hair and intelligent eyes.

The baby cradled in her arms looked at me curiously.

"His name is Liam," she said. "Liam, this is Officer Rupret. Say hello." The baby continued staring at me. He was probably wondering who let this guy into the house.

"How old is he?" I asked. I already knew, but what else would you say to a woman holding a baby?

"Five months," she smiled.

The Beadsworths lived in a very affluent neighbourhood. All the houses in the area resembled mini-mansions. After breakfast I strolled through the house. It was spacious, to say the least, and very opulent.

Fine carpets, marble countertops, exquisite chandeliers—it seemed no expenses were spared decorating.

I'd be the first to admit I didn't know much about big and expensive houses, but I did occasionally watch *Famous Homes and Hideaways*. And, this house looked like it belonged in that show.

How could someone on a police officer's salary afford this?

I went to the living room and placed myself on a stylish black leather sofa. Immediately my body became sucked into the softness. It reminded me of my brief affair with Cal Murray's sofa.

Amy Beadsworth came over and sat across from me. "Liam is sleeping," she said. "He wakes up early but, thankfully, sleeps in the afternoon. This gives me time to rest, too. I'm sorry about your house."

I gave her the *What-can-you-do* shrug.

"I think it's nice that you're staying with us. We have plenty of room."

I can see that. My eyes moved around the living room. "It must take a lot of time cleaning this place," I said.

She laughed, the way rich people do: proper, and not too loud. "With Noel and Liam I don't have time. Margarita, our maid, comes in the afternoon. She's so much help. She keeps this place spiffy. She's a wonderful cook, too. When I arrived from England, I didn't even know how to break an egg." She laughed. "Margarita has taught me a lot. I don't know what I would do without her."

I knew I'd tasted eggshells in my breakfast.

"You have family in Toronto?" she asked.

"A mother in Guelph."

"What about brothers and sisters?"

"I was an only child."

We heard the sound of the front door and Beadsworth came in, looking serious.

He kissed his wife and then sat down. She left us to talk.

"Did they find anything in my house?" I said.

"Nothing," he said.

"What about R.A.C.E.?" I said. "The address Joey gave us. Anything there?"

"Nothing. We found the location vacant. They knew we were coming."

“How?”

“How are you feeling?” he asked.

“Great, for a guy who just saw his house burned down and the kid he was supposed to protect, dead.”

Beadsworth had gotten used to my sarcasm so he made no comment.

“Aldrich must be really pissed?” I said.

“Yes. He was upset.” Beadsworth leaned back and unbuttoned his coat. He crossed his legs. “Not more upset than I was.”

“It was a mistake,” I said.

“Yes, a very fatal mistake.”

“I could have gone down with my house.”

“Perhaps.”

“Hey,” I snapped. “I know you told me to watch over Joey but Joey shouldn’t have been under my protection. If I remember correctly, you insisted he be left with me. Why?”

“I thought he would be safe,” he said. “I was wrong.” He sucked in air and blew out. “Officer Rupret, we are no longer investigating R.A.C.E., or whatever this organization maybe called.”

“We just give up?” I said.

“Indefinitely . . .”

He didn’t seem pleased about it either.

“This doesn’t make sense,” I said.

“Of course, it does. The RCMP investigation in to the wrongdoings of the drug squad will go to court within the next few days. The media will be focusing primarily on this event. The Chief does not want any more fodder for the press.”

“What about R.A.C.E. and Nex?” I asked.

“That is out of my hands. I’ll be going back to my divisional duties as of today.” He looked away. “Constable Barnes is making a speedy recovery.”

Knowing that made me feel a little better, but not a lot. Joey's death would be something I'd never get over.

Beadsworth continued. "Constable Barnes doesn't remember anything from that night, but the department's psychologist is monitoring him. If you require I can arrange one for you."

"No, I'm fine."

"Last night you mentioned you were with this woman, Laura Spencer. Is this correct?"

I nodded.

"We did a search and several names came up, but none live in Toronto."

"She doesn't live here. She was visiting her sister."

"Do you know her sister's name?"

"No."

"You also mentioned her sister lived around the block from your house. Do you have an address?"

I shook my head. I don't know what I was thinking yesterday. Maybe I wasn't thinking. Had I known Joey would be so vulnerable I would have acted differently.

"Can I see my house?" I said.

"Yes, of course. I can take you there. But there isn't much to see, I'm afraid."

I didn't care. I wanted to see for myself. And, I wanted to meet my dear ol' landlady.

The warehouse, located along the lakeshore, near the west end, was in a decrepit state. The multi-coloured—brown and pink—exterior bricks were fading, revealing white surface walls. The large rectangular windows were either tinted or broken, and those that were broken were boarded up with two-inch plywood. From the outside it looked like an unoccupied, rundown building, but inside it was anything but.

The warehouse was divided into four sections. One for the mixture of Nex, one for the production of the tablets, one for storage of the final product, and one for the distribution.

All the ingredients and equipment had been delivered. The blister packs, trays, liquid nitrogen freezing tunnels, refrigerators, and freeze-dryers had arrived early in the morning. They had everything to begin production of Nex.

Ms. Zee was surprised no alarms had gone off with these purchases. Someone could have alerted the police.

Kong entered the office. Ms. Zee had sent him to all her suppliers. It was an asset to have Kong in the negotiation process of a transaction. Suppliers were reluctant to overcharge.

Kong grunted.

She understood. He was unhappy with her. He'd wanted to be the one to snap Joey's neck.

"Kong," Ms. Zee said. "You will have other chances to help. I promise."

I found what was left of my house in total ruins. The second floor was black and charred, with the roof collapsed at an angle. There were a handful of investigators and a few clean-up personnel coming in and out of the house.

I stayed in the car, unable to generate the will to get out. Beadsworth was behind the wheel but said nothing. I wanted to go in, see with my own eyes, the state of my home. But I knew if I did I wouldn't be able to get the image out of my head.

So I sat watching from a distance. My house and my life had gone up in smoke. No home to go to, no job, per se.

I asked Beadsworth to drop me a block away. David was home and my landlady was there, too. I spent the next two hours at the house. While we chatted, my landlady cried.

She would live with her son until her house was rebuilt. I could live with them, if I wanted, but I declined. I was thinking about spending some time with my mother, but I didn't know how I was going to call her and tell her the bad news.

I left the house and headed for the Parking Enforcement Headquarters. Just as I entered the building people started coming towards me. They had seen the story on CITY-TV and asked me all sorts of questions.

"How did it happen?"

"Did you lose everything?"

"Will your insurance pay for it?"

"Where will you live?"

There was also lots of support.

"We're glad you're okay."

"If we can do anything, let us know."

I thanked everyone.

I found Staff Sergeant Motley in his office.

"Jon?" he said getting up. "Come in, have a seat."

I sat.

"I read it in the morning papers," he said. "I tried contacting you."

"I haven't been answering my cell phone," I said.

He waited. I stared around the familiar office. It looked the same. It was bare, but homely. I clearly remembered the times I had come in and had long talks with the sergeant. He always tried to solve my problems.

Now I had a big problem. I said, "I kind of screwed up."

He waited.

"And I was hoping I could . . ."

"Yes, of course," he said. "You can come back whenever you want. I'll talk to Sergeant Aldrich and we could arrange for your transfer back."

Sergeant Motley didn't even ask how I had screwed up. He knew what I wanted and he was there to provide it.

"But not now," I said.

"Whenever you are ready," he answered.

"Business good at my route?" I said, inquiring about my old shift.

"Not as good as it used to be," he smiled.

I got up. "I have to go."

He opened a drawer and pulled out a white envelope. "All the guys chipped in to help you get through." He handed it to me.

The envelope was thick and bulky. Without looking inside, I placed it in my pocket.

"Thank you, Sir."

I closed the door and found Roberta standing in the hall. Without saying a word she hugged me. "Jon, I'm so glad you're okay."

I nodded, feeling like a wounded warrior.

"Do you want to talk?" she asked.

I nodded.

We went to a deli across the street. A few minutes of silence had passed when she said, "Do you want to tell me everything?"

I nodded and told her exactly what had happened. She didn't understand most of it but she didn't interrupt me.

"I'm glad you are not hurt," she said when I had finished.

I leaned back and rubbed my temples. "I don't know what to do. This has been the worst time of my life. It's all happened so fast. This is not what I had expected my life to be. I'm homeless, Roberta."

"Don't say that," she said. "At least you're alive."

"You know, what I don't understand is why would they put me, the guy who gives tickets, on a so-called major drug team. On top of that, I don't understand how come no one has heard of R.A.C.E."

"What's R.A.C.E.?"

"Exactly. Radical Association of Criminal Ethnicities. Have you ever heard of it? No. Even Joey had never heard of it, and he was working with them. Cal Murray didn't know who we were talking about when we were at the House of Jam. Only people who actually thought this so-called group existed were Aldrich and Beadsworth. And . . ." I stopped. I went silent.

"Jon?" I heard her say.

I was staring at the table. I was trying desperately to remember everything that had happened. Exact words, certain body movements, precise images, they were now all important to me.

I looked up. "I have to go."

"Jon, are you okay?"

"I'm glad we had this talk," I said and walked out of the deli. I needed fresh air. I needed to recollect and reprocess everything in my mind. So much I had ignored before was so important now.

I stopped right in the middle of the sidewalk.

No. I couldn't start making any conclusions until I was certain. I needed to start at the beginning.

25

The first batch of Nex did not turn out as planned. The ingredients reacted negatively to the process. The combination had to be precise. After being frozen, the tablets formed a glassy solid, and once dried, the structure collapsed. Another batch was prepared immediately.

I knocked and a black kid opened the door. He looked at me attentively and then another, much taller kid, came rushing over.

"Theo, I told you never to open the door," said the older one.

"Hey, Voshon," I said.

I was back in Regent Park.

Voshon looked at me with searching eyes, "You're the guy with Officer Beadsworth." He stuck his head out into the hall. "Is Officer Beadsworth coming?"

"No, I came alone. Can I talk to you?"

"Yeah, sure, come in."

The apartment was pretty much empty, except for the sofa and a few other items.

"You moving?" I asked.

"Yeah, we got a place on Chester. One bedroom only, but the rent's good."

"I need some information," I started. "Has anyone suspicious come by here lately? I mean in Regent Park?"

"In Regent Park everyone's suspicious," he said, smiling.

I waited.

"Hey, man," he said. "I don't know nothing. You learn to mind your own business."

"When you moving?" I said.

"We'll be gone in a couple of days."

"Then you won't mind helping me out," I said.

He looked away. He looked at his little brother. "What're you looking for?"

"Anything," I said.

"There is this guy," Voshon said scratching his head. "Wears a large fur coat—even in the summer—tries to act like he owns the place. If anyone knows anything it would be him."

"What's his name?"

"Marcus, I think."

"Where do I find him?"

"I see him coming in and out of the building over there." Through the window I saw a brown building.

"Will he be there now?"

"Hey, I wouldn't go there alone. He usually has a bodyguard with him."

My mind started churning. I could stake out the building. Wait for this Marcus to come out . . . but then what?

I couldn't just walk up to him and say, "Hey, man. Have you been part of anything illegal or unlawful? If so, can you tell me where I can find R.A.C.E.?"

It wouldn't be that easy.

I thanked Voshon and left.

I stood across from the brown building, thinking hard. How was I going to get to him with the bodyguard hovering around? How was I going to make him talk?

I had no clue.

It was afternoon and the area was pretty much deserted, except for a couple of moms pushing strollers and chatting away. They were coming in my direction so I decided to leave.

Walking west, towards Parliament, I had an idea. Not a very bright idea—but an idea. I searched through my pockets for the number for Mahmud Hanif. I called him and, luckily, he was just north of Danforth, dropping off a passenger.

Ten or so minutes later a taxicab drove up. I got in the back.

"Hey, Mahmud," I said patting him on the shoulder. "Good to see you."

"Always good to see you, too," he said smiling. I swear this man smiled too much.

"How's business?" I asked.

"Good. I'm very sorry what happened to your house. I heard it on the news."

I shrugged, not knowing what to say.

"If you need a place to stay . . ."

"I'm fine."

"If you need any money . . ."

"No, really, I'm fine."

"If you need anything . . ."

"Yes, as a matter of fact, I do need something from you."

"Yes." His face became eager.

"I need your taxi."

There was a pause, and then a cry. "I understand."

"Understand what?" I said confused.

"Don't worry, Officer Rupret," he said reassuringly. "I know people that can help you."

"Mahmud," I said. "What are you talking about?'

"You don't need to drive taxi. You're still a young man. Driving taxi is not good."

"But . . ."

"I will call Lateef—he works downtown—a good man," Mahmud said. "He will help you find a job."

"I don't need a job," I nearly yelled.

"What?" he replied, eyeing me through the rear-view mirror. "You can't make money without a job?"

I started to laugh. "You think I want your taxi because I need money?"

He slowly moved his head up and down. "That is why I drive taxi. Why else?"

"It's for my investigation."

After a brief pause a smile crossed his face. "You want to go under cover. Yes?"

"Exactly," I said. "It's only for a short while."

"No problem. When do you need it?"

"Around six."

Mahmud dropped me off at the corner of College and McCaul. His fare, a middle-age couple, was waiting for him. I had insisted he take the fare; I was going to be using his taxi later. I waved him goodbye and then realized I was standing in front of the Toronto Police Headquarters. I doubled back and hurried around the corner. I moved as far away from the main entrance as possible. I had no desire to go inside. I was supposed to be recovering from my tragedy.

I was walking as fast as my feet would allow when up ahead a police cruiser emerged from the headquarters underground parking lot. I lowered my head and continued walking. I was not going to slow down and wait for the cruiser to pass me—that would mean stopping.

As I passed the cruiser, there was a loud honk that nearly threw me off my feet. I looked back and saw to my surprise, Constable Clara Terries. "Officer Rupret," she said.

I walked over to the driver's side.

"Hey, how are you doing?" I said.

"Not bad," she said.

A male officer sat beside her, and for some unexplainable reason I was glad he looked much, much older than her.

She introduced him but I didn't remember his name. I think I chose not to remember his name.

"I heard what happened," she said.

I shrugged, as if these things happened to me all the time.

"So what are you doing now?" I asked.

"I'm back on patrol," she said. "Get to wear my uniform again"

"I can see that."

The radio dispatcher cut through. There was a ten-something in progress.

"We should go," she said. "I was thinking, Officer Rupret, maybe we could talk some time, if you like?"

"Yeah, I would like that very much. And it's Jon."

"Bye, Jon," she said with a smile.

The sirens came on and the cruiser sped away.

Ed Burrows burst through the door. He was upset and he was angry. Ms. Zee looked up from her desk. He stormed toward her, his size threatening. Kong moved in his direction but Ms. Zee raised her hand. He retreated.

"This is unacceptable," he bellowed.

"What is?" she said calmly.

"Everything. How can I produce something as sensitive as Nex with this primitive technology."

She waited.

"The equipment is outdated. What we have are rejects from defunct pharmaceutical laboratories. The blender doesn't dissolve the active ingredients properly. One of the freezing tunnels refuses to stay at the required temperature. Several of the freeze-dryers discontinue functioning in the middle of the process—rendering large batches of Nex useless. It has to be precise. I refuse to work under these conditions."

Ms. Zee listened and then said, "Mr. Burrows, time and constraints did not allow us to acquire . . . state-of-the-art machines."

"Without them I cannot ensure a stable and functional product."

"You must try," she pleaded.

"It cannot be done."

"Yes it can, in experienced hands such as yours."

That was a boost to Burrows' ego and Ms. Zee continued. "You have the opportunity to create something that—" she was searching for the exact words, "will benefit so many people."

"But . . ."

"So much pain will be relieved because of your desire and determination."

He was glowing.

She smiled. "I promise. Soon you'll have state-of-the-art equipment. But right now you must use your energy in producing Nex."

He seemed more agreeable. "The building doesn't even have sufficient airflow systems to ensure product purity."

"I'll keep that in mind when we search for another location."

He thanked her and left.

26

I sat inside Mahmud's taxi not far from Regent Park. To fit the role of a taxi driver I had asked Mahmud to lend me his Blue Jays cap.

It had gotten dark very fast and the street was only occupied by the occasional passer-by.

I got out and went in the direction of the brown building. The poor lighting on the street concealed me. I found a white BMW in a lone corner spot. Earlier, Marcus had emerged from the vehicle and gone inside.

I looked around. There was a group of kids bouncing basketballs heading in the other direction. I knelt, took another look, and began releasing air from the tires. When I was on the third tire there was a sudden noise. Startled, I turned around, with fists raised, ready to fight. There was no one there. It was only the streetcar in the distance, going east on Gerrard.

I finished my task and headed back. Once I got inside the taxi I began to fully breathe again. My shirt was soaked from sweat and I tried to air it dry. While I was breathing deeply a man in a suit got inside the taxi.

"University Avenue and Edward Street," the man said.

I slowly turned.

"University Avenue," he repeated.

"Sir, I'm waiting for a customer," I said.

"Where is he?"

"Who?" I said.

"Your customer."

"I don't know."

"What do you mean you don't know?"

"Get out," I said.

"That's not fair," he said.

"What's not fair?"

"I shouldn't have to find another taxi if the guy you're waiting for doesn't even show up."

Actually, the man did have a point. My imaginary customer had no respect for my job as a driver, or for this man.

"How about this," I said. "I'll give you five bucks and you go find another taxi?"

He thought about it. "You're serious?"

I pulled out a blue coloured piece of paper and handed it to him.

"Thanks," he said. "I hope your customer comes soon."

I hoped so too.

I waited . . . and waited . . . and waited, until I could no longer wait.

Hours had gone by. No sign of Marcus. I turned the ignition and headed toward the building. I drove slowly. The BMW sat airless on the right. I moved past it, when suddenly the door of the brown building swung open and a suited man came out, followed by the unmistakable fur-coat-man.

I kept driving at a snail's pace, away from them. Through the rear-view mirror I saw Marcus look agitated. He began yelling at his bodyguard, for obvious reasons.

I was in the parking lot of an adjacent building when I saw Marcus look in my direction. He raised his hands and waved to me. I stopped. *Oh, crap.*

I did a three-sixty-turn and headed back.

I halted two feet from him. He rushed over.

“You here to pick someone up?” he said.

“Um . . . yeah. I got a call to come down, but all the buildings look the same,” I said.

“I’ll give you fifty bucks if you take me to Queen and Coxwell,” he said.

“Sure,” I said.

He turned and told his bodyguard to have the BMW fixed immediately.

He got in and I eased the taxi onto Gerrard.

“You’re not going to start the meter?” he said from behind.

I eyed the machine carefully and then pressed a button. Red numeric digits appeared.

We were going east when I said, “So, how about the weather, eh?”

“What about the weather?” he said annoyed.

“I . . . I mean . . . it’s nice,” I stumbled.

“Yeah, *so*.”

“I can tell you’re not a big weather fan.”

“It’s all the same.”

That’s probably because you wear a fur coat all the time.

“How about those Blue Jays, eh?” I said.

“You gonna talk all through the ride?”

“Just trying to make small talk,” I said.

“Don’t,” he shot back. “Just drive.”

I didn’t have much time. This wasn’t a long ride, anyways, so I dove in.

“You a drug dealer?”

Through the rear-view mirror I could see his face contort.

I said, “Yeah, you are. I saw you in the papers.” I lied.

“What’s your name, boy?”

I searched, "Abdul Karim—er, Hakim—bin Karim—bin Hakim Karim."

"That doesn't make sense."

"How would you know?" I said feeling offended. How dare this man insult my people?

"Mahmud Hanif. You don't look like Mahmud Hanif," he said.

"How would you know that?"

"There's a picture of him behind your head."

Damn. There was always a photo with the name and cab number of the driver on the back of the headrest.

Once we were past Broadview I had had enough. I found a spot and parked.

"What are you doing?" Marcus demanded.

I turned and looked him in the eye. "I need information."

"So?"

"You're going to give me the information I need."

"Kid, you're dead. You know that?"

"Shut up," I said. "You don't scare me."

"My boy will get you."

"Your boy is still pumping air in the tires with his mouth."

He moved for the door.

"I wouldn't do that."

"Why not?"

"When you're out that door I'm going to run after you and with that fur coat on you're not going to get very far. Once I catch you I'll beat the shit out of you." I was lying, of course. I was thinking more of my runing him over with the car.

"I'll call the cops. You can't touch me."

I rolled my eyes. "I'll say you bolted before you paid."

"Shit, kid. You got a lot of nerve."

I flared my nostrils boldly. *I was the man.*

He looked at me intently. "Wait a minute. Aren't you that parking cop who was in the papers a year or so ago?"

My nostrils deflated.

"Yeah, it was you." He started laughing. "What? You screwed up so bad now you're driving a taxi?"

"A man can't get no respect," I said.

He continued laughing.

"I am in the drug squad now." I flashed him my badge for good measure. "That is why you're going to help me."

He leaned back and spread his arms.

"Do you know anything about R.A.C.E.?" I said.

"Who?"

Whenever I mentioned R.A.C.E. people got that confused look.

"Do you know anything about Nex?"

"Kid, what are you talking about?"

"This new drug that's suppose to be bigger than Ecstasy."

"How'd you know about that?" Marcus asked, surprised.

"I'm in the drug squad."

"I don't have to tell you anything."

He was right. He didn't. It all looks so easy in the movies, where the hero demands answers from the villain and most often than not he gets them. In real life it's entirely different. I might have to beg.

"Come on, man," I said. "Help me out."

"I can't believe I'm hearing this," he said laughing. "The only way I'm talking is if you arrest me."

"Fine," I said. "Last time I do anyone a favour."

His eyes narrowed and he said, "What're you talking about?"

"I'm just saying," I started. "We know you're involved in all of this. Last week we saw them—" I had know idea what *them* looked like. "—at your place."

He said, "I'm gonna deny everything."

"Of course you are. But let me tell you. When these guys—" I was careful not to say R.A.C.E. "—Get busted, you're going down with them."

"What're you saying?"

"I'm saying we know they have the drug and it could be ready in a matter of days."

"You know about that?"

"Of course, man. We're the cops. We've got a huge team working on this case. You're a paper-reading-kind-of-guy so you must have heard about the RCMP's investigation into the drug squad?"

He nodded.

"To bring respectability back to the force we're going to get this gang of drug makers and we're going to make an example of them." I emphasized the next sentence. "We're going to make an example of *you*."

His face went serious. "The favour you mentioned. Why?"

"Let's just say, I want to be the one who breaks this investigation. Make up for the mistake I made."

A group of people stare at us. I guess they wanted a taxi. I started the car and drove.

"What will I get if I help you?"

"I'll tell them you were very helpful."

"I'll still go to jail. I sell drugs to kids, remember."

"That's *your* problem, but if you help us you won't go to jail for this new drug, will you?"

He thought about it.

"There is nothing to think about," I said.

"Okay, okay. They came a few days ago with their new quick-dissolving formula. You know about it?"

"Yeah, of course." *Quick-dissolving?*

"This thing, I mean, this tablet just disappears inside your mouth."

"You tried the drug?"

"No way," he snapped. "You crazy?"

"Where can I find these people?"

"How the hell do I know? The rule is you don't ask any questions. But they'll probably come back when they have the drug."

"Right," I said more to myself than him. "Once they come to you, we follow them."

"Yeah, whatever," he said.

"So we have a deal, right?"

He moved his head in agreement. "Yeah, sure."

I turned my head back, slightly. "You better stick to the deal or else—"

"Look out!" he screamed.

I twisted and saw a kid crossing the road. I turned the wheel sharply. The car veered to the right, went onto the sidewalk, and hit a large recycling bin. The heavy plastic bin flew over passing vehicles and landed on the opposite sidewalk, like a scene from a cartoon.

I turned to see if the kid was okay. He was walking in the opposite direction with his head low and bopping. His ears were covered with large pilot-style headphones. He had no idea what had just happened.

Teenagers!

I looked back and Marcus had horror written over his face. His eyes bulged out and his arms were spread apart. He looked as if he was going to fall and was holding on for dear life.

"You okay?" I said.

He was pale and his mouth was open.

"You must have seen worse," I said, unbuckling my seat belt.

He nodded and then quickly pounced out of the car.

"Remember our deal," I yelled as he ran away.

It's not pretty seeing a grown man in a fur coat run like that.

I got out to see the damage.

I nearly screamed, the kind of scream that even aliens on far away planets can hear.

There was a large dent, the size of a half watermelon, on the right side of the front. The headlight was smashed beyond repair.

This was not good.

Mahmud would kill me.

I pulled out my cell phone and called the one person I knew who could help in this situation.

Eight minutes later a brown coloured tow-truck parked behind the busted taxi. Out came Joe Coultier, his massive body moving toward me.

"Jonny," he said.

"What're you doing here?" I asked. "Why didn't you send someone else?"

"The boys are busy. This is our peak time, you know. Parking on the streets without residential permits, leaving cars in the parking lots of malls, the usual stuff."

"Who's watching the business?"

"Marcie."

“She’s back?” I asked.

“Yeah, I couldn’t run the place without her. I begged her and gave her a raise.”

“That’s too bad,” I said. “I was looking forward to opening my very own impound with her.”

“You know what? I like the coupon idea you had,” he said. “It would build customer loyalty and stuff. Anyways, you hit a taxi?”

“No. The taxi hit the recycling bin.”

“So what did you hit?”

“The recycling bin.”

“Both the taxi and you hit the recycling bin?’

“No. Only the taxi hit the recycling bin.”

He shook his head violently. “Okay, what were you driving?”

“The taxi.”

“What?” he said. “What’re you doing driving a taxi?”

“It’s a long story. You gonna tow or what?”

“I’ll tow,” he said getting down to business. “Just because you’re a loyal customer. No questions asked.”

“So how many tows have I got?” I inquired.

“Why?”

“This one could be free.”

Joe had taken the taxi to a mechanic he knew. I was going to cover the costs, of course, but that was not the problem. How was I going to tell Mahmud? He trusted me and I’d let him down.

Maybe I could deny it.

What taxi? I never borrowed any taxi? I don’t even have a license to operate one, must be someone else?

No. I couldn’t do that.

Mahmud was a good person, a decent person. I didn't know how I was going to tell him what had happened. This might even end our fragile relationship.

I got off and waited at the spot we had decided to meet. I looked at my watch and was surprised to see it was almost eleven. I paced back and forth, thinking of what to do next. Four long minutes later I saw Mahmud turn the corner and walk briskly towards me.

"Mahmud," I said. "Buddy, pal, how are you doing?"

"Good, Officer Rupret, how about you?" he said smiling. His eyes darted behind me, searching. "Where is the taxi?"

I scratched my head. "Well, Mahmud . . . maybe you should sit down."

He looked around. We were in the middle of the sidewalk.

"Standing might be better." I took a step back. I said, "Mahmud, something happened to your taxi."

His smile faded.

"There is a large dent on the right side."

He nodded, slowly.

"But I'm going to pay for the repair." I didn't know how much was in that thick white envelope Sergeant Motley gave me, but it would help.

There was a pause and then he finally said, "You are okay?"

"Yeah, couldn't be better," I shrugged.

"You hit another car?" he asked.

"No, recycling can."

"Recycling can?" He paused. "But recycling can is on the sidewalk."

"Yeah, well, I kind of . . . you have to realize there was this kid with these big headphones walking down the street and to avoid hitting him I swerved . . ."

He nodded, trying to digest what I was saying.

"Mahmud, I'm really sorry," I said.

Mahmud looked hurt. I understood. It was his only means of making a living.

His eyes narrowed as if thinking. He then moved his hand through his matted hair. He looked at me and then his eyes moved to the top of my head.

I pulled off the Blue Jays cap and handed it to him.

He put it on and then looked at the ground. "Maybe I made a mistake," he said.

"I know. You shouldn't have trusted me."

He smiled. "I made a mistake of not running taxi over you before."

I woke up in the middle of the night in the Beadsworths' guest bedroom. I tossed and turned and tossed some more. I was having strange dreams. First, I was in a taxi with Marcus being pulled by Joe Coultier—not towed, but literally pulled by his massive arms. Then, I'm back in the taxi and I hit a recycling can and out pops Mahmud. He demands why I hit his recycling can and not someone else's. Then I'm in the House of Jam and I'm being chased by Mahmud's taxi. Finally, I'm standing near a lake and I decide to jump into the water, and when I do the water turns into pills and I get sucked in like quicksand. I scream but no one is there to help except for Clara Terries. I call for her and she reaches out to help me, but before I can grab her I wake up.

It was 3:21 in the morning. My stomach moaned. I got up and went downstairs. As I turned in to the kitchen a boy leaped up, startled. He was holding a sandwich in his left hand and his right hand was covered in a cast.

"Hey, I'm not a robber," I said. Black guy in the house in the middle of the night can send wrong messages to white kids. "I'm your father's partner."

"I know that," he said. "I was surprised."

"You're . . . Christopher, right?" I said.

"No. Noel."

Damn. Close, though. "Mind if I join you?"

He shook his head and sat down. He took a bite of his sandwich.

"That looks good," I said.

"It's tuna. I'll show you were Mom keeps it."

He pointed out all the ingredients and I made myself a similar sandwich.

Once we were seated I said, "By the way, my name is Jon." I offered my hand as a late introduction. He shook it. "You couldn't sleep either?" I asked.

He nodded.

"I couldn't," I said. "I had nightmares."

"You did?" he said, looking up.

"Yeah."

"What kind of nightmares? Scary monster nightmares?'

"You could say that," I said.

"I get this nightmare where this humungous giant lizard with fangs and five tentacles comes out of the closet and eats me."

Humungous lizard? *I hope he doesn't come after me.*

"Are you a police officer just like dad?" he asked.

"Sure am," I said, in my police-like tone.

"You catch bad guys every day?"

"Sure do." I felt like John Wayne telling some whipper-snapper about his sheriff duties.

He then said, "You make lots of money like dad?"

Uh? "What?"

"Dad makes lots of money."

I paused. "Yes, he does."

I slowly took a bite of the sandwich, thinking. "Your dad told you he makes lots of money from his job?"

"No, but I hear him talk to Mom. He brings her money in an envelope."

"An envelope, eh?" I said, thinking deeper.

"Brown envelopes, sometimes white envelopes."

I began to eye the kitchen suspiciously: marble countertop, stainless steel dishwasher, two-door refrigerator, all top-of-the-line stuff.

"What else did your dad tell you," I asked, hoping to get more out of him.

He shrugged, suddenly disinterested.

I needed more information. "So, you broke your arm playing soccer?" I said.

He looked away.

I leaned in. "You didn't break your arm playing soccer, did you?"

He made no comment.

"You got into a fight."

He nodded, very slowly.

"Why?"

He looked up and opened his mouth into a wide smile.

I waited.

He pointed to his teeth.

"What?" I still did not understand.

He pointed more dramatically.

"Oh," I said. "Kids made fun of your braces?"

He closed his mouth and lowered his head, staring at the empty plate.

"Your parents don't know?"

He shook his head.

"Don't worry about what those kids think," I said. "When you're older you'll have a perfect smile and they'll have crooked teeth like cats."

He laughed.

Right then I should have told him an incident from my childhood, but I couldn't think of one so I let it go. "You know," I said. "You should tell your parents. Maybe they can help."

I suddenly realized the hypocrisy of what I was saying. Here I was giving Noel advice about being open and honest while I was hiding my career from my mother.

When this was all over and done I was going to have a long talk with her. She would understand. She always did.

"Talk to your parents when you feel you're up to it," I finally said.

27

At the breakfast table I sipped coffee while eating toast with marmalade. Beadsworth sat across from me with a newspaper. He was going over the front-page stories. Amy was upstairs with Liam. Noel had already gone to school.

I stared at Beadsworth intently. Something about him made me irritated. It wasn't his trimmed beard, or his perfect ironed shirt, pants, or tie. It wasn't even the way he was reading the paper, folding each page precisely to avoid any creases. It was what his son Noel had told me last night. Beadsworth gave his wife money in brown and white envelopes, and large sums of it, at that.

Where did he get that kind of money? Not as a police officer, I was sure.

I glared at him.

Maybe, Phillip, it's because you're a corrupt cop, taking money from drug dealers so you can live a life of luxury.

He flipped the page and glanced at me. I chewed my toast.

Think about your wife and kids, Phillip. Wait, your wife is in cahoots with you. Where does she keep your money? Maybe, she is a victim. Yes. She has no choice but to follow you. You fiend!

He flipped the page again. "Breakfast okay?" he asked, smiling.

"Oh, yes. Perfect."

Yes, keep smiling, you well-dressed dictator.

He scanned the last page and placed the neatly folded paper on the table.

"Everything satisfactory yesterday?" he said. "Amy told me you came home last night looking distressed."

Why do you care?

I said nothing.

"I've been made aware that Constable Barnes is now at home," he said. "He's doing much better. He doesn't remember much, I'm afraid. But the force is not placing *any* pressure on him until he has fully recovered. If you like you can visit him."

I nodded.

Hearing about Barnes, my mind drifted to Laura Spencer. I hadn't thought about her after my house burned down. She had gone to Connecticut and now, who knows where else. And I'd left in a hurry, worried about Joey.

I cringed. Joey still had not been found. First Barnes, then Joey. Maybe it was better that Laura was not near me. Lately, whoever I associated with got hurt, even my landlady. Because of me, she'd lost everything.

It would be nice to see Barnes again.

Ed Burrows stormed into the office. He was smiling from end-to-end. "We have it!" he said.

He placed a small navy-blue tray with a dozen square white tablets in front of her. Ms. Zee leaned over to pick one up when Burrows stopped her.

"Not with your fingers," he said, handing her a small instrument that looked like a tweezer.

She plucked one up and brought it close to her. Her hand trembled at the thought of finally holding Nex.

Burrows spoke, "This is our finest batch. The ingredients acted positively to the process. I feel we should have compliance." Ms. Zee knew that meant the drug would give the result they required. "But we do need to test it. Until then we cannot be one-hundred per cent certain." What that meant was they needed a guinea pig, someone who would voluntarily or—involuntarily—test the drug.

She thought about Joey. With a little persistence he would have been popping down the tablets like M&Ms. But he was no longer available. It then suddenly dawned on her, Regent Park.

"I'll send Martin," she said. "No—wait. I'll go." She wanted to personally see Marcus' face when he saw she had the drug.

In Thorncliffe Park searching for a parking place, I wished I had my parking enforcement cruiser. I could have parked anywhere.

A purplish van exited a spot and I immediately took it. I went up the elevators to the fifteenth floor. I found Barnes' apartment and knocked.

A pretty girl, in her early twenties, answered the door.

"Hi," I said. "My name is Jon Rupret . . ."

"Yes, Michael mentioned you were coming," she said. "Come in."

I went in and the smell of something cooking penetrated my nostrils.

"Michael is in the bedroom." She led me down the hall and into the room.

I found Michael Barnes propped up in the bed watching TV. He looked up and a smile crossed his face.

"Hey, man," he said. "How are you doing?"

"Better than you," I said.

"Have a seat."

I sat on the single chair opposite the bed.

The girl behind me said, "Michael, can I get you anything?"

"No, Honey, I'm fine," he said and she went away.

He leaned over to me and whispered, "So what do you think of her? She nice?"

She seemed polite and was very pretty. "Sure," I said.

His smile widened. "My mom told me she was at the hospital every day. She was at my bedside hoping and praying for my recovery. I didn't realize it but I love her so much." He faced the television and waited for the commercials to come. "I'm going to ask her to marry me."

"That's great," I said. I paused and then said, "I'm sorry about what happened that night."

"That's okay," he said. "You know what's strange? I don't remember much."

"Yeah, Beadsworth told me."

"But you know what?" he said glancing back to the TV. "I do remember going there with you but I don't remember anything after that except for . . ." he trailed off.

"Except for what?" I asked trying to get his attention.

"Uh . . . yeah. Except once in a while I see a bald head."

"Bald head?"

"A big shiny bald head. I don't know why."

"Is there a face attached to it?"

"I hope so. But I don't see it. It's blurred." He shut his eyes and opened them. "At the hospital I was on some heavy-duty drugs and I got these funky dreams where I'm at the House of Jam—but, it's not really the House of Jam but a weird, psychedelic kind of club. I'm either with you or my partner, Carlos, or sometimes even with Detective Garnett."

"That's not a dream. That's a nightmare."

"But every time it's like this bald head is coming after me. Chasing me."

"Does it catch you?" I said, fishing for some clue.

"I don't know—I guess so."

His mind was going back to the TV.

I had decided it was time to go, when he said, "What happened to R.A.C.E.? Did you guys catch them? Carlos never talks about them."

I didn't know where to begin. Operation Anti-R.A.C.E. was no longer operational and our main witness was dead. For all we knew, Nex was already out on the streets. But I couldn't tell him all this. Not in his condition.

"We're making progress," I said. I got up and gave him a pat on the shoulder. "You make good progress too, okay?"

He smiled and thanked me for coming and then went back to watching TV.

I got back downtown, called Cal Murray, and after a few rings he answered. I told him I wanted a talk with him. After a little begging he agreed.

I waited behind the House of Jam until he showed up. "I don't have much time, but come," he said.

We went up the flight of stairs, through the narrow hall and into his office.

"This hot rapper from Scarborough will be coming down to promote his new CD and we've got a lot of promotional stuff to do."

"What's his name?" I asked.

"Altar Boy. You might not have heard of him yet, but he'll be the next big thing."

He went around his desk and sat down. "Have a seat," he offered.

I saw the oh-so-familiar sofa and my mind flashed back to the time I had nearly lost my heart to it.

"I'll stand," I said.

Cal said, "It was nice of you guys not to launch an investigation after the attack. It would have given this place a bad rep. How's he doing, anyways?"

"Constable Barnes is recovering," I said. I was about to ask him a question when he interrupted me.

"Who was it that did it?"

"I'm sorry?" I said.

"You guys did catch whoever attacked the officer?"

"Not yet—that's not why I'm here—"

"—That's not possible," he said, taken aback. "You have the videotapes from that night."

"Not all," I corrected him. "We're missing the one that recorded the attack."

He puffed, "I handed all the tapes to the police."

"All of them?"

"Yes, all. Even before I had a chance to view them, someone came and took them."

"Who? Can you remember?"

His eyes darted from one end of the desk to the other. He was thinking hard. "Yes, of course," he said. "It was your partner."

"Sorry?" I said startled. "Who?"

"Your partner. With the beard and the slight accent. I gave both of you the tour of the club. Remember?"

I found myself losing breath and getting dizzy. "Do you mind if I sit down?" Before he answered, I fell on the sofa. My mind was reeling. This was too much. I had suspected Beadsworth was up to something illegal but this was tampering with evidence.

I spoke with laboured breath, "Are you sure it was Phillip Beadsworth?"

"Yes," he said, recognizing the name. "He came up to my office and demanded I give him all the camera tapes, and assured me there would be no investigation if I did that."

I grabbed my head. Everything was making more sense. I strained. Yes, it was getting clearer. Joey had mentioned there was a mole in the police department. Beadsworth. I remembered Beadsworth's words, "*Things were happening before you arrived and they will continue to happen after you leave.*" He meant his involvement with R.A.C.E. He was part of R.A.C.E. He was the one who had insisted Joey stay with me. Why me? Joey should have been in the witness protection program. Beadsworth knew if Joey was under me he'd have access to him.

My mouth dropped.

"Is something wrong?" I heard Cal say, but I ignored him.

Beadsworth must have joined Operation Anti-R.A.C.E. to keep an eye on the investigation. He was leaking information to R.A.C.E. In return he was paid well; that explained the envelopes he gave his wife. That also explained the huge house and everything inside it.

I had to talk to Aldrich. I didn't like him, but I had to do something.

"Hey man, you okay?" Cal said again.

"Yeah . . . I'm fine." My phone rang. It was Marcus from Regent Park. He sounded nervous. R.A.C.E. was on the way to meet him.

I got up, "Thanks, man." I went to the door. "Oh, by the way, there's a tiny little tear on the sofa. If you want to get rid of it and get yourself a fancy one—especially for this new rapper, you give me a call."

The Lincoln turned into Regent Park. Hause was driving with Ms. Zee and Kong in the back. Martin didn't accompany them. He was too busy with the logistics of the operation.

They found Marcus in the laundry room. Ms. Zee sensed he looked uneasy, almost nervous. It could be that she now had the drug and he had no choice but agree to all her demands.

The smell of detergent and fabric softener was very strong.

"Do you have it?" he said. "Or is this another sample?"

She eyed his bodyguard in the back, a skinny guy with a menacing face. He had his eyes fixed on Kong. Kong in return had his eyes fixed on him.

"Do you have it or is this a waste of my time?" Marcus said. His right hand shook slightly.

She pulled out a plastic prescription bottle and placed it on top of one of the washing machines. "It's there."

Marcus motioned and his bodyguard walked over, picked it up, and handed it to him.

Marcus scanned the bottle and then looked at the cap.

"It's child proof," Ms. Zee said. "You have to push—"

"I know how to open it," he said, annoyed. He twisted the cap off and dropped a tablet in his right palm. The tweezers were inside Ms. Zee's pocket but she wasn't going to offer them to him. "It's square. Clever," he said. He flipped the tablet over, examining it from all sides and angles. He then half-closed his palm and did a motion as if he was weighing it. He felt a jolt in his hand and then it went numb. "Shit." He looked down and the tablet had almost completely disappeared. Three blinks later he regained feeling in his fingers. "What happened?" he said, looking at her.

"You were sweating," she said.

I parked at a spot from where I could see the brown building. I couldn't see much from this distance but I didn't want to blow my cover by getting any closer. During the ride I had hatched a plan.

Once R.A.C.E. was done with their business they would come out. When they did, I'd follow them to their hide-out. I'd then notify Aldrich and with a task force we'd swoop down and apprehend them. When we had all the members of R.A.C.E., we'd go and get their main accomplice: Detective Phillip Beadsworth.

I felt a lump in my throat. I thought about his wife and his children, specially, about Noel with his crooked teeth and metal braces. He was a good kid with so much potential. What would happen to him after he saw his father go to jail? Maybe he'd drop out of school and end up a drug dealer. It would be ironic, like father like son.

Ms. Zee said, "When the tablet made contact with your sweat it dispersed into your skin."

"You mean it went into my body?" Marcus nearly screamed.

"Don't worry, your skin didn't absorb all of it. I'd advise you to remove it from your hand immediately."

Without realizing it he wiped his hand over his coat. A white powdery paste attached itself to the fur.

He screamed.

She couldn't help but laugh.

His bodyguard pulled out a cloth and tried without success to remove the residue from the fur. He made it even worse by smearing it. Marcus cursed and shoved him aside.

Ms. Zee was now laughing harder.

"I'm glad you're enjoying this," he spat. He glanced over at Kong, whose face stayed the same the entire time. "At least someone doesn't find this funny."

"He doesn't find anything funny," Ms. Zee answered.

Marcus straightened up and faced her. He needed some of the drug so it could be analyzed and copied. He knew people who'd be happy to help.

"We need to test the drug," Ms. Zee said.

"What're you talking about?" he said. "Didn't you see what just happened?" He lifted his right hand.

"Nex was not meant for sweaty palms. We need to see the effect when it is placed on the tongue." She knew he was satisfied. But she wasn't.

He eyed her hard. He then motioned his bodyguard. The bodyguard hesitated; he didn't want to leave his boss alone with them.

"I'll be all right," Marcus said, turning to Ms. Zee. "We're business partners now. Isn't that right?"

Ms. Zee hated his smugness but didn't say anything.

The bodyguard left them.

From my spot I saw someone come out of the building but I couldn't tell exactly who. He went around the corner and disappeared. I got out and crossed the street, careful not to get too close.

The man came back, and I realized it was the bodyguard. Another man was with him. They went inside the building.

I immediately turned around and went back to the car. Something was happening inside, but I had to wait for R.A.C.E. to come out.

The door of the laundry room swung open and in came the bodyguard with a short skinny man.

The bodyguard went to Marcus and whispered something in his ear. Marcus nodded approvingly.

"We have a volunteer," he turned to Ms. Zee.

She eyed the short man. He was wearing a ragged jacket that was so stained that no amount of washing would do it any good. He had stubble on his chin that looked more like dirt than hair. His eyes were vacant, as if he didn't know why he was here.

"Give it to him, then," she said.

Marcus gave the bottle containing the tablets to his bodyguard. He wasn't going to touch it again.

The bodyguard reluctantly took it. He then offered it to the short man. The man's eyes widened.

"No way, man," he said. "I am not taking no shit. You guys cops? I don't do drugs, man. I've been clean for months."

Ms. Zee said, "We're not cops. We just want you to try it."

He looked at the bottle. "Not for twenty bucks," he said.

Twenty dollars? Ms. Zee shook her head. Here they were on the brink of something enormous and Marcus was being cheap.

"I'll give you a hundred dollars if you try it," she said.

"Hundred bucks?" he said. "Sure, I'll try anything for a hundred bucks."

"Your hands dry?" Ms. Zee said.

The man wiped his hand on his dirty coat and then showed it to her.

She nodded to the bodyguard who dropped a tablet on the man's hand.

"Do not swallow," Ms. Zee said. "Place it on your tongue."

The man held the square tablet between his two fingers and then stuck his tongue out and placed it on it. He wanted to follow her orders precisely. He wanted his hundred dollars.

Instantly he grabbed his chest. He closed his eyes so tight that deep lines etched his face. He fell to his knees.

Agonizing seconds went by as the man, with his head bowed close to his chest, stayed still on his knees.

Then he lifted his head and a smile curled his face. He opened his eyes.

"What happened?" Ms. Zee demanded.

"Shit. That was awesome," he said, showing his stained teeth. "Can I get another?"

She pulled out a hundred dollar bill and shoved it to him. He took it, but said, "Please, one more."

"That'll cost you now," said Marcus, seeing a business opportunity.

"Just give him another and throw him out," Ms. Zee said.

"Outside," Marcus waved to his bodyguard. He didn't like seeing goods being given away for free.

"So what do you think?" Ms. Zee said once the two had left.

Marcus spoke with superiority. "It has potential. Fifty-fifty sounds reasonable."

"Let's stick to our deal. Shall we?"

"Thirty-seventy it is," he said, realizing who had the upper hand. "When will I get a shipment?" he said eagerly.

"Within forty-eight hours."

"That long?"

"The process requires time."

"All right, all right. Just as long as I get the first shipment."

Kong and Ms. Zee left.

When the bodyguard came back, Marcus said, "He swallow the tablet?"

"Yeah."

"And?"

"He wanted another one."

A huge smile crossed Marcus' face. Even his deal with the police officer fit into his plans.

26

When Ms. Zee and Kong were inside the Lincoln, Hause turned and said, "We're being followed."

"Who?" Ms. Zee demanded.

"The black officer whose house we burned down."

Jonny Rupret, she realized. What's he doing here?

"Where is he?" she said.

Hause motioned to the back. Ms. Zee turned slightly and saw a gray car parked in the distance.

"How long has he been there?" Ms. Zee asked.

"After you went inside."

"Try to lose him." She hoped the officer hadn't recognized her.

Two people came out of the building. I couldn't see clearly but I had a hunch it was the bodyguard with the same man I saw going in. A few minutes later two more people came out. I squinted, trying to get a clearer picture, but they quickly entered a white Lincoln.

I couldn't believe I had missed the Lincoln. It was right there in front of me.

I started my car and waited.

The Lincoln backed up and turned in the direction of the street I was parked on.

I ducked, then peered over the dashboard, and saw the Lincoln enter Gerrard and drive past me.

I did a U-turn and followed.

The Lincoln sped ahead. I was only half-a-block behind. I didn't accelerate. I didn't want them to think they were being followed. My purpose was only to find out where they were going.

They continued on Gerrard, passing Broadview then Greenwood and then they turned left on Coxwell. They were going north when they turned right onto O'Connor. It was when they entered Eglinton that I realized we were going toward Scarborough.

They went left, right and then left again. I had a feeling they were trying to lose me. *How could that be possible?* I hadn't even been close to the building. I'd been so far away that I couldn't even see anyone come in or come out.

I kept chase.

They entered a one-way street and accelerated. I did, too. They turned into another street but I was right behind them. A highly qualified parking enforcement officer was following them—me.

We'd done this cat-and-mouse chase for almost fifteen minutes when they exited onto a main road and began going at the required speed.

When we were back on Eglinton I found myself getting a familiar feeling. My Civic was only two cars behind when I recognized where we were. The LLPM Import & Export building was a traffic light away.

Maybe R.A.C.E. *did* do operations at that building.

I expected the Lincoln to turn left into the building's parking lot, but instead it turned right. What the. . . ?

Hesitantly, I did so too.

The Lincoln went into an alley beside a shop.

It hit me like a thunderbolt.

They went behind the Bubble T Shop.

What was R.A.C.E. doing at my—now favourite—tea shop?

I found a parking spot in front of the shop and got out. I pulled out my cell, ready to dial a number, but stopped.

I wasn't going to call Beadsworth. I was now certain he was part of their operation, maybe not as a full-fledged member but as an accomplice.

I wanted to call Aldrich but first I had to be sure this was where R.A.C.E. was operating. What if Marcus had given me the wrong information? What would happen if I called Aldrich and he came down with half the force only to find out they weren't producing Nex but making delicious bubble tea? How would I save face then?

My face would surely be splashed across all the major newspapers: *Ex-PEO screws up, yet again. Force humiliated with raid at quiet bubble-tea shop. John Rupert does it again!* NO. I could not let that happen.

I had this heavy feeling that I should make sure first.

I peered through the window. As usual, Susan was behind the cash register. A handful of teenagers sat in one corner and a guy was reading a magazine in another.

I decided to go around into the alley.

Garbage and old cardboard boxes littered the pathway. When I was at the end I took a peek and saw the white Lincoln parked to the side. There was a door open, with sounds coming out. The sounds were probably from the staff of the Bubble T Shop.

I scanned the back area. There was no one around. They must have gone inside the shop. But what were they doing?

I carefully entered the open door and found another door on the left somewhat ajar.

I grabbed the door handle and pulled. A flight of stairs went down.

This was absurd. I wasn't going down someone's basement.

I turned, when something hard hit me across the cheek. I reacted and fell forward, stumbling and then rolling down the steps. I realized I was on the ground when my head thumped on concrete.

I was still conscious when I heard footsteps come down. I lifted my head, felt dizzy, then decided against it. Maybe if I closed my eyes for a second it might help. I felt a shadow over me and I opened my eyes

A huge bald Chinese guy stared at me menacingly.

"Hey, man," I said. "I know how this looks. But I wasn't trying to steal nothing. I'm a c—"

He grabbed my collar and lifted me up like a doll.

"Thanks," I said once on my two feet.

The guy didn't say anything; he just towered over me, threateningly.

My right cheek stung when my fingers touched it. It was going to leave a bruise. My nose hadn't healed entirely from the last time, and now I had to worry about my cheek. I hoped make-up would cover the mark.

I sucked air and looked up. The big guy had his arms crossed. The bulges underneath his shirt told me this guy worked out. I had to be careful.

"I know it was a mistake," I said raising my hands as if these things happened all the time. "You saw me snooping around and you thought I was going to steal something. So you . . . kind of . . . *bumped* into me." I winked at him. He didn't wink back. "So it's no problem. I won't charge you with assault—if you're worried about it." He didn't look too worried.

He stared silently.

"I'm Officer Jon—R before E—Rupret of the Toronto Police Service."

In a blink of a second a hand shot out, grabbed my throat, and pulled me closer.

The grip was immense. Blood rushed to my head and my eyes bulged out.

He brought my face closer and I could feel hot air come out of his large nostrils.

I tried to say something, but I needed air to do so, which was now suddenly in short supply.

I grabbed his wrist but I couldn't even circle it with my fingers.

I was about to kick him in his privates when I heard a voice.

His fingers released my neck and I flopped on my bum.

I knew sucking air quickly would be hazardous so I closed my mouth and inhaled slowly through my nose.

My neck was raw. I would need more makeup to cover that, too.

I looked up and nearly lost my breath. Again.

Laura, with her red hair, was standing beside the big guy, who I was now going to charge with assault and attempted murder. She had a smile on her face.

"Laura, wh—what are you doing here?" I asked.

"I should ask you the same question," she answered.

"I'm here for the tea," I said, collecting myself. "What about you?"

She smiled the smile I had earlier found endearing. Right now it felt intimidating.

I managed to get up.

"Shouldn't you be in the States?" I said.

"You don't get it, do you?"

"Of course, I get it." *Get what?* I narrowed my eyes.

She laughed, rolling her head back. "You have no idea."

"I have many ideas, but I can't discuss any of them with you . . . at this moment." I looked around.

She motioned to the big man, who moved toward me.

I moved back but hit what felt like a metal door.

Feeling cornered, I pulled on the handle and fell back into darkness.

I looked around and everything was black.

Someone switched on the lights.

"Better?" she said.

There were several machines, all covered with blue plastic, at one end of the basement. Equipment—the science lab kind—was scattered everywhere.

"This looks like a clan lab," I said, turning to them.

Then it hit me.

"You," I pointed. "You're making Nex." It suddenly dawned on me that I had infiltrated R.A.C.E. Something else dawned on me.

"You're part of R.A.C.E.?" I said to Laura.

She smiled, "Good. We are finally making progress. Kong, tie him up on that chair."

The big guy moved toward me. I doubled back and planted myself on the chair. If this gigantic bone-crushing-type-of-guy wanted to tie me up, who was I to protest? I placed my hands behind my back and smiled.

He looked disappointed. He was looking forward to roughing me up. I wasn't going to give him any satisfaction. I may be a wimp, but I was a partially damaged wimp.

He bound my wrists.

She walked over and leaned down. I could smell her perfume.

Was that Elizabeth Taylor's Black Pearls?

"I liked you," she said. "But you had to follow us and then enter our establishment."

"Your name isn't Laura Spencer, is it?" I said.

She shook her head.

"You never had a sister in Toronto, did you?"

"Everything was a lie, Officer Rupret."

I had opened up to her. I couldn't believe I had told her about Nigeria and my grandfather. I felt used.

"Don't feel bad," she said. "At least you didn't burn in your house."

What?

"Why didn't I?" I said.

"Think. You're part of the police."

Yes, I was part of the finest police force in the country, and at this moment I was damn proud of it. "I have seen where you produce Nex. Why don't you give up? You won't get away."

"Yes, you have seen everything." She looked at Kong. "But *you* won't get away. Alive."

Up until then I had had the feeling that I was not in any life-threatening danger. But suddenly I was feeling differently. I had to do something.

"Half the police department is outside," I bluffed.

"No, they are not."

"Yes, and I'm wired. You're being recorded."

"Really?" She ripped my shirt open—the buttons flew everywhere. "You're lying."

"Code red. Code red. Abort mission," I mouthed to my armpit. "Officer down. Officer down."

"Oh, shut up," she said and slapped me. Hard.

That would leave a mark.

"Don't you understand," she said, getting agitated. "The police will not come to help you."

"Why is that?" I said.

She said nothing.

Then it hit me. "The mole," I said slowly.

Her face betrayed nothing.

"Yes," I laughed. "You wouldn't think I would know. Would you?"

She licked her lips.

"You thought I wouldn't find out who your mole was?" I said. "But I did. I put two-and-two together."

"You know?" she finally said.

"I know." I was proud of myself. Seeing her squirm like that made my chest inflate. It deflated immediately when I caught sight of Kong.

She said, "I didn't think you were—"

"—Clever or intelligent enough," I said.

"Bright was the word I was looking for. I didn't think you were bright enough."

"Well I did. Your mole was part of Operation Anti-R.A.C.E. so that he could spy for you. He fed you information so you could be a step ahead of us. Whenever possible he misguided us. But he didn't misguide me. I was onto him from the beginning. The way he talked. The way he walked. It wasn't normal." She listened attentively. "Then the incident with Officer Barnes at the House of Jam—" I stopped. I turned to

Kong. The *bald head* Barnes was talking about. Kong was the one who'd hurt Barnes. I wasn't about to start pointing fingers at anyone, seeing as I was immobile. I ground my teeth and continued. "The missing camera tape was my first indication."

"What camera tape?" she said.

She was testing me.

"The missing camera tape from the House of Jam. So he doesn't tell you everything, does he?"

"Only what is necessary," she half responded.

"He had insisted Joey stay with me after he had run away from you." This part was difficult for me but I wanted it off my chest. "He insisted Joey stay with me. You! You kept me away so that your goons could get to him. Isn't that right?"

Her eyes betrayed her.

Anger rose in me. "He was just a kid."

"He was a stupid kid," she said.

My whole body was energized with rage. I roared and with all my might tried to break free of the restraints on my wrists. As I did so the rope cut deeper into my skin. The pain was immense and soon all my energy faded. My shoulders slumped and I lowered my head. This would have worked in the movies.

"The money," I finally said.

"What?" she said.

I lifted my head. "The money he gives his wife at night. Why would someone do that if they weren't hiding something?"

"He's married?" she said confused.

"Oh, so you don't know?"

"He only tells me what is necessary."

"Well, let me tell you. He also has children. You didn't know that either?"

"I was not aware," she said, clearly taken aback. "He doesn't seem like the fatherly type."

"You also wouldn't know anything about his mansion, would you?"

"Mansion? I thought he lived in a condo."

"He has a tiny little mansion in Forest Hill." I was working on the make-the-partners-enemy-ploy. After I was done she was going to hate Beadsworth. She was then going to free me and help me stop the production of Nex just to get back at Beadsworth. Well, maybe not exactly like that, but I was working on it.

There was a sound in the back. She turned. I tilted to get a better view. There were footsteps coming down. All three was of us waited anxiously. At least, I did.

Once I saw the shoes, I relaxed.

"Speak of the devil," I said.

29

Beadsworth came down with his hands in his pockets and a grim look on his face. Behind him was a man with blond hair.

"Hey, Phil," I said. It's always better to refer to your enemy by his first name; gives them less credibility. "Tell her about your mansion."

Beadsworth shot me a look.

I didn't care. "Also, the money you give to your wife at night. You know, in brown and white envelopes."

Beadsworth said, "Officer Rupret, please be silent."

I wasn't going to stay silent. "Tell her about your children."

"Officer Rupret. You don't realize—"

"—No! *You* don't realize. Playing everyone like a fool so you could get rich. You did it just for money, didn't you?" I was visibly upset.

Laura looked at me, then at Beadsworth, and then at me again. She then started to laugh.

Villains! They were all crackers.

When she was done she said to me, "You're not as bright as I gave you credit for."

What was she talking about?

"You think he is the informant?" she said, pointing to Beadsworth.

Then I saw the gun, wedged in Beadsworth's back by the blond man. Beadsworth's head was bowed low—in defeat.

"Where did you find him?" Laura said.

The blond man answered, "He was snooping around the back."

"A big mistake, Detective Beadsworth," Laura said. "Tie him up."

Beadsworth was tied up—wrists and ankles—and placed ten feet behind me. We sat in silence. Our captors had left us. They had probably gone off to some meeting to decide our fates. I didn't care. I was wrong about so many things. It hurt.

I was glad Beadsworth was behind me. I couldn't face him. Here I was, ready to tell everything I knew about him, to the one person who had deceived me.

I heard footsteps and saw Laura emerge from behind the metal door. Right behind her was the owner of the shop.

"This is not good," he said nervously. "We can't have police officers here. We have customers upstairs."

"Get rid of them," she said.

"They are police officers," he said.

"Not them. The customers."

"That might be—"

"Tell them you have a gas leak and the building must be evacuated. Give them a voucher for a free drink. Just get them out."

He didn't look happy.

She said, "We are so close. We keep them here for a few days until—" she stopped when she realized I was eavesdropping. "Kong will watch over them."

I cringed.

When they were leaving, I said, "I never liked the wallpaper. The colour was ugly."

The-so-called-owner turned to me, then gingerly walked away.

It was quiet again. The metal door was shut tight to prevent the outside world from hearing our screams. I *was* prepared to scream.

At least they didn't shut the lights off and left us in darkness.

I could hear Beadsworth breathing in the back. Ever since he was bound, he had not said a word.

I didn't know what to say. But I wanted to say something.

"I'm sorry," I said.

No response. Only breathing.

"I was wrong, okay?" I said. "I thought you were the mole."

"And how did you deduce that, Officer Rupret?" he finally said.

"You were acting strange. It was a mistake. I'm sorry, man." I tried twisting my head but could only manage up to a certain extent. "How did you know I was here?" I said.

"I've been following you," came the answer from behind.

"Following me? For how long?"

"Since yesterday."

"You were behind me when I was trailing the Lincoln?" I asked.

"Yes. Three cars back. I saw you park and disappear behind the tea shop. I waited, but when you didn't come out I decided to take a look. That's when the blond gentleman pulled a gun on me."

"But why follow me?"

"So you wouldn't do anything perilous."

"Like this."

"Yes." There was silence again.

"I need some answers," I said.

"You are entitled to them." There was a brief pause. I think he was sorting out his thoughts. Then he began. "As you may or may not know, it was Sergeant Aldrich who instigated the investigation into the drug squad."

I didn't know that.

"What you also may not know is that Sergeant Aldrich was once part of that very same drug squad."

I didn't know that either. *But why investigate your own team?*

"I will not go into the details of the misappropriation in the fink fund but I will say that there were certain officers who were not following all the rules. These officers were noted for bribery, money laundering, assault and various other offenses. Sergeant Aldrich was not, by any means, part of those corrupt officers. No. While in the drug squad, Sergeant Aldrich was clean. But, eventually he became depressed by the legal system; drug dealers and pushers were receiving insignificant penalties."

"How do you know all of this?" I said.

"Detective David Longfoot."

"Who?"

"You met him in Scarborough on our stake-out."

I remembered. He and Beadsworth had had a private chat in Beadsworth's car while I was forced to go for a walk.

Beadsworth said, "One night, when Detective Longfoot was under cover, he stumbled upon this group—"

"R.A.C.E.," I spoke in.

"Actually, Officer Rupret, the name R.A.C.E. never existed until . . ." he trailed off.

"Until what?" I asked.

"Until Sergeant Aldrich invented it."

I was taken back. "So Aldrich gave R.A.C.E. the name R.A.C.E.?"

"Precisely."

Wow. "So this Radical Association of Criminal Ethnicities—"

"Invented."

"And the stock market bullshit about Nex—"

"Invented."

Beadsworth continued. "Once Detective Longfoot realized this group was onto something big, he contacted his supervisor, Sergeant Aldrich. The information provided to Sergeant Aldrich stated R.A.C.E.—we shall still call it that—was working on this new drug, which was going to be bigger than Ecstasy. Sergeant Aldrich saw an opportunity. I believe it was then that he made contact with R.A.C.E.

"He would provide R.A.C.E. with information and in return they would give him a piece of, as they say, the action."

I was partially correct. It *was* about money.

"Detective Longfoot was told to suspend his investigation into the group, but he felt this could one day pose a real threat, so he continued privately. Seeing that R.A.C.E. might be exposed, Sergeant Aldrich involved internal affairs, citing improprieties in the squad. The RCMP then launched a full-blown inquiry into the now-missing fink fund. Some drug-squad officers were re-assigned and others were suspended.

"Detective Longfoot was suspended with pay pending the inquiry. Prior to this he had sent a report directly to the chief, highlighting the seriousness of this new group. She in turn ordered that a team look into this. Sergeant Aldrich volunteered to head this new team along with Detective Garnett."

"Hold on," I said. Something didn't make sense. "Why put Aldrich in charge of a team that would investigate a group he was part of?"

"At the time, Detective Longfoot was not aware of Aldrich's involvement. Even the chief does not know."

"Then who knows?"

"Five individuals: Detective Longfoot, Detective Garnett, Detective Nemdharry, and you and I."

"So that's why we weren't allowed to talk to any members of the drug squad?" I said more to myself than him.

"Precisely," he said. "Detective Longfoot and I go back many years. He suspected something and informed me of this. I then volunteered to be part of Operation Anti-R.A.C.E."

"So you could keep an eye on the team."

"Yes."

"Then why bring me in?"

He went silent.

"Why involve me in Operation Anti-R.A.C.E.?"

Again silence.

I twisted, straining my neck. "You didn't answer my question."

"Officer Rupret," he said. "You were brought in to . . . complicate our investigation."

"Complicate?"

"Yes."

"You mean screw up? *Right?*" I snapped.

"Sergeant Aldrich had no intentions of this operation being successful. It was only a façade. Set up to please the chief. That was why you were brought in. Sergeant Aldrich remembers well what had transpired between you—then a parking enforcement officer—and the drug squad."

"It was a mistake," I said, as always explaining my actions from that night.

"An error in judgment. Yes. Sergeant Aldrich thought you to be a loose canon. Naïve and incompetent, if you pardon my saying, perfect to nullify this investigation." There was fidgeting. "But I had insisted you be put under my supervision—"

"I'm under no one's supervision," I retorted.

"You made that quite clear."

There was silence again. I couldn't believe I was brought in to jeopardize the operation. Here I was thinking Aldrich only wanted me because I was young, handsome and creative.

"So it was Aldrich who told you to watch over the LLPM Import & Export building?" I said.

"Precisely," Beadsworth answered. "He was certain we were closing in on R.A.C.E. So he placed the entire team to watch over that one building, hoping to buy some time."

"Putting all the eggs in one basket," I muttered to myself.

"Sorry?"

"Nothing. What about the videocassette you took from the House of Jam?" I asked.

"You're aware of it?"

"I met Cal Murray in the morning."

There was a noise and then Beadsworth said, "The tape is safe."

"Does it show Barnes' attacker?"

"Quite clearly."

"Then why take it?"

"We did not want R.A.C.E. to become alarmed and end their operations. We wanted to confiscate the Nex production equipment and we did not want them to leave our jurisdiction. We did not want the OPP or the RCMP involved. Also, by securing the videocassette I was able to hold some leverage over Sergeant Aldrich, in case it was justified. And, if the videocassette had gone into Sergeant Aldrich's hands, it would have disappeared."

It was simple and it made sense.

"Is that why you left Joey with me and not with Aldrich?" I asked.

"Yes . . . but I shouldn't have."

"I screwed up," I said taking full responsibility. "It was my fault. Okay?"

"Perhaps. But . . ." He paused. "They did not find a body in your house."

"What?"

"No burned or charred body, I'm afraid."

"He's alive?" I said.

"We don't know."

I felt a little better. There was still hope.

There was something else I wanted to ask. "I spoke to Noel the other night; he mentioned that . . . he saw you give your wife money."

"Yes."

"Large amounts of money . . . at night."

"Yes."

"Large amounts of money in brown and white envelopes at night."

"What's your point?"

"Is it drug money?" I blurted.

There was a pause, then laughter. "Is that what you think? That I've been giving my wife drug money?"

"I mean . . . the house . . . the furniture . . . the swimming pool . . . your wife doesn't even work, I mean. How can you afford it?"

"She doesn't have to work. The money I give to her is hers."

I didn't understand.

"It's her money," he said. "On my way back from work I withdraw money from her account, seal it in bank envelopes, which do come in brown and white, and give them to her. Our main bank branch is in Toronto." There was laughter again, and then he said, "My wife is what?"

I thought hard. "She is a woman."

"Yes, a woman. But . . . where am I from?"

"England."

"Where do you think she's from?"

I hope this wasn't a trick question. "England."

"Precisely, she's from England, hence her English accent."

He wasn't making any sense.

"Have you heard of the House of York?"

I shook my head.

"My wife is Lady Amy Dowling of York," he said boldly. "She's royalty."

"You're kidding, right?"

"No. The money I give to her is from her estate."

He was laughing hard. "Do you think I would buy an expensive house if I was laundering money? I work for the police. I would be caught the next day."

"The force knows your wife gets money from England?"

"Of course they do. How do you think I justify my lifestyle with a police officer's salary?"

It was all a misunderstanding. We were two grown men, bound to chairs, laughing hysterically.

"So are you . . . like a prince or something?" I asked.

"No, no. I'm just an ordinary bloke."

"Even if you were . . . I wasn't going to call you, Your Highness."

"Your Highness." He started to laugh again. Hearing him, I started to laugh, too.

We stopped when our stomachs couldn't take much more.

"How do we get out?" I said.

"I'm not sure," he replied.

It was impossible for either of us to move without tipping over and falling on our sides. Even if one of us did manage to get closer to the other, there was no way we could gnaw at the ropes with our teeth.

As I was churning escape possibilities in my head, the metal door swung open. It was Kong.

Oh, shit.

He shut the door and moved toward me. Being ahead of Beadsworth, I knew I was first.

"Hey, Kong," I said, trying to be brave. "I know what you're thinking but I'm not into big muscular Chinese men. I prefer gentle little Chinese men."

A fist shot out and hit me squarely on my left cheek. I jerked and fell sideways. It stung, as my cheek and my head smacked into the cement floor.

I closed my eyes and pretended to die. Maybe, he would go over me and attack Beadsworth instead. It doesn't sound noble but I was in pain.

But that wouldn't be. He grabbed me and sat me up again.

"Let him go," I heard Beadsworth say.

I now had more respect for Beadsworth. He was willing to sacrifice himself.

But Kong wasn't interested. He was going to have his fun with me.

This was the time I should do something heroic, but what? I couldn't kick him, karate chop him or even head butt him. I could . . . spit at him. Yes, that would do it. My highly corrosive saliva, once aimed and fired accurately, would burn his eyes.

I began to gather all my fluids, even the reserves down my throat, for an aerial assault. After much snorting and sucking I was only able to manage enough for a spray.

Kong readied himself for another assault. I closed my eyes for the impact. He hit me straight at the top of my mouth. My chair and I toppled over and onto my back.

I opened my eyes and from my vertical position saw Beadsworth look away. My lip was cut and I was bleeding.

A shadow came over me and Kong once again sat me up. I was getting the feeling he would hit me, sit me up and then hit me again. How long was this going to go on? I think until he got bored or until I expired. The latter made more sense. He seemed to be interested in hitting me.

It stung when I licked my upper lip.

Kong cracked and rubbed his knuckles.

I was glad the joints in his fingers were getting stiff.

Perhaps his fingers wouldn't be able to take much more and he would leave me alone. I couldn't take many more hits—not from him, at least.

"Let him go," I heard Beadsworth say again.

Kong merely glanced at Beadsworth. He flared his nostrils and he prepared for the finish.

Beadsworth tried again to get Kong's attention but he was too focused on me.

Wait your turn, Phil. It'd soon be over.

I closed my eyes. Any second now the hammer would come down and leave me for dead.

There was a metallic screech. I opened my eyes. The metal door swung open and in came Ronald Garnett holding a gun.

"Police," Garnett bellowed.

Kong, with his fist still in the air, glanced at Garnett, and then turned his attention back to me.

Garnett moved toward us. "Release them."

Kong let go of me and faced Garnett. Garnett was as tall and massive as Kong.

If both had decided to battle right now, my money would have been on Garnett, not because he was the good guy but because he had a gun.

Several more officers came down. It took four of them to handcuff Kong.

One officer came over. Officer Moro.

"You look terrible," he said, cutting my restraints.

"Thanks," I said. "We almost had him."

"Sure you did." He smiled.

"Get paramedics," I heard Garnett say.

He came over.

"Are you all right?" he asked.

Without saying a word I threw myself at him. "I love you, man. I take back all the rumours I spread about you."

"What rumours?" he said pushing me aside like a rag doll. He went to Beadsworth.

"I'm fine," Beadsworth said. "Officer Rupret kept the assailant preoccupied so that no harm came to me."

Garnett looked at me with admiration.

I smiled weakly, before fainting.

30

The Sundance braked and then turned sharply into another parking lot. Ms. Zee had sent Suraj to the Bubble T Shop. She knew Kong would have no problem in killing the two officers but would need help in disposing of their bodies. It was no longer possible to let the officers live, since they had seen her.

From behind the wheel Suraj saw a cluster of police cars in front of the shop. He dialed Ms. Zee's number and told her. She was not pleased. She told him to get back.

I was sitting in the passenger side of my car. I had four first-aid stitches on my upper lip from the paramedics and I was given painkillers. I had refused to go to the hospital. We were getting closer to R.A.C.E. and I wanted to be part of the big bust. I didn't want to see it on the news while lying in a hospital bed.

I saw Beadsworth talking to Susan, the cashier of the Bubble T Shop. It looked as if he was thanking her. A moment later he came over and slid into the driver's seat.

"You should have a doctor look at you," he said.

"Naw, I'm fine," I said, which would be true until the painkillers wore off.

“How did Garnett find us?” I asked.

“When I was following you, I notified him of my whereabouts. When he didn’t hear from me he came down. He found the Bubble T Shop closed. He tried my cell phone but the blond gentleman had stripped me of it earlier. He then questioned the neighbours. Inside the coffee shop across the street was that girl.” Beadsworth moved his head in the direction of Susan. “She told Garnett she saw you earlier, looking in. Garnett returned with other members and broke through the door.”

“I’m glad you called Garnett,” I said.

He turned and looked me straight in the eyes. “That’s what we do, Officer Rupret. We’re a team. We look out for one another.”

“Hey, I didn’t know which side you were on.”

He didn’t say anything. He just nodded.

“We hope our assailant is more talkative,” he said. “Perhaps, we can finally break this case.” He looked across to the many vehicles littering the parking lot. “We are now searching for the owner of the shop. He goes by the name of Martin. But no matter, we’ll find him.”

“What about Aldrich?” I asked.

“Nothing yet.”

“What do you mean, nothing yet?” I said. I could feel the pain coming on. “We know he’s working with R.A.C.E.”

“What do you suggest?”

“We go and bust his ass.”

“It’s not that simple. Sergeant Aldrich is our superior. There will be a formal complaint filed and then an investigation by internal affairs. Meanwhile, we need to find R.A.C.E.,” he raised an eyebrow toward me. “And persuade them to come forward with evidence against him.”

"You need witnesses." I smiled.

He smiled back.

Ms. Zee was furious. Aldrich was on the other line and she was giving him an earful. Operation Anti-R.A.C.E. was supposed to be shut down. How could he lose control of his team? Why didn't he reprimand the officer who had followed them? Why didn't he know about the raid at the Bubble T Shop? Why didn't he do anything to stop it?

Aldrich pleaded that it had all happened behind his back.

He was supposed to protect them, she insisted. If she went down she would take him with her.

Now it was Aldrich's turn. Why wasn't Nex produced and distributed by now? Did she think he was going to fool the squad forever? She had told him she would have it in a matter of days, not several weeks. She was naïve to think he could always clean up after her.

"They have Kong," she yelled and slammed the phone down. She covered her face. What was she going to do?

Martin entered.

She looked up, more composed.

"We have to move," she said.

Martin understood. "Burrows isn't too happy," he said.

"I don't care," she snapped. She then bit her lip and said, "Why not?"

"I'll get him," he said.

Burrows entered the office, followed by Martin. "We cannot move," Burrows said. "Not now."

She waited for him to explain.

"Our finest batch is in the freezing process," he said. "If we take it out now the tablets will collapse."

A lot of money was riding on that batch and she didn't want to see it go to waste.

"Mr. Burrows," she said as carefully as possible. "Our situation has changed. We have no choice but to find another location—perhaps a better one. We have to move tonight."

"We could wait a few more hours," Martin spoke. "That should be enough time to take a prepared batch with us."

Burrows agreed.

Ms. Zee thought about it. "Fine. But start clearing the warehouse. The freeze-dryers will be the last to move."

A sweet melody woke me up. I was inside my car, which was being driven by Beadsworth. The melody was coming from Beadsworth's cell phone. Garnett had found it at the Bubble T Shop. We were the last to leave Scarborough and were on our way to his house. Beadsworth had insisted I get home and get some rest.

He answered it, spoke a few words, and hung up.

"Who was it?" I asked.

"Detective Garnett has been unable to get any information from your assailant. He won't talk."

That wasn't a surprise. The man hadn't spoken two words when he was smacking me around.

"He will talk," Beadsworth said, assuring me. "Detective Garnett can be very persuasive."

We were in Forest Hill; the magnificent houses gave that away. We entered Beadsworth's driveway and parked.

Amy opened the door and her face turned to horror. "Oh, my—"

"I'm fine," I said with a weak smile. I had bruises all over my face and stitches on my upper lip.

Noel was in the living room watching whatever show kids his age watch.

Amy looked over at her husband. He kissed her. He would fill her in on the details later.

She took our coats and asked if we wanted anything. I shook my head. I'm not sure what Beadsworth said.

I went into the living room and flopped on the sofa. Noel was too mesmerized to see me come in. He was watching some weird cartoon. The characters had big eyes and small mouths. Every so often they would fly in the air and make a pose. Their lips weren't even in sync with their voices. What ever happened to high-quality cartoons like the *Looney Tunes*?

Beadsworth and Amy were in the kitchen.

I closed my eyes. I tried to tune out the sounds from the TV. I should go up and straight to bed. In a minute, I promised myself.

I was falling asleep.

A shadow came over me and I jolted awake.

Noel was examining my face.

"Did you get into a fight?" he asked, examining my bruises.

"No," I said. "What's makes you say that?"

"You look hurt," he responded.

"You mean this." I pointed to my upper lip with a laugh. "This is how I look when I don't take my vitamins. I'll be fine."

He looked like he didn't believe me. I really didn't know why. I guess I don't give children much credit. They're much smarter than the cartoons they watch.

"Yeah," I said. "I kind of got into a fight. But don't tell your parents, okay?"

He nodded. It was our little deal. I wouldn't tell his parents how he broke his arm and he wouldn't tell *his* parents that I got into a fight.

Beadsworth came in with the cell phone in his ear. He said something and then hung up. He smiled.

"It was Garnett," he said.

"Garnett got him talking?" I said.

"Better than that. We know where Nex is being produced."

Moving through smaller streets we finally saw a familiar Toyota parked to one side. Garnett got out as we stopped behind it.

"It's in that warehouse," he said, pointing to a rundown building around the corner. I assumed many years of neglect had assisted in the building's current state. Graffiti covered a good portion of the walls. The windows were cracked or broken, and some were boarded up. There was light coming from inside. "A large moving van came and took some equipment. And we know where it's going."

"How?" I asked.

He bobbed his head toward the Toyota. It was then that I realized someone was inside his car. I tilted my head. It was Martin, the owner of the Bubble T Shop. He sagged in the backseat with his head low.

I went over, tapped on the window and waved. He raised his eyes to me. I then made a fist. He turned and sagged even further.

I heard Garnett's voice from behind. He was speaking to Beadsworth, "He's willing to make a deal."

I looked around the corner. Opposite the warehouse, a man walked past the front entrance and came towards us—Nemdharry.

"There is a main entrance in the front but it's bolted. There are two fire exits on either side—those won't be any problem. We can cover the narrow paths easily. A large loading dock is in the back. On the northeast side there is a closed gate that leads to the dock. Terries is watching over it."

"Clara is here?" I said and then realized I shouldn't have referred to her by her first name. I didn't even know her.

Nemdharry paid no attention to my slight. "Yeah."

Two minutes later another car pulled up. Herrera came out. "I hope he's not pulling our balls," he grunted.

Ever since Barnes was hurt, Herrera had been on the edge.

Garnett and Beadswoth said nothing.

"He better not be shitting us." Herrera looked in the direction of Garnett's car.

Garnett finally said. "Carlos, you okay?"

"I'm fine," Herrera said. He pulled out his gun and checked to see if it was loaded. "What're we waiting for?"

I was thinking that too.

Her makeshift office was bare, save for the lone desk and two chairs. Ms. Zee placed her elbows on the desk and her face in her palms. There was so much running through her mind, but in the end it was all directed towards one man. Peter Stankovich. Her ex-husband.

Peter Stankovich had stolen over four millions dollars from the clients of the insurance company he had worked for. It was supposed to be a perfect crime. A crime so easy to accomplish that he wondered why no one else had thought of it.

He sent one hundred of his clients false invoices regarding their policies. In them, he inflated their monthly premiums. With the help of the funds accountant, he opened another company account, where the money was directly deposited. After taking the excess, he then forwarded the actual premium amount to the correct account.

At the end of each year, he sent each client an annual policy statement with the excess premium figures. For three years, no one noticed. The correct amounts were coming in from policyholders. Everything seemed normal. Until, one year the insurance company quietly hired an external company to prepare and send annual policy statements to its clients.

When clients received their correct statements they were outraged at the difference from what they were actually paying.

The insurance company received many calls, and all those calls were from clients of Peter Stankovich.

Peter Stankovich and the accountant were convicted of fraud and embezzlement in excess of $5000 and each sentenced to six years.

Peter Stankovich was cocky, arrogant, and cruel. That was the way Ms. Zee remembered him.

She clearly remembered what he had said to her the last time they had dinner together in their home. "You're nothing but a stupid spoiled slut. Without me you'd be greeting customers at Walmart."

She wasn't stupid. Spoiled, yes, but not stupid. She knew what he was up to and she did what he had done to his clients. She opened a separate account, one hidden from him, and each week deposited small amounts into that account. In the end she had a large sum.

With Martin, her lawyer, she took the divorce papers to Peter in jail and had him sign them. He wasn't happy. It wasn't the divorce that bothered him. It was the fact that she stole money from him. He tried to get her charged too, but, as he had once, the police thought she was just a spoiled housewife, incapable of anything devious.

It was at the jail visiting Peter that she saw Kong. He was in for assault, pending a trial. Through Martin she posted Kong's bail. Then, she met Armand, and the possibility of outdoing her ex-husband came into being.

She lifted her head up and saw the empty room. She hadn't had time to furnish it, which was a good thing. The only valuable object was the design of Nex.

Ms. Zee placed the papers in her briefcase and kept it close to her. She understood the situation. She was going to take the samples, which Ed Burrows would bring to her any minute now, and leave the country. She had many contacts and those contacts would be very useful in her escape.

With the process in her hands she could start her operations anywhere—in any country.

Burrows came through the door. In his hands was a sealed white container, the size of an icebox.

"There are five thousand in here," he said.

Five thousand tablets of Nex, she smiled. This wasn't a waste, after all.

"Where's Martin?" Ms. Zee asked.

"I haven't seen him," he replied.

She quickly ordered Hause to go find him. Martin was going to arrange for everything. He was going to arrange her escape.

Hause came back shaking his head. Martin was gone.

Now she was worried.

31

I was getting nervous. I didn't know what Garnett was waiting for. Weren't we ready? I gave Beadsworth a *Let's-go* look. He shrugged.

A Volvo pulled up beside us. The only person missing from Operation Anti-R.A.C.E. was Barnes. Then the door swung open and out came Sergeant Aldrich.

This was going to be good.

"Good work, Detective," Aldrich said, speaking to Garnett. "Fine work."

Garnett made no comment.

"Are you certain they are in there?" Aldrich said.

"Yes," Garnett responded.

Aldrich smiled but it didn't look natural.

I wanted to punch him—on his upper lip.

Aldrich came over to me. His blonde hair was perfectly combed. He looked cool, calm and collected. "Officer Rupret, I hear you're the one who cracked open this case. I'm quite certain the intelligence unit will receive a letter of recommendation."

Martin was sitting inside Garnett's Toyota. I looked at Aldrich and then at Martin. I did this, maybe three or four times. I then winked at Aldrich. The wink that said, *I know*.

For a split second there was a twitch under his left eye.

"Thank you, Sir," I said, ever so politely. "I'm thinking more about joining internal affairs." I didn't know if I was qualified, or capable, but who cared.

Aldrich's other eye twitched. It was entertaining to see the volley of twitches from one eye to the other.

Garnett's voice interrupted my fun. "Sir, should we proceed?" Garnett said.

I admired Garnett for keeping himself professional, even though he knew Aldrich was a criminal.

Aldrich coughed. His twitching ceased. "Yes, go ahead, Detective."

Aldrich was about to move away from me when I said, "Sir, you were right. I *am* young, imaginative, creative and bold. I used all these qualities to solve this case."

I think he wanted to hit me but he just walked away.

When Garnett gave the signal we were at the front of the warehouse in less than a minute. Both Beadsworth and I got out of our vehicle at the same time.

I followed as Beadsworth raced along the side of the building and toward a door. With all his might he kicked the door. I was amazed at how much strength those legs of his had. Maybe the door was in bad shape with the hinges wearing out. In any case, the door went down.

Beadsworth moved in.

We were inside a small area no bigger than two elevator shafts. On my left were empty pizza boxes. It smelled of onions and anchovies.

We were faced with another door. Like a fly, Beadsworth attached himself to the right side wall, his gun tightly gripped to his chest. I wanted to do the same, but the pizza boxes got in my way.

Beadsworth motioned his head toward the door.

I gestured. *What?*

He moved his leg and motioned again.

I was to kick the door down.

I shook my head and touched my upper lip. I was not in good shape.

He nodded, abruptly turned, and with one kick knocked the door down.

Kicking down doors was not my thing. I could manage breaking windows with baseball bats, if the windows were thin and I was guaranteed no flying glass would hit me.

We heard voices echo from inside.

Police.

Get down.

Stop.

Don't move.

We entered the warehouse, the fluorescent lights high above us. The place felt cold.

We were confronted with large baffles that ran along one side, with occasional openings that resembled doors.

A man peeked out from one of the openings.

"Stop!" I yelled, my gun trembling before me.

He ducked back in.

I ran after him.

Inside the opening I found a disorganized room. It looked like it was in the process of being cleared. Monitors, keyboards, cables and wires were scattered everywhere. There was other equipment, too. Your chemistry lab type: beakers, test tubes, flasks, and instruments I did not know the names of.

The man disappeared around another door. I heard a voice. When I turned the corner I saw Beadsworth on top of the man. The man was sprawled on his stomach. He had brown skin and a punched in nose.

From the corner of my eye I saw a man with blond hair holding something that looked like a computer monitor. It was the guy who had pulled the gun on Beadsworth at the Bubble T Shop.

When he saw me he dropped what he was holding and ran behind another baffle.

The place was a maze.

I wasn't going to run after him. Let Garnett or Nemdharry do it.

But Beadsworth had seen me see him, so he was expecting me to run and arrest him.

Reluctantly, I did.

As I spun around the corner and through a door draped with long strips of plastic, I felt a sudden chill.

I was inside another room. Huge racks that went up at least eight feet now surrounded me. The racks held empty trays. As I moved past them I realized some were full. Most of the trays contained individual white tablets.

Curiosity pushed me to pick one up. I applied pressure, and there was a weak jolt, not enough to cause any alarms, but the tablet crumpled between my fingers, leaving behind small crystals that looked like sugar.

I was about to lick it—that's what they did on TV, when I heard steps further up. I wiped the white stuff on my pants and with my gun ready, went deeper into the room.

There were maybe two-dozen of these racks. I crouched, and through the racks tried to spot any legs.

There was movement on my left.

I turned.

Nothing.

This was absurd.

"Hey, dude," I yelled. "You're surrounded. Come out and we'll go easy on you."

Go easy on you? Who ever says that?

I eased forward, my eyes darting around. I wasn't going to let this guy surprise me. No sir. I was like a tiger sneaking up on its prey.

Nothing got past these radar ears.

A shadow came over me, as a huge rack tipped. I rolled sideways, missing it by inches, but several of the trays flew out and hit me squarely on the face.

That hurt.

I was covered with hundreds of white tablets.

I stroked my hair and tablets fell out.

I got to my feet, but lost my balance on the scattered tablets. I scrambled up and composed myself.

This was really absurd.

I tiptoed over the sea of white tablets and stomped ahead.

I was now pissed. "I'm going to shoot you," I said. At this point I would have.

As I was getting further, it was getting colder.

I was shivering.

I knew why.

Many of the freezer doors were left open. *Purposely*.

He was trying to freeze me.

I don't think so.

He didn't realize how resilient I was.

I sneezed. And then sneezed several times more.

I wiped the snot with the back of my sleeve.

I must be coming down with something.

I did a full circle and when I was certain I was alone I gently shut one of the freezer doors.

I went along doing this.

When I pulled the last door to close it, out came a fist from behind. I reacted, but not fast enough. It smashed into my chin.

I lost my footing and fell on my back. My gun, already too cold to grip, flew out and landed underneath one of the racks.

I had to get back on my feet, but he was on me like a tiger.

He raised his fist but stopped in midair.

I was confused.

He looked to his left and I did too.

Garnett stood with his gun aimed squarely at him.

This was the second time Garnett had saved my life. It was embarrassing.

I got to my feet as Garnett handcuffed the blond man.

The blond man had the *I-almost-had-you* look.

I hated it.

Garnett pulled the blond man away by his collar.

I was standing alone in the cold room.

I had had enough. The warehouse was secure and the occupants in custody. I took the first exit out onto the street.

Three members of the Clandestine Laboratory Unit brushed past me. They had their hands full with all the chemicals and stuff inside.

It was the middle of the night but I could still make out a dozen or so marked and unmarked vehicles around the warehouse.

The media would be swarming in any minute.

I couldn't believe it was finally over. We had R.A.C.E. and Nex. But I didn't feel cheerful or happy.

I was relieved, though.

Maybe, I was expecting more.

I guess I was hoping I would be the one to solve this case all by myself. Instead, it was Beadsworth who'd made sense of everything that had happened.

There was a noise that made me turn. I saw Herrera escorting Laura, whose real name, I later found out, was Zeena Stankovich. She was handcuffed and her head was bent.

As they got closer, I stopped them.

"I knew it was you all along," I said.

Her face contorted. She was ready to spit.

"Take her away," I said.

Herrera was more than glad to.

I saw someone *I* was glad to see. Clara Terries. She had just turned the corner and was walking with another officer. I was relieved to see it was Nemdharry and not some young, good-looking fellow.

Not that it mattered . . .

She smiled as she came closer.

"I guess, we did it, Jon." Her smile widened.

Jon. I blushed. I lowered my voice, "Ma'am, I'm also referred to as Jonny."

"Is that right?" she said, playing along. "I'm referred to as Clara. Not Officer Terries or Officer Clara. Just Clara."

"It's a deal. Clara."

We both went silent. I glanced at the warehouse.

"Are we still on?" she asked.

"I'm sorry?" I said.

"When we first met, you asked if I liked bubble tea. I'll take you up on that offer."

My face dropped. It was the last place I wanted to go—not that I had anything against bubble tea. As a matter of fact, I still cannot stop praising the strawberry kind.

"Uh, I . . . if you really want . . ." I started.

She leaned closer and whispered. "I'm only kidding. I heard what happened."

I was relieved.

"Maybe, somewhere else then?" She winked.

I nodded and smiled.

I sat on the cold pavement and leaned back on my palms, trying to soak up everything. Reporters, followed by cameramen, approach the secured area. More people were led in handcuffs to marked cruisers. Aldrich talked to reporters as if it was *he* who had stopped this new and unknown threat.

I later found out it was Garnett who had called Aldrich here.

Apart from Longfoot, Garnett, Beadsworth, Nemdharry, and me, of course, no one knew Aldrich's ties to R.A.C.E., not even the other members of Operation Anti-R.A.C.E.

Aldrich would be disciplined but it would all be internal, I was later told.

Garnett emerged from the warehouse. I waved him over.

Reluctantly he came.

I didn't bother getting up. "Detective Garnett, shouldn't you be talking to the media instead of him?"

Garnett looked in the direction of Aldrich and said, "That might be his last time. Let him talk. He's good at it."

Was that a joke?

"Sir," I said. "I would like to thank you for saving my life. *Twice*."

He looked at me intently. "Officer Rupert, I had no choice. I didn't want any mess on my hands. Remember clearly what I'm about to say. If I had a choice you wouldn't be talking to me right now."

That, I knew, was not a joke.

Beadsworth was bending down to a cruiser window. He was talking to Zeena Stankovich, the mastermind behind this operation. He said a few words and then approached me.

"I'm glad you've found a good spot," he said, referring to the side pavement.

"Only one available, I'm afraid. If you want I could probably find a spot for you," I said looking around.

"I'll pass."

"She give you any trouble?" I said, jerking my head toward the cruiser.

"As a matter of fact, no," he said. "She was very cooperative. She knew we were coming."

There was a moment of silence when he said, "Are you still interested in being a drug enforcement officer?"

"It's too dangerous. Right now I'm not sure about anything."

Beadsworth said, "I've just spoken to Joseph Lenard. He is alive and staying with a friend. He said something that didn't make sense, but he said you would understand. He said he was watching television when he heard gunshots, bullets ripped through the window, and . . . I'm not sure if this is correct, but that they hit Michael Jordan?"

I grinned. "A friend."

"He then saw a flaming bottle come through the window. He didn't know what else to do but jump through the back window to the porch roof and escaped. We'll clarify his statements later."

Joey was alive.

There was silence and then Beadsworth spoke. "Officer Rupret, you're still welcome to stay at our home until you decide what to do."

"Can you stop calling me Officer Rupret," I snapped. "Haven't we gone through enough? Can't you call me Jon or Jonny?"

He paused and then said, "Jon."

Wow. *I was making progress with him.*

"Then can I call you Phil or Phillip?" I said.

He thought about it.

"No," he said, and walked away.

The sun came up. I was the last person to leave the sidewalk and the area. Beadsworth had offered me a ride but I declined. I wanted some time alone. I didn't know whether I was going to stay in the force or not, but there was one thing I did know for sure. I wanted to go back home and, over tea and biscuits, have a long talk with my mom.

WAJEEHA QURESHI

WWW.MOBASHARQURESHI.COM